TEXAS PAST

A novel of the Old West

Brevia Publishing Company
101 W. 75th Pl
Merrillville, IN 46410
http://westernfiction.com

Texas Past

ISBN 978-0-9628531-2-8

This book printed on acid free paper

Printed in the United States of America

Contents

About the Author

Voyle Glover has spent most of his years practicing law. His early years were spent in Arizona where he learned to love all things Western. His love of the Old West and the many stories about the outlaws, settlers, Indians and pioneers captured his imagination.

In the '70's, Glover wrote his first western story and it was published in *Far West*, a western fiction publication that was located in California. He went on to have several more of his short stories, and two novellas published by *Far West*.

Law School interrupted his writing career and it has only been in the last few of years that he's been "back in the saddle" writing westerns. His favorite western fiction author was Louis L'Amour, whom he calls "The Dean of Western Fiction."

Glover admits that L'Amour has influenced his writing more than any other writer. He insists on writing his stories and adhering to the traditions of L'Amour, to wit, a strong, rugged and self-reliant hero, with historically accurate settings, and characters that jump right off the pages of the history of the Old West and into his stories.

Glover says of L'Amour: "There is no writer of western fiction to match Louis L'Amour. He's the only western fiction writer whose books I'll read more than once."

He tells of the time when he wrote a letter to L'Amour asking his advice about agents. L'Amour actually replied to him in a typed letter, replete with some typos. He congratulated Glover on getting his first story published in the premier issue of *Far West*, then noted that they'd be sharing that issue. L'Amour was featured on the first page and Glover found himself listed on the cover page with his writing hero.

He says of the that moment: "I was really shocked that he actually took the time to reply, but wow, what an honor to be on the cover page with the Dean of Western Fiction, Louis L'Amour."

CHAPTER 1

I've seen some big men in my day, but the man I was looking at was one of the biggest I ever laid eyes on. I had to squint on account of the bright sun as I looked up at him. He sat his saddle with one leg thrown across the big Montana, silver-wrapped, six-inch saddle horn, leaning forward slightly, with his hands folded on top of one knee. He had a bushy, coal-black mustache hanging down the corners of his mouth, and one of them long, twisted cigars sticking out of one side of his face. A dark grey *Mex'* sombrero rested on the back of his head. It gave shade to all his head and half his body. I don't recollect ever seeing a hat that big before.

He was wearing a pair of bandoliers, which isn't much else but a couple cartridge belts slung over the chest. His were crossed over each shoulder, and around his waist he had belted a pair of guns that looked expensive. The handles were white with some speckles of silver on them. But, it was his eyes that made me feel kind of weak and puny. They were black as a 'Pache buck and real shiny, like they were made out of glass; and just now, they were boring a hole right through me. He was just about the toughest, meanest-looking man I ever come on.

I stood there on the porch looking up at him and feeling foolish, with a trickle of bean juice from a tortilla running down the corner of my mouth. The kid that had run inside just a minute earlier and told me a *senor* outside wanted to buy my riding horse, edged past me and moved out of the way to one side. I had told the kid to inform the *senor* that I wasn't interested. Right after the kid ran outside, I heard a shot and heard a cry of pain from my horse. I ran out just in time to see my horse fall to his knees and then tumble over.

Since I was just south of the border, I wasn't anxious to have trouble. They can make it awful tough on a *gringo* in these parts, and all I wanted to do was make a little deal on a pair of wild horses I had caught, eat some good *Mex'* food, and ride out. I didn't want trouble, especially with a man who looked to be about twice my size and a whole lot meaner. I reckon if he'd gone about it right, I'd have sold him the horse if I'd seen it was going to bring this kind of trouble. It was a little mustang I'd picked up wild and we'd only been together a couple months. We'd taken a real likin' to each other.

But, he'd gone and made it impossible for me to side-step him. I didn't feel up to him, but I knew when it was over, he'd be wishing he'd went and stole a horse somewhere instead of shooting mine.

I stayed in the shade of the porch and said, "Reckon you bought my horse, mister." I moved the tortilla to my left hand, took another bite, then wiped my right hand on the front of my shirt. I didn't want any slippery fingers if I had to reach for my gun.

He showed me a lot of white teeth and said real friendly, "*Senor*, when Hernandez Vaca asked to buy your horse it was alive." He shrugged his shoulders and said, "I do not want to buy your horse, now. It is dead." He gave a funny little frown, like he was some kind of actor on a stage and was trying to show some kind of sympathy.

If I had been in Texas, there wouldn't have been any patience in me at all because we got a way of dealing with these kind of men, and mostly it's sudden. The Mexican soldiers can get pretty rough on Americans over here who shoot their citizens, so I wasn't anxious to spend a good part of my days in a Mexican jail. I forced myself to be polite.

With my teeth showing through a smile, I replied, "Mister Vaca, I ain't too sure why you shot my horse but I'm willing to let things lay, long as you pay me for that horse. I reckon you owe me one hundred dollars,

'Merican." I took another bite of my tortilla. My eyes never left his, and I found myself getting a familiar feeling deep down inside. I didn't like that feeling, but it always came on me when there was danger. It's like everything around me slowed down, and inside, my gut always goes hollow. It was like I'd never eaten three of those tortillas.

He was grinning now, and I could see he was enjoying this. He wasn't going to let things lay. I expect he was a man used to having his way in life and probably, was one of those men who enjoyed killing. I've met a few now and again. They all got a certain way about them. I saw it in this one's eyes and in his face. He had it in his mind to kill me and take my horses.

He pushed his sombrero forward and it covered his forehead and put shade over his eyes. Then, he swung his leg back in place and sat up straight in the saddle. The grin left his face, and all the mean in that big man came out in his eyes and on his face. His voice took on a husky tone and he said, "*Gringo*, I suggest you finish your meal and leave. If you need a horse to replace the one that died on you, I will sell you a nice one."

He pointed across the street at my two horses that I'd shut up in a little corral. "Take your pick, *gringo*. You may have either one for three hundred of your *gringo* pesos. They are fresh from eating the beautiful *Tejas* grass." The mocking tone of his voice was matched by his eyes. He was enjoying this, supremely confident that he'd cornered a *gringo* grub-line rider.

I wiped the bean juice off my mouth with the back of my left sleeve and said, "I kind of like the horse you're riding. I think I'll take your horse and maybe fifty dollars for my troubles." All the polite had dropped out of my voice and I wasn't smiling any more, either. I had my thumb hung in my belt right near my Colt.

He dropped his pretending and said, "*Senor*, perhaps you shall die today and not see your *Tejas* again, eh?

I'd been raised in some hard country, and had ridden with some of the hardest men that ever sat a saddle. And some I'd ridden with were mean men. They loved to kill. I don't know if it was from the power they felt from being able to take the life of another human being, or the pleasure they got in watching someone weaker than them beg for his life. But, I knew I was looking at one of those kind of men. His streak of mean ran deep, and it was obvious he'd played this game before. The man was a killer and he was set on murdering me.

I waited there in the shade for him to move.

He was an explosion of dark movement as he drew. I give him credit that he was maybe the fastest I ever saw before. Not the smartest. Just the fastest. I couldn't see his eyes real good because he'd shifted in the saddle, and the shade from his sombrero hid them, but I reckon they were wide with surprise when my shot slapped him hard in the center of his chest. His gun was just clearing its holster. He fell backwards, then jerked forward, trying to line up his gun on me.

Maybe my second shot wasn't necessary, but I was raised some different than most folk. My pa always told me that when a man is shot and is as good as dead, that's when he's most dangerous. That's when you don't expect a man to shoot you, when he's supposed to be dead. My second shot threw him sideways and out of the saddle.

I moved back against the wall and stood there for a long moment, not looking at anything in particular, waiting for any sounds that might mean an attack from a partner of his or from someone in the town. I didn't hear a thing and not a soul moved. It wasn't like that in Texas. There, soon as the shooting stops, there's a whole passel of kids and folks all wanting to get a good look-see at the dead man. I reckon maybe these folks were different that way.

I moved out into the street and stood over the body. I gave him a quick glance, still wary, looking around the place, and not trusting that he was alone. He was sprawled out on his back, a gun still in one hand, his eyes staring empty at the blistering hot sun. It wasn't pretty, but then I never saw a dead man that didn't make my stomach get tight.

I stepped back, turned slowly in a circle, looking around for any signs of friends. As loud as I could, I yelled, "Hey! If any *amigos* of this

Senor Vaca are around, then come on out! We'll go ahead and take care of our fight now, like a man's supposed to do." I didn't want anyone sneaking along on my trail.

An old man came out of the *cantina* where I had been eating. He was the man who'd been setting way off to one side giving orders to the women where I'd ordered my food. He held up a hand, palm facing me, and with a head shaking like a man does when he says "no," said with a big smile on his face: "*Senor*, this one has no friends." Then, the old man walked over and spat right smack into that dead man's face.

He looked at me and with a look of complete disgust on his face said, "That is what we think of Hernandez Vaca!"

I smiled at him and asked, "Who is he?"

"He was a thief, a *bandito*. Vaca would come into our village, force us to feed him, force our women to drink and laugh with him, would humiliate them, and their husbands and children, and then would ride off and never pay for what he took." The old man spoke with a rasp and his hatred of this Vaca was plain.

"Why didn't the village just up and shoot him?"

He looked at me like I was a crazy man, then said, "Shoot him? Vaca? *Senor*, there is not a man within a hundred miles who would have ever dared to try and shoot this one. We all thought he was protected by *El Diablo*, the devil. Vaca has had many fights, and has slain many good men."

He paused, looked me up and down careful, then added, "You do not look to be what you are, *senor*."

I laughed at that. I've been told that before, and maybe for different reasons. I grinned at him and asked, "Just what do I look like?"

He said, "You have the look of a brave man, but a brave man who knows when to be a coward. You do not have the look of one who rushed into danger as you did."

Well, it was a pretty smooth way of telling me he thought I was a mite foolish. Brave, but foolish. But that man didn't grow up with his pa knocking him in the head every time he did or said something foolish. Pa had his own ideas about what was foolish, and for me to let that Vaca shoot my horse and then sell me back one of my own horses while he stole the other would have been plumb foolish to his way of thinking. Pa would have crawled out of his grave and whopped me alongside the head if I'd let that man do me like he wanted. My pa wasn't an educated man, but he was the smartest man I ever knew, and he taught me all about good and bad, and about how to handle folks that try to ride over the top of you. Sometimes a man has to fight, Pa always said, and sometimes a man has to run. I've run a time or two, walked away more times than that, and now and then, I've stayed to fight.

I had my first taste of that when I was just a kid, right after Ma died and I left home for Texas. I had a run-in with a man who tried to choke me to death in a little town along the way to Texas. I cut him with my knife and he nearly died. I came near to hanging over that, but I never have let a man ride roughshod over me. There were a few that had tried, and them that tried were either dead or tired of trying.

I walked back to the dead man and dug into his pockets. He had a little leather pouch and it was heavy with coin. I cut it free and opened it. I calculated there was most of seven hundred dollars worth of gold coins in the pouch. That Vaca must have been doing pretty good at his robbing and killing. I took out a few gold coins, stuck them in my vest and jerked the pouch shut. Then I stripped him of his guns. I tried the action on them, but they just didn't feel right to me. I stuck his guns in my saddle bags. I knew I could sell them over in Texas. I'd have taken his boots, only they were way too big.

But, his sombrero was a perfect fit. I sailed my tattered Stetson across the street. Some kid would likely snatch that up. Wearing that sombrero was like wearing the top of a cook wagon. Wasn't much else but me and shade under that thing, though it was a mite too heavy. Figured I'd get used to it, and if I didn't, I'd trade it off somewhere when I got back to Texas.

I cleared my voice and yelled, "Hey! All you come on out here! I got something for you!"

No one moved, so I asked the old man why they wouldn't come out. He said, "They are frightened of you. You have slain the *amigo* of *Diablo*, so they think you may be a better *amigo* of him than was Vaca."

I laughed. I suppose I never thought of myself as a bad man, but these were superstitious folk, and I could see the old man's point. I said, "And what about you? Do you think that?"

He smiled for the first time and said, "No. I think you are just a man. A *ver'* dangerous man, but *jus'* a man. There *es* more of good in you, *senor*, than there was evil in Vaca."

I asked, "Will you call the people? I want you and your people to have Vaca's money. I already took out what he owed me."

He called them in their own tongue, and they came out real slow, each wanting the other to be just a step or two ahead, just in case I was the friend of the devil.

I took out the sack of coins and began counting. I announced the figure to the people and had the old man repeat it in their tongue. Then, I told them that I wanted them to share it all. He explained what I said and I saw some of them get real excited and begin to talk at each other, hands waving around and their faces all screwed up with excitement. Then, I told them that the old man would distribute it to them because that money would have to be broken down at a bank somewhere so everyone could get his share.

After the old man told them that, I dropped the sack into his hands, picked up the reins of that black and swung into the saddle. That *Mex'* saddle felt pretty good, so I just left it on, but as soon as I got to Texas, I'd sell it and get another one. I knew the one I'd get, too. It was in the livery, was used, but was the most comfortable saddle I'd ever straddled. I had borrowed it once on a horse I'd rented there. The *Mex'* saddle was too heavy, and I never was one for fancy things on a saddle, especially a saddle that glistens. Such things get a man killed, and the extra weight on a horse on a long trail will make for a much slower trip. I swung back to the ground, walked over to my dead horse, stripped off the saddle and carried it over to the little corral. I got it on one of my horses, cinched it tight, then led them both back, and got the old man to get their attention again.

I pointed to the horses and said, "Here's two fine horses, one with a saddle. Make a fine pair for somebody. I'll take two hundred-fifty dollars for the pair, and I'll throw in the saddle, free!"

I think there was one or two in that crowd that understood 'Merican, because they didn't even wait for that old man to explain what I said. Two young men in sandals come up to the old man and talked at him for a little. The old man turned to me and said, "They say that for two hundred pesos, they will buy your horses."

I agreed, took the money from the old man, swung back into the saddle and left. I guess some would call me a fool for not taking all that coin because there wasn't a soul who could have stopped me, but Pa would have been mighty upset to see his boy turn out greedy, and I reckon Ma would have cried. Those people had more a claim on that coin than I did. That crook had stole their food, their women, their time, and I reckon their manhood.

As I rode out of that little village, I saw a couple little brown-skinned kids jerking the pants off Vaca's body. Another was already setting in the street and shoving his feet into Vaca's boots. I had to stop and tell him to take off his sandals. He didn't understand at first because I could only tell him "no," and then point to his sandals, but pretty soon he got the idea. He gave me a grin, shucked those sandals and shoved his feet into the boots.

In a few hours I was near the border.

Texas was looking real good.

CHAPTER 2

I made it back across the border in a day, and in another day I was home in Keyhole, Texas. It was a tiny, dried up town that served about five ranches nearby and wasn't much more than a bunch of claptrap shacks that let the dust blow through. Nothing ever stayed long in Keyhole, not even the dogs, and I found out my time had come to an end when I got back.

I had a job as a kind of marshal there. I got fourteen dollars a month, a room to sleep in, which I had to give up if I arrested anyone, and meals provided. It wasn't much, but there wasn't much trouble, either. I never had any mean kind of trouble, just some rowdy cowboys now and then. It gave me a lot of free time, and I used it to find wild horses which I'd sell to local ranchers, and if they were all full up, to anyone I could find. This last time, I couldn't find nary a soul who'd even look at my mustangs, so that's why I'd ended up south of the border. There were a couple ranches I'd sold to down there in the past, and if I couldn't have sold them in the towns along the way, I'd have sold them to one of the ranchers.

I put away my horse and walked to my room. A few minutes later, a knock sounded and Williams, the mayor and owner of the only store in town, walked in. I gave him a friendly howdy and noticed he didn't look right at me in the eye like a man should. He was a man with something on his mind.

He fidgeted with his apron, then said, "Luke, I've some bad news for you."

"Spit it out, Williams." I hate to fool around with folks who can't speak their minds right out. I've got no patience with them.

He sighed, then said, "Luke, I've been elected to tell you that we don't need you any more."

I grinned at him. "You mean you're all getting wise to the fact that there's not much need for a lawman, here?"

He blushed, then said, "Luke, I like you. I wish you could stay, but they won't listen to me."

"What's the problem, then?"

"Luke, you remember that cowboy you had to knock down and throw in the horse trough a couple weeks ago?"

I remembered that one. He'd been kind of rowdy, and I'd have let him go on, except he got to shooting his gun and I was afraid he might hit someone. I nodded.

He said, "Well, that was the ramrod for the Bar-T. That's the spread run by..."

"I know who it's run by. Russ Meyers isn't exactly a stranger to me, Williams."

"Yeah. Well, Meyers came into town a day after you went across the border and told the town that unless they got rid of you, that he and his riders wouldn't be coming here anymore, and instead, they would ride the extra ten miles to Red Bluff." He cleared his throat and continued, "The town figures it can't afford the loss, Luke."

I walked to the back room, threw my few rags into my bag and slung it across my shoulders. I stopped as I passed Williams and said, "It's been nice knowing you all." I left and went over to the saloon and got Brady, the barkeep, to pay me off. It was only seven dollars, but we fussed some because I'd figured it out to be nine dollars. But, I gave in finally because he got to throwing numbers at me called fractions, and I couldn't argue those kind of numbers with him.

I knew I'd been there too long. Some of them hadn't wanted me in the first place on account of my being handy with a gun, but they'd give in when a scare had gone around on account of some *Mex'* raiders nearby.

I had run the job for nearly a year, and had a little trouble from Meyers in the beginning, but after I run a *hardcase* out of town, things quieted down and Meyers quit pushing at me. But, I guess he was just waiting for a good excuse to run me off. I had given some thought to leaving before because the job had got to be pretty dull, and the pay wasn't as much as I could get riding herd, but I'd kept putting it out of my mind. This had been a job where I could take off just about any time I wanted, as long as things were quiet.

I headed for a ranch over near the Brazos, the Slash-Bar outfit. I'd met a few of that bunch once while selling horses in a town near there, and they seemed to be a good bunch. The owner, a man called Blackjack Reston, was the owner, and he was supposed to be a real tough *hombre*, but fair as any man. I know being black or white didn't matter much to him because I'd seen two black cowboys, and one or two *injun* cowboys in his bunch. I knew he took on men with a past because one of his riders who bought a horse from me was Tyler Coom, the Kansas City gunman. Being handy with a gun didn't matter to Reston. Only question with him was whether a man could chase cows out of the brush.

It took me a couple days to locate the ranch. I'd have made it there sooner, only some kid give me a bum steer on where it was at. I don't know if he was just mixed up or if he did it on purpose, but it cost me a half a day's ride. I pulled into the ranch in the late afternoon when everyone was eating, and I guess my temper was wearing just a little thin. I was still aggravated at that kid.

The cook saw me walk in and slung another tin plate out onto the table. I sat down with a nod at everyone, and in a minute he was slopping beans out onto my plate. I reached out, took a big hunk of cornbread to go with it and got to wondering if this was the daily fare. I been on a ranch once where the only thing we ever got was beans, biscuits, and now and then some beef. I already had my share of those kinds of meals. I was grateful for this meal, but I wasn't too fond of beans. Not steady, anyway. Me and beans could part company and I'd never miss them.

One of the men spoke to me in between mouthfuls. He asked, "Looking for work?"

I nodded, and he said, "Ain't none to be had around here. We got all the drifters we want on this ranch. Eat up and ride out."

I asked, "You the boss, here?"

One man cut in, "Latimer's a boss alright. He bosses his old lady—when she lets him!"

They all got a good laugh out of that, and I watched the red come up from his neck. He jerked a bite out of a piece of cornbread, and suddenly, I had the feeling he was wishing I was the one who'd joshed him. I saw right off that he was just one of those kind of men who wants to be taken serious all the time, only everyone knows him and they always do the opposite of what he wants. He glared at the other man and then looked back to me.

"I ain't no boss, but I'm telling what he'd tell you." He took another big bite off that chunk of cornbread he was holding, and I think he was wishing it was me he was taking a bite out of.

I smiled at him and said, "Reckon I'll do my asking anyhow."

One huge black man sitting way to the rear said, "Aw, don't let Latimer bother you none. Boss was talking about getting some new riders on just the other day. If you can set a saddle and sling a rope, he'll hire you."

Latimer got red in the face again and stood up. He moved away from the bench and walked to where this man was sitting. The other man looked up to him and said, "Now Latimer, I done whupped you once. I can do it twice if you've a mind for it."

That cook come in with a big stick and whacked it on the table. It startled most all of us, and he said loudly, "Ain't no fighting done at my table! You boys take your troubles outside."

Latimer glared some more, this time at the cook, because I think he was ready to take advantage of that black cowboy, only maybe he was remembering some things about that whuppin' he'd gotten. Then, he glared at me and as he walked back, he said, "I'll take care of you later."

I figured things was done with and went back to chewing that cornbread and beans, but Latimer had a different idea. Some men are like that. They got to try you,and got to see what their position is going to be in the grub line.

He was silent for a few minutes, but he kept looking up from his beans and glaring at me. I could see it working in him. Finally, he glared at me and said, "You best be riding cowboy." He chewed some more on his beans, then, with a gruff, angry tone added, "Now! You've had enough to eat."

I kept on chewing and ignored him. He leaned forward and his breath like to have chased me from the table. It smelled like he had a wad of 'chaw' in his mouth, mingled with cornbread. It was awful, and I waved a hand in front of my nose and made a face.

I leaned back, trying to get away from his breath, and he said, "You ain't off this ranch in one more minute, they're gonna carry you off!"

I looked down the table at the others and asked, "He try this with every new man?" No one answered. They were all curious, I knew, about how I'd handle him. I'd sat in on a few incidents just like this, only with me one of the bunch watching while one of the boys tried to rawhide a new rider. Now, it was my turn.

I shrugged my shoulders, stood, and moved back from the table. I said, "Looks like I got to finish this meal later." I walked to the door, stopped, turned back and said to Latimer, "Soon as I beat some manners into you!"

He blinked a time or two like he didn't believe what he was hearing, then shoved himself away from the table and stomped to the door. I got out in front of the corral and waited. He moved up slow to me, fists held up and kind of out in front, like I saw a real boxer do once. I wondered if maybe I hadn't got mixed up with more than I could handle. The room had emptied behind him, with most staying on the porch in the shade, some still holding their tin plates and eating. They were enjoying this.

We circled, careful of each other. I was thinking of how I hated to move around much just after a meal, more than I was thinking of how to punch on that man. Probably, I should have been paying more attention, because suddenly, he threw a couple of wicked punches at me and caught me with both of them, one in the chest and the other on the right side of the jaw. I woke up a second or two later in the dust staring at the cloudless, Texas-blue sky. I rolled over and was coming up when he got me another good one, only I saved it from being as bad as it could have been by falling with the punch. It was one of those punches a man swings from behind his back, and if I hadn't fell with it some, I'd have went all the way down and for certain, out.

I come out of the dirt mad, now. I had a mouth full of dust, and he had hurt me, plus he'd spoiled my supper. I felt blood splashing down from my nose and hoped he hadn't broken my nose. It had been broken three times already.

I wiped at it with my sleeve and moved slowly towards the man. He was enjoying himself, feeling certain he'd put enough hurt and fear in me to win the fight. Funny thing about me, though. I'm not much in a fight unless I'm good and riled. I've lost a couple fights on account of that, and almost lost this one before I even threw a punch because of it.

But, I was mad, now. I came at him, ducked as he threw a right fist over my head, then I straightened and slammed him hard in the gut twice, backed off, then leaned one into his face as hard as I could. He squalled loud like a steer being branded and ended with a roar of pain. He staggered back holding his face, blood spurting from his nose and from between his fingers.

I moved in and hammered two hard ones to his gut, and slammed him with a left that caught him flush on the jaw. He toppled like a big tree that met a saw, landing hard on his back. He rolled over moaning, then struggled to get to his knees. I had to admire him. I never had a man get up from a punch like that. It was my best shot, and he wasn't out.

I was all set to level him with another punch as he got up, when this powerful, booming voice sounded, "Let him go! He's beaten."

I turned towards the sound, and this short, barrel of a man came walking down the steps of the house. He had one of those calf-skin vests, all white and brown, and was bareheaded. The top of his head was slick and shiny, like a brown rock that's seen a million winds and an ocean of rain.

He walked up to me and stuck out his hand, "I'm Blackjack Reston." He gave me a long hard look deep in the eyes, then glanced at the man I'd licked, then back to me.

I took his hand. "Luke Adams, sir, and looking for a job."

He looked over at Latimer and said, "Good! I can use a couple good riders. You handle cows before?" He stepped back and looked me over again.

"Yes sir. I worked cows at a couple places, and even went on a drive or two. Once to Kansas, once to Colorado. Me and cows ain't exactly strangers."

He laughed and said, "Have Slim get you a couple horses. I'll put you in the book. You'll draw thirty a month and all the beans you can eat, plus all the horseflesh you can use up." He paused, looked over to Latimer and called out: "Latimer! You're done. I won't have a man working for me who picks fights and then can't win them!"

Reston turned back to me and said, "My ramrod is 'Red' Conners. He'll be in late, so he'll give you your orders in the morning." He glared at everyone a few seconds, then turned and stomped back into the house.

I got along with all those men. There were a couple who would get *proddy* now and then, but it usually had to do with being tired, or it being early in the morning. There wasn't a mean man in that bunch after Latimer left. And old man Reston never fussed with us much and left most of the bossing to Red, who was the best ramrod I ever rode for.

I probably would have been happy enough to stay at that ranch for a longer time than I did, only some trouble came up. It was shooting trouble and it even got the Texas Rangers after me. Worse than that, it put a shadow on my trail that followed me, and when it found me, brought death.

CHAPTER 3

I had worked there a couple years when I had some bad trouble. Up to then, about all I had was a couple fights, one was sort of friendly, and the other more a shoving match, with neither one of us wanting to expend the energy on a fight. Mostly, life was riding, chasing mossy backs, and eating hardtack that was flavored with crunchy beans, and now and then, some beef.

My bad trouble came about on a bright, eye-squinting Texas day. The boss gave out orders as usual that morning. Me, and a black rider named Spoon, called that because of a big spoon he always carried in his pocket, were to go up to the north section and chase some strays down towards the ranch. It was going to be a two or three day job, and Spoon wasn't too keen on spending that much time with me, even though we got along all right. I think it had to do with my cooking, which was just a shade better than his, which is to say, it was terrible.

Spoon had swore he'd never eat my cooking again after the time my stew turned his spoon black. I never figured for sure what done his spoon that way, unless it was those hot peppers I threw in. I do remember neither of us could eat much of it because it was too hot, and they hurt my stomach. I swore off hot peppers after that.

As we rode out, Spoon was grumbling and I was whistling, because I liked getting away from everyone else for awhile, even if it was chasing old mossy-backs through sagebrush and thorns sharp enough to slit a good pair of chaps, or your horse's leg, if you weren't careful. It was hard, but a cowboy was on his own, never hearing a boss yell at him, no branding or fence jobs, and none of the ordinary kind of work.

We got to this little line shack in the early afternoon, riding slow and remembering the times we'd been this way before. Spoon hobbled the horses, slipped off the saddles, then gave them a quick rub-down while I scrounged around for some wood for a fire. Then, Spoon led the other two horses we'd brought for changes into a small corral. We planned to give our mounts a blow, then, that late afternoon, ride on over to get a quick count of cows and maybe move them down closer to us. That's all we'd do for this day.

We both sat up against the side of the shack where it was shaded, because the insides of that place was like an oven. We hadn't rested there more than two snorts of a tired horse when we spotted three riders coming our way. They were coming at a kind of lope, not in a hurry, but headed our way for certain. I noticed them fan out slightly as they spotted us. They also slowed to a walk.

I stood, and so did Spoon. I could tell he was nervous because he kept wiping his hands on his pants. I didn't let on, but I was some worried, too. It's not often a body will see another rider this far out, let alone three of them, and when you do, the chances are good they're hard riders looking back on their trail for a lawman or a posse.

Spoon asked, "What they want, Luke? What you think they want?" I could feel the fear rising in him and his voice was pitched a little higher than usual.

The leader, the one riding out front and looking like he belonged there, walked his sorrel over to us and swung out of the saddle. He moved careful, and his step was soft, not even making the leather creak. That man had some cat in him for sure. I glanced at his gun holster, which was not ordinary. It was well-worn, but with the kind of wear that comes from practice—lots of it.

I knew he was more than just good with his gun. He had the look. The grips on the big forty-five Colt was black, and it looked like a well-used tool. Lot of cowboys have guns, but most don't use them. They carry them for snakes and coyotes and such. His hung at his side at just the right distance, and I could tell from the way he carried himself, he was ready.

The other two sat still in the saddle, spread out just a little. I wasn't scared, but my gut was tight, and I was primed. Pa always said that a man who didn't smile when he came onto you was one to watch close. Not one of these riders had a smile or even a howdy— just some hard stares.

The Cat Foot man spoke up: "We got word you boys been moving some beef now and then that don't belong to you." He pushed his hat back a little and I could see enough hard in that man's eyes to know he was ready to do us harm. He was just waiting like a cat watches a bird.

I think they all thought we were going to try and talk about it and explain how they had the wrong men and such, but I been raised different than most folk. That man had accused us of rustling, and there's just one thing they do to rustlers in Texas and that is string them up high, unless they can shoot them first. Beside that, I knew that a couple of rag-tag punchers' word was worth about as much as a spent bullet three feet in front of a deer.

It's easy to criticize what I did next, because I'll admit I was awful sudden, but these were hard times and those was hard men, and they were set to hang us both or shoot us. Only thing, they figured on taking a couple of riders who could sling rope. They weren't ready for somebody who growed up slinging a gun. Shuckin' a gun was something I'd done most every day of my life since I was a *yonker*, when my Pa stuck his old forty-four down the front of my pants and said it was mine to carry when we were on the trail.

I didn't waste words with denying his charge. One minute I'm standing polite and the next, I had my Colt shucked and lined up on Cat Foot with the hammer eared back. Surprise washed over their faces. I'd shucked that gun pretty fast, and I could see they were doing some re-thinking about who I was.

I'd worked on jerking my gun out every day of my life when I was just a kid in Kentucky. My Pa used to make me carry my gun shoved down the front of my pants, and I had to get that big gun shucked sudden-like in order to hit them rabbits and squirrels. He reckoned that having to hunt like that would help me learn to shuck a gun sudden. It did.

Cat Foot, he didn't move, but he just watched me with them green eyes. He was hard, that man, and not scared a bit.

I looked him square in his green eyes and said, "Boys, I'm not real certain where you got your information, but whoever gave it to you almost got some of you dead. I never rustled a cow in my life and neither has my friend, here." I smiled, showing my teeth, because I wanted to let them riders know I didn't hold a grudge against them.

One rider, a kid of maybe twenty, with a squinty way of looking, spoke up and said, "You ain't but one and your partner there don't even count. You're all alone, mister." He smiled, squinted at me and added, "We got you."

I took the smile out of my eyes and off my face. "Kid, in ordinary times I'd just take one of your ears off, but I'm peaceful and I'm letting it slide. But if you get any ideas, you'll be leavin' your saddle backwards."

I moved to the side where I could get a good view of the kid, where his horse's head was not in my way, then I added, "Kid, don't think I can't be pushed into a war, here." I paused a long moment, looking directly at him, then said softly, "Might be I'll miss and take more than your ear off, though."

The kid looked at the man on his right, then to the Cat Foot man, then back to me. He wanted someone else to take it up, but nobody said a word.

Then, the Cat Foot man held up his hand and said gently, "Back off, Ben. The man's holding all the aces, and this man isn't one to push. Take my word on it. He doesn't need the other one for help, here."

I put my smile back on and said, "Glad you see it my way. I don't want no war." I moved to one side, my gun not wavering off the man with the green eyes, then added, "We ride for Blackjack Reston. Have for years, and we're chasin' strays down. You can check it out. You got the wrong boys."

Cat Foot sighed, gave an angry glance at the kid called Ben, then said, "We don't want a war, either. I'm thinking we were a bit sudden, here. One of us had a bad idea." He was staring hard at the man called Ben as he spoke.

I saw him relaxed around his eyes watched as the tension left him. He fiddled some with the bridle on his horse's head and said, "We're trailin' a couple riders. We'll get some water and keep lookin', if it's all the same with you."

What happened next was pure foolishness on my part. I got taken with that Cat Foot man, got to liking him. And, when he eased off, I did the same. So, in spite of my instincts, I slid my Colt back in the holster at my belly.

My pa would have reminded me right then, if he was alive, about the time we met a she-bear and her cubs on a morning trail back in Kentucky. We was both some surprised, and Pa and me just stared at that old bear while she reared up and stared right back. Pa didn't make any move with the rifle, just held it pointing her way like it was when we come on her. She stared a long minute, then jumped off into the bushes and was gone. I was all for following, but Pa took me by the shoulder and said, "Son, when you meet up with a mean critter, if you can have peace, have it. Don't be laying aside your gun to have it, but don't be chasing after trouble either."

Well, I didn't chase this trouble, but I did lay aside my gun, and I never should have done that. I knew the Cat Foot man didn't want a fight. He was like that she-bear, not scared, but wise enough to know when to move off the trail. That kid though, he was like a dog when you take away a piece of meat he's about to sink his teeth into.

He just went mean all of a sudden.

Even though I'd put away my Colt, I was still watching close. Hadn't been that I was still watching, I might have missed the kid's move because he drew his gun without me seeing it. All I caught was his wild eyes and the twitch of his right shoulder, and I dove for the dirt, yelling for Spoon to do the same as me. That kid got a shot off, but it went into the dirt right beside his own horse because my shot took him clean out of the saddle backwards, just like I promised. I heard him scream and heard him hit the ground with a heavy thud. He made no sound after that.

Cat Foot put a shot that clipped the top out of my ear, only I didn't know that until later. I put two shots his way quick, rolled fast and put one at the other rider. I heard the soft chunk as it smacked into the rider, and he grabbed for the saddle horn, but missed and piled into the dirt. It didn't kill him though, because he was laying there yelling that he was hit. I was rolling in the dirt again even before he hit the ground and was about to line up on Cat Foot when I heard him yell for me to hold up.

I got out of the dirt and edged over toward the shack, my gun still out and pointed towards the Cat Foot man. Spoon was on his back with a big smear of blood all over his chest, and that Cat Foot man was holding onto his saddle with one hand and wincing with pain. He still had his gun lined up on me, and I saw the dark stain all over his pant leg. Spoon had put one in him and he'd put one in Spoon.

Cat Foot called out, "No more, cowboy! No more war." He holstered his gun to show he was for peace, and I slid mine back into the holster, but still keeping an eye out. There was no way he was going to get that gun lined on me before I got one in him. I'm not bragging. I just know what I can do with a gun, and it was just him and me, now.

I watched him limp over to the rider who yelling about being hit, then I went over to Spoon. He was crying, and I got to admit I was kind of ashamed at him because I was raised different, I guess. I suppose I shouldn't have held it against Spoon, because he was dying and he knew it.

His eyes rolled up, focused on me, then tears began running over. I looked away, because like I said, I was raised different and it made me ashamed. He said, "Luke, I ain't ready to die." He choked some, then in a voice that would have broke his mama's heart said,, "God, you ain't gonna let me die out here, is you?"

I tried hard to comfort Spoon, but I never was very good with words in such cases. I did say a prayer for him and he calmed some after that.

Spoon talked about being bad and about doing some things he wished he hadn't done in his life, and he said he wished he'd stayed on the Jesus road. I talked to him some about Jesus, remembering some of the things my Ma used to tell me. That gave him comfort, I could tell.

I stopped, and he said, "More, Luke. Tell me more. Tell me about Jesus."

I told him how the Good Book said he was going to be going with Jesus. My ma used to make me go to church with her, and though it never really took with me, she was a Bible quoting woman. I wished now I'd remembered some of those verses she used to quote at me. I told him a few stories I remembered, like the one about Samsom and a couple others, though I probably didn't get them right. I was quiet for a long time and he looked up at me with them deep, dark eyes full of pain and said, "Go on, Luke. Tell me more." His voice got down to a whisper.

I told him about the time Jesus got beat up by a bunch of men like the ones who had shot him, and how Jesus had come down and died to take care of all the bad we'd done; and I told him how a sinner had to quit his hard living and had to pray to get into heaven. At that, he wanted me to pray with him, but I didn't know what to say. Then, I remembered the story about the crook that died with Jesus, so I told him that story, and how the crook went to heaven even though he was a bad man, too, like me and Spoon, and all he done was ask polite to be remembered. He really liked that story and asked me to tell it to him again.

Spoon told me he used to read the Good Book, and once, when he was a young man, declared that he was going to be a preachin' man, but soon after that he'd had gotten away from God and the church, and got to drinking and running with some bad company. I told him he was about to get into some real good company. He smiled at that, then died. I laid him back against the side of the shack. It had taken him about fifteen minutes to die.

I stood, then walked over to Cat Foot and his partner. I was sad, but I was also mad. I stopped and just stood there, looking at the two of them. Cat Foot stood there easy, waiting to see which way the wind blew. The other man laid there moaning some, the scared showing all over his face.

I said, "We both lost a partner and I'm for letting things lay as they are." I know if it hadn't been for Cat Foot talking peace before that kid started shooting, I'd have started the war all over. But, we both knew the kid had set off the war and that neither of us had really wanted it to happen.

Cat Foot look at me and said, "I owe you this much, mister." He jerked a knot tighter in the neckerchief he'd wrapped around his leg, then continued, "You shot the son of Amos Briner. Now, even though it was the kid's idea to come up here and it was his fault for startin' the ball, you best be ridin' because Amos Briner will take this hard." He winced as he shifted his weight, then added, "He'll hunt you." He paused a long moment, then added, "He'll hunt you hard and when he gets you, he'll hang you."

He wiped the sweat off his brow with the back of his shirt sleeve, put the hat back on and said, "Amos has some riders on the payroll that are snake-mean and sleep with their guns. Fact is, some of them have seen the insides of 'dobe walls with bars on the windows for being too handy with their gun. They'll be the ones after you."

I had to ask him, "What about you? You gonna be riding after me, too?"

He gave that hard smile of his and said, "No. I'm certain my days of riding for Amos Briner is over. I let his kid die and didn't bring back the one that did it. Amos will never forgive that." He looked at his partner and added, "Only reason I'm ridin' back is to bring Tuck and the boy home and tell him what happened. I'll leave after that."

"Will you tell him how it happened? Tell him I never wanted to kill anyone?"

He nodded. "Yeah, I'll tell him exactly how it happened, but knowing Amos, truth won't much matter. Ben never could do wrong in the old man's eyes, and Amos couldn't see the side of the kid you and me saw today."

They rode out and I stood there looking down at Spoon for a long time, thinking about things. Finally, I went in the shack, threw a couple cans of beans in a sack, filled my canteen, and made some coffee. I gave serious thought to riding over to Briner's spread and facing up to it, but I gave up on that thought. I've known too many men like Briner. They're tough and hard like the land they fight every day of their life. He'd likely have me hanged on the spot and never give one minutes listen to my side of it.

In fact, likely it wouldn't matter to him that his kid was wrong. Probably, that was why the kid was mean. His pa never took him to task for his wrongs like mine done. Pa whipped me more times that I care to recall, and my ma was no piker when it come to handing out *lickins* either. My pa once told me that if I ever went bad and they set out to hang me for my crimes, he wouldn't come and watch, but he wouldn't be there to stop it, either. I don't think Amos Briner saw things like my pa did.

After I buried Spoon, I left a note to the boss explaining things, then I stocked up and made ready for my long ride out of Texas. I figured that once I got to the New Mexico Territory, I would be safe. I took my horse and one of the horses Spoon and I had brought with us. I didn't figure the boss would hold it against me on account of what had been done and because of wages I was due. In an hour, I was five miles from the line shack and in four days, I was near the Canadian River.

I was resting up in some hills when I spied some riders coming slow. I've been trailed three times in my life, and this looked to be the hardest run of them all because the riders in this bunch weren't ordinary. This bunch was good at trailing, and it seemed that they might have an *injun* with them because I never met a white man could track like they were doing me. I'd taken real care to cover my trail. No ordinary rider was going to track me this quick, I knew. I figured the tracker to either be an *injun* or someone who used to scout for the army. Whoever it was, he was good.

I wondered if they talked with the farmer I got some water and milk from a couple days ago. Texas is one dry place in the summer and I had no choice but to get something wet in me. It was mighty sweet milk, that water was cool, and the biscuits that were thrown in were tasty, but it looked like it was going to cost me more than the dollar I'd given.

After another day of riding, I knew it was going to be impossible to shake those riders. There was seven of them, and one was riding without a saddle, so my guess about the *injun* was true. Also, they were trailing a nice string of remounts along behind. They'd come for a long trail and they weren't likely to have to turn back on account of tired horse flesh.

I began planning for my war ground right then. Pa always told me that if I had to get in a war, that I should do as best I could to get on grounds that was good for me and bad for the other side. So, I scouted for good ground. I also began to rest my mount, walking alongside him part of the time. I shucked my boots and tugged a pair of store shoes from my saddle bags. I'd gotten those a few years back and always carried them for walking. They were soft on the feet and had a good feel to them.

In a couple of days, I found some ground that was favorable to my side. There was a tumble of boulders large enough to give shade and to hide a couple horses in, and just right to make my ambush. Them boulders were sprawled around like God took a handful and just tossed them at that spot, letting them fall whichever way they wanted. It gave shade around, with grass for the horses, and there was water in a couple places. I knew they'd follow me in here and I hoped they'd make camp here because of the water. It was a likely spot for a camp, and I'd have made one myself, but I was afraid of the scout coming up on me there.

That *injun* would surely know about the water, but just in case, I made a couple little mistakes so they'd be sure and spot my trail. It wasn't the kind of mistake most men would make. That tracker would get suspicious if I started leaving clear sign when before, I'd been making it hard. So, once I scraped my horse's dung off the ground and hid it under a bush just like I'd done all the time I'd been running, but I left a little trace of it that most men would miss. I knew that *injun* would spot it, though.

I also made sure that I slopped some water around on the ground as I wiped my horse's nostrils out. That was mighty cooling for any horse, and mine appreciated it. The water would evaporate, but it'd leave the dirt looking different, and that *injun* tracker wouldn't miss it. Later, I urinated on the side of the trail and made sure I splashed around some on a bush. He'd notice the dust missing off that bush.

I rested a couple hours, then I rode out of that bunch of rocks on a dead run, like I was scared. They'd think I spotted them and was in too big a hurry to worry about my trail. Then, getting back in control, I walked both horses over some rocks in one place. You get a tracker with savvy, and if you throw a change at him, he'll suspect something right off. If you had been hiding your trail good, then you start making it easy, that tracker is going to know something isn't right. I wanted that *injun* to think I rode through that bunch of rocks, got some water, headed out scared, then got a hold of myself and went back to hiding my trail. He'd spot the long stride and the deep prints of the run and figure I was scared.

I was counting on that.

After most of three miles, I circled wide and headed back, aiming to come back into those rocks from the south side. I wanted to be on the far side of where that bunch rode in. I figured them to be a few hours or less behind. If I was lucky, they'd reach this spot late in the day, but if they came through here early in the day, I'd just have to let them pass and try for another ambush, unless they decided to camp early in the day.

It was late that afternoon when they come riding in, moving slow, that *injun* way out front, leaning over now and then as he eye-balled my trail. He was skinny, but the meat that was showing was all tough. That man could have tracked me down on foot. I got a lot of respect for what those *injun* trackers can do.

I eased back into the rocks, because I got this feeling in me that one of the riders, especially that *injun*, might sense that I was there looking at them. I've done felt too many looks, and I just got to figure some folks can feel it like I can, especially if I'm all primed for trouble. Time to watch a man is when he's not expecting trouble, when he's relaxed and off-guard. Then, you got a good chance he won't sense you. But, there's a lot of men who couldn't tell you were looking at them if you were breathing on their neck. These riders weren't like that. They had that look about them that said they were ready, had been hunted and they been hunting, too. I would take no chances with men like that.

All the riders pulled up and began walking the horses, except the *injun*. I heard him trot off and I knew he'd be following the trail on out for a mile or two, satisfying himself that I was gone. The rest began slipping off the saddles and making camp. That *injun* must have told them of the water, because they got to looking around for it. I got worried that they'd stumble on me by accident, but as luck would have it the *injun* came riding back and told them where to look.

They settled down in various spots, talking soft, and now and then some cussing would cause their voice to get louder. I figured that was for me and what they were having to go through chasing me across half of Texas.

The sun finally dropped out of the sky and cool settled in the rocks. Mighty strange how it can be so hot and then get so cold in just a short time. I just laid back in them rocks enjoying the cool, because that sun had dried me out real bad.

I waited until long into the night, way after all those rider except one, had settled in their bed rolls. Only one I had some worries over was the *injun*. That one looked more and more to me like part mountain lion, and I was going to have to move real quiet to keep him from getting my wind.

When I finally stirred, it was with some slow, careful movements. What I had in mind was to slow them riders up some. There was no way I was going to take them all out, but I'd make them a whole lot more careful on my trail. They'd learn what it meant to hunt Luke Adams.

I crawled on my belly down next to the camp, trying to look like a rock, or a dark shadow. I got to admit, it was a help having a skin that was burnt by that Texas sun to a deep brown. I looked almost the same as a shadow does. A body would have had to have looked close and hard to have spotted me.

I went in among the horses easy, not spooking a one, rubbing a nose here and there, never standing up all the way. On each horse's back, right where the saddle would sit, I made a careful, shallow slit in the skin with my knife. I always keep my knife honed sharp as any razor, so them horses didn't do more than wiggle their skin, like if a horsefly would bite them. It wouldn't take too much sweating and rubbing to work those slits open wide and make a sore. It was a low down, mean thing to do, I know, but when a body's in a war, there's just one rule*: win it.*

What I had to do next was almost as hard, because I never, in my born days, least until then, had shot at a man from ambush, and worse, in his bedroll. It went against the grain, and maybe Pa didn't squirm none in his grave, because he'd understand, but I know Ma rolled over a time or two. It had to be done, though, especially to that *injun*. I had to take him out. They could get more horses from a ranch, but good trackers like that *injun* would be hard to come by.

I aimed my rifle low because there was no sense in killing that tracker. I held no grudge against him. He was just doing what he was paid to do. Likely, he wasn't getting more than a cow for his family for all his trouble. Whatever he was getting, I knew it wasn't worth what I was about to give him.

The shot split open the night and busted that camp fast. I saw the *injun* roll toward cover, holding onto his leg where I'd popped him. Most men would have squalled like a calf at branding, but he never whimpered or made a sound. The others were jumping and hollering so much you'd have thought they were the ones hit. Bodies were diving for cover and rolling in the dirt. I never heard such carrying on since Pa tried to clobber a weasel after our chickens.

I got in a couple more shots, missing one rolling blanket, then I hit someone running and he squealed like a scalded dog, fell across the campfire and began rolling. He wouldn't die, but he wouldn't be riding soon, either. The others just fell into the night, and suddenly, it was as quiet as a Texas rain in the summer.

I slid off the rock I was on and made it back to my horses. It was no place to be hanging around. In minutes, I was traveling away into the night, and I figured it would be a couple hours, maybe even daybreak, before they were able to decide I wasn't around no more. By then, I would be long gone. They might trail me, but no sore-backed horse was going to catch this rider. They might not be scared of me, but I had their respect, now. And, they'd be sore-footed by the time they got back home.

CHAPTER 4

First ranch I spied, I nosed my horses that way. I was getting lean from eating jackrabbits and quail, plus a little jerky I had. My ponies were feeling the pinch, too, and I noticed that one was taking me shorter than before. She put me to mind of Fred, the old mule I come to Texas on. He'd go until he didn't feel like going no more, then he'd stop cold. I'd kick him in the ribs, he'd go a little further, then stop some more. He was a mighty stubborn mule, and I wasn't too sorry the day he got stole by some *injuns.*

It was a nice looking little place, setting there on a high mesa with a few scrawny pines around it. There wasn't a bunk house so I figured it was a family just getting started, or else a man trying on his own with the family waiting for him to make it. Met a couple of men who did that, and it makes good sense, because a body doesn't know what hard times are until he starts to run cows. You got to fight rustlers, drought, *injuns,* and *northers* that'd blow your cows right onto the next ranch.

I rode up slow, enjoying the wind as it snapped my hat back and billowed out my shirt. I pulled up in the yard and helloed the house. I saw the door crack open. A man hollered, "Who are you and what do you want?"

When a man greets you like that, it isn't natural. Mostly, when a man rides up into a yard, he gets a "howdy" and an invite to eat. Most folks are hungry for talk, especially those stuck way out miles from any town or neighbors, like this one. I folded my hands on the horn of my saddle so he could see I was peaceful, then answered, "Just a tired cowboy looking for water, food and work, 'bout in that order."

A man walked out onto the porch, and I guess he was the biggest man I ever laid eyes on, even bigger than that *Mex' bandito* I had trouble with a few years before. He would have made two of me, and I'm not exactly small. It looked to me when the good Lord made that man, he forgot for a minute what he was doing and instead of putting human meat on them bones, he threw some steer meat into the mix. The man was Texas beef in boots if I ever saw it. He was wide and he was high, and a carbine dangled from his right hand, pointed down but in my general direction.

"Who'd you work for last, stranger?"

The way he said it wasn't so much like asking a question as he was commanding me to answer him. He reminded me of my pa. I said, "Rode for the Slash-Bar outfit near the Brazos." I looked at him a second, then added, "Texas."

He frowned and said, "Blackjack's spread?"

I shouldn't have been surprised that he'd know my boss because old Blackjack rode enough trails and pushed enough cows out of Texas so that a lot of men might know of him. But, here I was so far off and a man standing there who knew him. It was a pleasant surprise. I said, "Yeah, that's the one."

He said, "I used to ride for him. Meanest piece of flesh in boots I ever knew."

"Yeah, he could be mean," I agreed.

"Why'd you leave?"

I hesitated. Out here, most men don't talk much about where they come from or why they left where they were on account of so many of them being on the dodge, or running from some kind of trouble. But, he'd asked, and I had a feeling that if I didn't tell him I'd be riding on by with nary a bite of grub and barely a drink of water. It took me about a couple minutes, with him standing on the porch, rifle dangling from his hand, and me setting on my horse with the wind snapping my hat brim back and blowing out my shirt.

He grunted, then said, "Reckon I'd have done the same." Then, he invited me in for some food.

I stripped my horse, the black I'd got in Mexico, and hobbled both horses. I'd taken a real liking to that black, except for one bad habit he had, which was to try and mash my foot every time I stood close by him. I named him 'Mash' on account of that.

The inside of that house was a lot like the outside, mostly bare and unpainted. Cracks in the boards let the wind come sifting through, and come winter, I reckon that shack wouldn't be much on keeping a body warm. He had some can labels stuck up over some of the cracks, along with a few old newspapers spread across the walls, hung by old nails and splinters. When the cold came blowing across the rim of the ridge, that paper wasn't going to stop too much of anything.

He turned from a big iron stove where he'd just lit a fire, stuck out a giant hand and said, "Name is Smith. John Smith."

I told him my name and he said, "You might have the Rangers after you. Ever think of that?"

I said, "It was a fair fight and wasn't no reason for the law to mix in. You think they're in on this hunt for me?"

I liked Smith right off. He was a plain speaking man, direct, and without that way of sidling up to a point like some men have. If something was on his mind, I had a feeling it didn't rest there long. He'd just drag it on out.

He shook his head, frowned at me and said, "You've got to understand that there's some things working against you that can't be beat. It's a stacked deck, and there ain't no way you're going to change it." He walked over to the stove and stirred whatever was bubbling in his big black pot.

"First thing you have against you is who you killed. If it was just some drifter, you'd likely be all right. But, you had to shoot the son of a man most everyone in Texas knows. I know Amos Briner. Met him twice. He swung a wide loop when he first rode into Texas, and I reckon his roundups weren't always carrying the right brands, but he was a man of his word. If he made a promise, the devil wouldn't change his mind. He's known to be a hard man, one of the early men into that part of Texas. His daddy rode with Austin to Mexico, and Amos knew Houston personal. He'll spend every penny he's got to get you hung or shot, legal or otherwise."

The big man stopped stirring, and without even using a rag, took the heavy, steaming pot off the stove and brought it over to the table. I kept looking for the smoke to start coming from his hands, but he must have had steer hide for skin as well. He plopped it down and threw a battered tin plate at me.

"Dig in!" he ordered.

I lit into that stuff, whatever it was, because I was as starved as a wolf on the far side of winter. I gulped down three heaping spoons of whatever it was and quickly decided Smith never had to eat his own cooking for long, else he'd have been dead by now. It was the worst stuff I ever sunk a tooth into, but what got me to gagging and blinking was that it tasted like he accidentally got some of the fire wood in it. My mouth was on fire and my eyes were brimming with tears. Suddenly, I got the hic-cups. That was when I bolted for the door, heading for the well. I couldn't help but think of Spoon and the time I put all those hot peppers in our food and it turned his spoon black. Maybe him and Jesus had got together after all.

Smith came out on the porch and stood there watching, feeding his face. In between chews, he talked. "Guess I ought to have told you. This here is my Half 'n Half Stew."

I swallowed another dipper of water, glared at him and said, "Don't tell me. It's half of hell and half brimstone."

He though that was pretty funny and got to laughing so hard he choked on a mouthful, then got to spitting and stomping. It stuck me funny, so I got to laughing at him, and there we stood, me laughing like a fool, blinking back the tears from the fire in my mouth, and him choking, stomping and laughing.

Finally, with tears streaming down his cheeks, getting soaked up into that big black beard of his, he stopped and said, laughing as he spoke, "Stranger, that's called Half 'n Half Stew. That stew is half a pot of green chili peppers and half a pot of red chili peppers. I throw a little flour in for flavor, and some chunks of mutton or beef, if I got it. Today, it was mutton." He took off laughing again, which set me off to laughing, too. We were worse than a couple of *yonkers*.

That evening he took out his pipe, stretched out on the porch, and when he had it going, said, "You got something else working against you, boy." He peered at me real keen, took a puff off his pipe and went on: "Being good with that gun don't help you none. There's some good folks down in Texas who don't fault a man for a fair fight, but they look at a man who is handy with a gun a little different than other folks. Likely, they got you down a a real bad *hombre*, a *hardcase*."

I grinned at him in the dark. "I know what you mean, Mister Smith. Some of...."

"Now you be calling me John. I don't like 'mister'."

I smiled, then went on. "I knew some of those hard *hombres* you tell about. Had to tussle with a few, but never understood them. I growed up thinking a man was a man and got called by what he done, not by how good he was with a gun. And, if a man's jerkin' a gun out on another man, he best know what he's doing. That kid made a fool's play, jerkin' his gun on a man he saw plain was more than handy with a gun. I growed up jerkin' a gun out of my pants, sir, and I had already showed what I could do to that kid."

"I see it same as you, stranger, but...."

It was my turn. Stranger would have been alright, since he didn't know much about me except what I'd told him, but I wanted this man to use my given name because I had took a liking to him. Figured if I was beholden to use his, then he ought to use mine.

"Hold up there, John. I'd sure be pleased if you'd call me Luke. Sounds kind of funny, you calling me a stranger after I done told you my name and all."

He laughed loud and deep. "Sure, Luke. Habit of mine."

Then he stretched out his legs and continued, "Like I was saying, I see it like you, but then I was raised by a little band of Comanche. They were family, if you know what I mean. Man was expected to be a warrior one day."

"How come you to leave?"

"Raiding party left one day and just never came back. I was still too young for fighting, so I had been left behind. There wasn't anyone left among us after that but some women and a few old men. I drifted off a couple months later because the rest were bound to locate friends, and I was busting my buttons to see the white man's world I'd been hearing about. I knew I was white and I wanted to see what my kind of people were like." He snorted, knocked his pipe against a rail, then added, "From all I learned in school and since, I got to admit there are some days I wish I would have stayed with the Comanche."

We talked late into the night, then he went inside , but I laid out my roll on the ground away from the house. He didn't ask me in, but I'd have refused anyway because it suited my back more on the ground than on them hard boards in the house. My saddle made a nice pillow and I enjoyed the stars and the sounds of the night until I drifted off to sleep.

I woke early to the sound of boots getting stomped on. It put me in mind of the way my pa used to get his boots on. He'd bat the top of a boot against the wall in case some critter crawled in, then he'd slide his foot down aways, then he'd stomp until the boot was on firm. He'd repeat the process for the other boot, then he'd stomp a couple extra times after they were on. Used to drive my ma crazy, and I wasn't too fond of it myself, especially since my Pa got up a couple hours before the rooster woke up.

I sat up, slid my boots on and made for the well. After I got a good drink and a face wash, I headed for the house, but not before I grabbed some dried beef in my sack. I ate the dried beef because I sort of had an idea that he was going to have some of that stew for breakfast, and I wasn't up to it. Sure enough, I walked in and he was spooning it down like it was hoecake and larrup.

He grinned and said, "Thought you'd be awake soon, so I put on the stew."

I waved a hand at him and said, "Aw, that's mighty nice of you John, but see, I ain't wanting to fry my insides out this early in the day. Reckon the sun will take care of all the frying I need today. You just eat it all up."

He smiled, then said, "We'll ride into Reata and pick up some supplies." He paused, gave me a real serious look, then said, "I am kind of low on my peppers."

I grinned, then asked him about the job he'd offered me. It wasn't punching cows, and I wasn't too sure what he wanted of me.

He wiped his plate with a piece of moldy bread, tore off a bite, then said, "Well, I was coming to that. Wanted you to get to know me better, first. Probably best if we get it ironed out now." He sighed, then said, "I been holding out on you some, boy."

He run his finger through his beard and said, "Luke, I don't run cows. I run sheep, and I've a few hundred head over near Taiban Creek with a *Mex'* herder."

I jerked up hard at that. I was a cowboy, and there was just no way I was going to push sheep. I held up my hand and said, "Look here, John. I appreciate the offer, but you're asking this Texas cowboy to do something that is awful unnatural."

He nodded his head in agreement, then said, "Luke, I understand that, but I'm not asking you to touch a sheep. Just stand guard for me and my herders."

"You asking to hire out my gun?"

"That's one way of putting it, but yes, I'm hiring you and that gun you wear, and seem to be so good at pulling. I hope you can shoot as good as I saw you handle that gun."

I hadn't known he was watching me this morning. I'd been limbering up, practicing like I try and do most every day. I said, "I can shoot straight enough, I reckon." I thought a minute, then asked, "You sure I won't have to get around them sheep?"

He laughed. "Certain, Luke." He stood and went over to a tub and threw his plate into it. I had an idea the water in that tub was probably a week or two old.

He said, "Ranches all around me are running cows, and although I can't say for certain that every one of them is behind my troubles, some riders have been paying me regular visits. They've driven off three of my herders, shot a few of my sheep, and put a few well-aimed shots near me twice. Just warnings, I'm sure. Then, last week, four riders came in and told me I had until the end of the week to clear out. They were plumb serious, Luke."

My pa always told me that if work was offered and was inside the law, that I should take it and not be too proud, no matter what it was. This wasn't what he had in mind when he said that, because I know he was thinking of one time he had to dig up stumps for a farmer. But, this was work and it was inside the law. And besides, I wouldn't have nothing to do with them sheep. Pa had told me about his bad times when he had taken any kind of work he could find. I remember him saying, "Son, them was hard days, but we never went hungry."

I could use the rest and knew my horses could. If I worked here a couple months, maybe I could put together a stake and move on farther from Texas. I was still too close. I didn't like the idea of shooting at some cowboys on account of a bunch of sheep, but I figured that as long as they didn't carry it too far, maybe just shooting a few sheep now and then or scaring the herders a little, why I could get along in this job real good and not have any trouble.

I looked at him and said, "Well, I'm your new hand, Boss, but you got to loan me some cartridges, because I had to use most of mine. I got four in my pistol and six left for my rifle.

My new boss leaned across the table, grabbed my hand and shook it real hard, and said, "Luke, I'll buy you a whole box when we hit Reata. In fact, I'll buy you two boxes." He stood up, grabbed a dirty black hat off a peg, crammed it down on his head and clomped out of the door.

He headed for the small corral and I followed. We were silent as we saddled up. I threw a roll on behind. It could be a long ride, and the clouds said maybe some rain. I wasn't sure where Reata was located. I'd never heard of it.

We came to the sheep camp and I almost gagged. The stink was terrible. I never had taken to the smell of sheep. Something about them makes my nose wrinkle, and I'd sneeze. Sure enough, I gave a good loud sneeze and Smith looked back and laughed. I hauled up short of the camp and he went on in to talk with the herder. He was a slim, dark Mexican, and he was jabbering and waving his hands about, obviously upset at something.

The boss waved me in, but I just shook my head. Pretty soon he came back. "Gets better with time, son."

I made a face and said, "I'd rather smell cows, boss. Something about them sheep gets to me."

He turned serious and said, "Miguel said some riders came by camp this morning. They told him they'd be back at the end of the week and either he or the sheep had better be gone."

I didn't say anything. Things like that didn't need talking about. Time came, we'd both know what to do. Smith turned his mount around and headed out for the Pecos, muttering about high water. I wasn't too partial to riding wet, so I hoped the water was down.

It wasn't.

CHAPTER 5

Crossing the Pecos wasn't as bad as I thought it might be. It wasn't down like I hoped, but it was down considerable from what it had been. I could see the high mark on the banks. Time we got back, that river would be lower. We swam part way, rode the other part. I held up my guns, tied my boots on the end of my rifle, and trailed my horse, hanging onto her tail. The boss just swam alongside his horse, one hand on the saddle, the other holding his gear up. Big as he was, I got to wondering if maybe he wasn't doing the swimming for the both of them.

We stripped down under a tree near the bank and wrung out our clothes. I was for laying there awhile in the sun, but the boss didn't want to be wasting time, so he jumped into wet clothes and I was forced to follow. I've rode wet many a time, and there just isn't anything I know that is more uncomfortable. Your tail itches and it's just a real terrible feeling. Even when you dry out, it's a long time before you feel right.

Until that sun dried us, it was the most miserable ride I ever had, except the time on a drive to Kansas. I got real wet then too, but at least I had a slicker, and part of me stayed dry. The misery that time came from the terrible lightening storms we hit. I'd never seen what they called *sky-fire,* and the first time I saw it, I got about as spooked as the cattle we were driving.

Near the end of the first day on the trail, we spotted two miners walking up the side of the mountain we was coming down. They were leading a couple of burros loaded down with supply packs of food and stuff. It took us most of an hour to come up on them.

They were leery of us. One held a shotgun, and it was no accident that it was pointing in our general direction. One thing about a gun like that is that's all a body has to do—point it in the general direction. A sane man won't go up against one of those guns when it's up close.

We pulled over to the side of the trail to let them pass, but they pulled up. It was pretty clear they were troubled over having to give their backs to us. I couldn't fault them none for that. A man can't be too careful.

I rested both hands on top of my saddle horn to show I was peaceful, and the boss tipped back his hat and give them a howdy.

He said, "I'm Smith, and this here is Luke, my partner. We're going into Reata. You boys come from there?"

The one with the shotgun never smiled, just watched us real close. The other spit a long stream of brown over the side of the trail and said, "Thought you boys might be part of the Horrel gang. They been holdin' up just about everything on the trail, in or out."

I said, "I don't blame you. Long as you keep that scatter gun handy though, I reckon that gang will stay clear of you."

I saw the miner with the shotgun crack a grin at that and he said, "I blowed away a good horse and half a man just yesterday. Him and his partner never learned about these kind of guns. Likely, that partner ain't stopped ridin' yet."

His grin widened, and I grinned back. I cotton to a man who wastes few words and knows when to fight. They both looked as tough a pair as I ever come across. The one with the shotgun told us there was a herd near town, and some of the riders was drinkin' hard in town. Told us it was part of a Texas bunch of beef headed for the Army and some *injuns*. First time I ever knew we were feeding *injuns*. I was glad to know that. It always troubled me the way we run the *injun* here and there, when they was here first. We ought to be feeding them.

We didn't talk too long, because it was getting on in the day. All of us wanted to get off that mountain trail before dark. I glanced back as we rode away and sure enough, that pair was hidden off the trail. If we'd have ridden back that way anytime soon, we'd have been blowed off the side of that mountain, for certain. I grinned, because I liked that. I'm careful that way and it pleases me when I meet careful folk. I've got no use for fools and those two weren't fools, I could see.

As we came down, Smith said, "Luke, be careful around those Texans. Might be Briner's crew, for all we know."

I smiled and replied, "I was thinking the same thing, Boss. I'll be careful."

We reached town with no trouble, not even seeing another rider on the trail. We rode in near dark and put the horses away. The boss went into the hotel and got us a room, then we went to get a good feed. I looked forward to that because I hadn't had a decent meal in so long I'd forgot what food tasted like.

It wasn't a big place where we ate, but it was the fanciest place I ever ate in. There was these pretty red and white sheets spread over the tops of all the tables, and the window curtains were the same color. That place had smells in it that I never smelled in my life. I took to grinning and rubbing my hands against my vest. I was like some kid about to ride his first pony, and my mouth was watering from the smells of food in the room. There was a whole mob of folks at tables in there, all talking at once, it seemed, and one little lady was running around to those tables and bringing big trays of food out.

When we sat down, the boss give me a piece of paper with a lot of writing on it. I looked at it, put it down and took to admiring the place. After awhile, he looked up at me from another piece of paper he was studying.

"Well, what are you having, Luke?"

I chuckled and said, "Reckon I'll have everything that smells so good."

"You ever been in a restaurant before, Luke?"

I frowned because I wasn't too sure what that word meant. I shook my head. I'd have remembered being in something like that, I know.

He laughed and said, "No matter. That smell is fried chicken, steak, coffee, apple pie, and a couple other things."

I grinned and said, "Well, just have the cook trot it all out, Boss. I'll have some of everything."

He chuckled like I said a joke, then he saw I was serious and shrugged them big shoulders. Right then a beautiful lady walked up in this bright green dress and asked us what we'd be having to eat. I think she smelled as good as that food. She was the first woman I'd laid eyes on in a year, at least. I could feel the blood rising in my face.

The boss ordered himself a couple of steaks, hot peppers, coffee, and some biscuits with brown gravy. The lady asked me what I wanted, so I repeated what I told the boss already. She smiled big and said, "I've had a few like you in here before. Been living on your own cooking. I'll bring you out the works."

She started to walk away, then stopped and said, "How about taking off your hat, cowboy. Keeps the dirt from falling into your food." Then she pranced off.

I grinned and drug off that big old hat and shoved it under my chair. I could see what she meant about the dirt falling in my food, because it was plenty dusty, and I knew my head would be bobbing when I lit into that pile of food.

I rubbed my hands along my thighs, leaned forward and asked, "Say, Boss, what's this works she's talkin' about?"

He grinned and said, "I ain't never seen it, but I heard about it. Just have to wait and see, Luke. I got a feeling you are going to have yourself a feed even your mama never gave you."

Well, the boss never spoke no truer words. She brought back a plate as big as my hat. If it had sides, I could have taken a bath in it and had room left over for my elbows. There were things on it I never saw in my life. There was a whole chicken done up brown and crisp, like I never had before. A big chunk of beef was laying there, and when I forked it that meat fell apart and melted right in my mouth.

On one side of the platter was a pile of green beans, some kind of funny green things with a point to them, a little dish of some kind of red and white things in it, some boiled tomatoes, yams that was sweet as larrup, and right smack in the middle of all that was a pile of the softest potatoes I ever tasted. Brown gravy run off the side of that pile and was so creamy I like to have ordered a bowl of it all by itself. The biscuits were soft as a calf's belly, and the butter had soaked into them till they were yellow, like gold nuggets in a pile.

I must have ate over an hour. The boss finished long before and sat there smoking his pipe, picking at his teeth now and then with a small sliver of wood, and grinning at me. I'd look up at him now and then and grin back, but mostly I was too busy to pay attention. Finally, after I had eaten that first plate down to the white and was moving another plate full of potatoes, yellow squash and some more of them green pointy things in front of me, I paused to take a slow sip on my fifth cup of the best Arbuckle's coffee I ever tasted.

While I was slurping at my coffee, I caught the eye of this old man at the table near ours. He was staring at me like I was part of a side show. I leaned back to see him better and to give him a stare right back, then noticed that there was a lady right along side of him that was staring too, only she glanced away when I looked at her. Then, I saw that the whole room was staring at me, including that lady who brought the food to us. She was standing to one side with her arms folded, smiling real big, and so was most everyone else. I looked down real quick to see what I had spilled on me. I thought maybe I had dropped a piece of that chicken on my lap, but I was clear of any droppings.

Then it came to me. Here I'd been eating like a starved wolf at the innards of a dead cow, paying no mind at all to manners. If my skin wasn't so dark from a couple thousand Texas suns, I reckon it would have turned as red as those squares on that table sheet in front of me. I just hung my head down and slowed my eating.

I didn't dare look up until that lady walked over and plopped down the biggest piece of apple pie I ever saw. That was half a pie all by itself. The boss waved his piece off, but I dug in. It was tart, hot as a branding iron, and with a crust that melted soon as it was in my mouth. If I hadn't been so embarrassed, I'd have asked for the boss' piece of pie, too. But, I figured I'd order a whole pie some time when I was in this town again. I knew for sure, I'd be back. No sense making a pig of myself this time.

The lady in the green dress came over again and said, "Well cowboy, how'd you like our special?"

I grinned at her, swallowed the last bite of that pie and said, "Ma'm, if it was any more special, I'd wonder if I'd died and gone to heaven."

She smiled and said, "Well, I've seen many men come in here, and even a few who ate as much, but I never saw one who enjoyed it as much. This meal is on the house, cowboy!"

I tried to thank her, but she moved off saying something about me being good for business. We left and I headed for the hotel because when I eat like that I get powerful sleepy. The boss headed for the saloon. I wasn't partial to *likker* and have always had trouble in saloons, so I told him I was bedding down for the night. Besides, I figured I might run into some of those Texas punchers in there, and one of them might know me.

Next morning I woke up hungry as a catamount eyeballing a calf, and I felt alert and alive, almost restless. That feed had done me a lot of good. The boss snored on, so I decided to take in the early sun on the porch. When I eat big, I sleep long and hard, but always wake up hungry. Don't know why, but I do.

I stepped out into the cool of the morning and took a deep breath. It smelled good and felt even better. There were a few folk walking about, but mostly it was quiet. I always liked the early part of the day. Getting up early gives a man the chance to work the kinks out of his body and his mind.

I spied a chair that looked to be built especially for comfortable setting, so I dragged it over near a post and sat down, propping my feet on the post. I had in mind to wait for the boss to wake, and then we'd eat. I closed my eyes and relaxed, enjoying the golden splash of sun as it took the edge off the cool and reddened the backs of my eyelids. A good day was in the making.

I'd been there a short time when I heard some steps. I looked up and saw a man standing by me in a frock coat, the kind you see a preacher wear, only he was no preacher, I could see. A black, twisted cigar stuck out of one side of his mouth, and a shiny, pearl handled pistol rested snug in a holster at his side. He coat tail was laid back behind the gun so it could be got to in a hurry. I'd have thought he was a dude except for the mean, hard look behind his shiny, black eyes. They were boring a hole right through me.

His voice had the same hard in it that his eyes had. He said, "Boy, you are setting on my personal chair."

If he had spoke nice to me, I probably would have moved without a word, or even a hard look. I know what it means to a man to have a special place and a certain chair. My pa used to sit in a big rocker on the porch in the evening. He always had to have that chair, and ma made sure it was kept it in the same place. We'd watch the sun go down and the stars come out, and we'd talk, him rocking, Ma in her chair sewing, and me laying on the porch. Probably, this man liked the morning as much as we liked the evening, and here I was, a stranger using his favorite chair and his spot. I could understand that.

Instead, I looked up at him and said, "Mister, if you ask me with a please, I'll give up your chair."

I saw the surprise wipe across his face. He must have been a mighty big man in these parts and wasn't used to back talk from anyone, especially a heel-worn, trail-rough cowboy. He took that cigar from his mouth with his left hand, and I took note of that, then he looked at me close and hard.

Finally, he said, "I enjoy sitting in that chair at this hour, friend, but I'll enjoy killing you more than sitting in that chair."

I smiled. "Mister, we aren't friends and I don't want to kill any man over a chair. I reckon I'll give you the chair if you want it bad enough to kill a man over it."

He smiled, but not with his eyes. His voice raised a bit and he said, "I can see you don't understand the way things are in this town. You see, you've ruined my day." He put his cigar back into his mouth and sucked on it some, then said, "You don't honestly think I'd allow you to get away with ruining my day, do you?"

I knew then he was primed and ready to go, because he was talking funny. I don't understand it, but a lot of men's voices will change when they're ready to fight. Some will get real husky. That's the way I get. Others will get a higher pitch or maybe a bit of a quiver in it, but every man I ever had a fighting matter with got his voice troubled first. I know that when my voice gets husky, I also get to grinning and saying things that aren't generally said with a smile.

Suddenly, I stood up. It wasn't a jump, but an easy, quick move. One minute I was relaxed there in the chair, and suddenly, I'm standing right in front of him, eye to eye. He stepped back and let that cigar drop to the porch.

I asked, "You goin' to burn this hotel down?"

That threw him off and he frowned, then answered, "Time it takes for that to catch, I'll have it back." His eyes never left mine, and just when I thought he was ready, he asked, "What's your name, boy? I ought to know who it is I'm killing, especially since I'll be paying for your burial."

"I'm Luke Adams. What you want put on your marker?"

He smiled at that. "Langley. Bill Langley." He stood there, proud and mean looking, like I should have come to attention when he said his name. It didn't mean anything to me.

I made one last try. "Mr. Langley, you think I ain't got much chance of takin' you down, or even of getting a shot off, but I got to tell you that I don't think there's a man alive I couldn't get a bullet into face to face. He might get one in me, but I'll put one in him for sure, and it'll be in his brisket. I hit what I aim at, sir, every time."

I paused, then added, "Now, you take your chair and I'll walk away from you. Otherwise, I'll kill you where you stand. I ain't the boy you think, Mr. Langley."

He didn't say a word, but just stared hard, his eyes searching mine. Then, he lost that killing gleam in his eye, puckered his lips, bent down and got his cigar, and said, "Something about you is mighty convincing, boy. Mighty convincing. You got a way about you. I've faced enough men in my time to know when to walk away." He nodded his head at the chair and added, "You enjoy that chair."

Then, he give me a little salute, turned and walked away. I was glad to leave things lay. Some men I know would never have been able to walk away like that. I had to admire him for that. I'd met a few men who liked to kill, and I think he was one of those kind of men, but he was the first one I'd ever faced who kept his control. Most men like him are like mad dogs. I watched him disappear into the hotel, then sat back down in the chair.

The boss came out a little later and we had us a quick feed. I never mentioned what had happened, but during our meal that Langley fellow came in and went to a table. The boss sat up real straight and whispered to me, "Luke, you know who that is? That's Bill Langley! Worst killer ever rode across Texas."

I looked at the boss and saw he was real taken with this Langley. The boss never struck me as being that way, but I reckon it was the reputation he carried that made the boss look at him like a calf to its mother. I started to mention our meeting, but decided not to. I had the feeling the boss wouldn't believe me, and even if he did, I had the idea he wouldn't be that happy. There's something about finding out that somebody isn't what you thought him to be that rankles a body. It was that way with me when Spoon died. Made me feel bad inside.

We ate and left. Langley looked over at me once and gave a little smile. I just nodded and the boss caught it. He asked me about it, but I just told him we'd met this morning early. He asked some more, but I made little of it and he give up.

We got shells for me and some grub. I made sure he got some things I could eat. He loaded up on fresh peppers the Mexicans sold there in town. Now, I like peppers, but not like the boss did. I think he could have lived steady on them. He said he liked to flavor his peppers with a little food. He was joking but I believed him. I made sure he knew I wasn't partial to them; and in fact, I let on like I had a stomach problem and wasn't able to tolerate them too well, which was true. Once any man put one of the boss' meals in him, he had a stomach problem. I did give some thought to cooking, but I reckon I hate cooking worse than riding drag. Everything I cook burns, smells better than it tastes, or comes out hard as my head.

We agreed on the way back that he'd leave out the peppers from my stuff.

CHAPTER 6

We were loading up our stuff on the mare we brought along for packing, when a whole slew of riders come boiling into town. There must have been ten or more of them, and they were riding like they was trying to turn a herd of cows in a stampede. Just before they reached us, they slid to a stop, all of them, and began piling off their mounts, yelling and whooping. I could tell they was just off the trail and set to howl.

I was a bit surprised that the trail boss would let that many riders go into town, especially during the day, but he must have had a good reason. I know when I trailed up into Kansas, we never left those cows once that whole trip. We passed a town or two, but the boss told us he'd shoot any man caught sneaking into town. One old timer snuck in, but he never got caught.

Then I caught sight of a familiar face. Something about the way he set his horse made me look at him, and the fact that he wasn't whooping and yelling like the others. He wiped the hat back off his face, and sure enough it was that Cat Foot man from Texas. He nosed the big bay horse he was riding towards the hitching rail nearby, then swung from his horse with that soft, easy way of his. I noticed that even in a friendly town, and with all his partners standing around, he still left one hand stay free and near the big .44 on his side.

Walking soft and staying alive. The thought came suddenly, and it was a fit description of how that man lived.

I hollered out at him and he turned quick as a flash. He was as primed as he had been that day when we rode up on me and Spoon. When he saw me he relaxed, but not them green eyes. They stayed cool and alert, watching for any kind of wrong moves.

I gave him a smile and he walked up to me, the reins of his horse dangling from one hand. He wasn't a smiling man, but he cracked a little one for me. I didn't reach out for a handshake because I knew it would embarrass him not to. It wouldn't be for any reason except maybe that he was a man always keeping that one hand free as possible.

"You should have kept ridin' *amigo*." He said it low, so the others wouldn't be hearing.

I smiled, then replied, "I lost them riders way back. I don't figure on 'em findin' my trail any time soon."

He shook his head, looked down at his dusty boots and then back at me. His green eyes were shining bright and he gave me that funny little grin again. "Reckon you've got some learnin' to do about the kind of man Amos Briner is and the kind of men who ride for him. He's got cows in this herd, son."

"Any of them riding special for me?"

"Well, I can tell you that you're a wanted man in Texas, and the Rangers have orders to bring you in. If Briner ever gets word you're in these parts, he will show up with some guns. He'll stretch your hide over his fireplace, son." He smiled that funny little smile of his, then added, "But no, to your question. There's only men along to help push the cows. Two of the riders belong to Briner. But, all of them were told to keep an eye out for you."

I liked this man. He knew that talking to me was dangerous for him, for word has a way of traveling in this country. It might be someone would take word that he recalled seeing me and Cat Foot having a conversation. But, maybe Briner knew that the day he took on Cat Foot was the day he'd die with his boots on. That Cat Foot man was probably the most dangerous man I ever met in my life.

If Briner was that determined, he'd nose me out one day. The only way a body can hide out in this country is to stay out all the time in the hills. I don't mind spending long times in the hills, but I got to get into town sooner or later. I'm not one of those hermits. Now that I'd had a feed in a place with the red squares on the table, I knew I'd be coming back. That was certain. I'd have fought an army to get another one of them feeds and a look at that pretty girl that served.

A few riders were standing about, not knowing what was up, likely watching to see if some trouble might be in the making, and maybe a few wondering if I was the one Briner had said to look out for. I saw the quick little side glances. We went on talking there in the sun. I asked Cat Foot what he was up to and he told me he'd hooked onto a big herd that was thrown together by about five ranchers down near where I came from.

Even Blackjack had a hundred head in it. Briner had nigh unto two hundred head mixed in. Cat Foot said he'd told the ranchers there were too many cows to drive, but they were overstocked, some of them, and some needed the cash, so they were trailing close to a thousand critters up to the soldier boys near Sante Fe. It had been a troublesome drive so far, with the herd spooking on them once. Cat Foot calculated they lost a hundred head on that run. And now they were getting uneasy on account of some stories of Vitorio and his band raiding around.

Finally, Cat Foot give his gun belt a hitch, turned to go, then said, "Oh yeah. Briner offered me $1000.00 cash to put you over the back of a horse."

I smiled my thanks, then asked, "Lot of money. How come you to pass?"

He give that funny little smile again and said, "I like livin', son."

I knew that wasn't his real reason, but he wasn't the kind of man who wanted to tell another man he liked him or held respect for him. We both knew that in a stand-up gun fight that it'd be a hard day for both of us.

I wasn't doubtful of putting lead in him, but I figure he'd put some in me, too. He was one of those men you don't usually stop with one bullet.

The boss was standing over near the horses, looking like he was busy tying down the packs and stuff, but I knew he'd been watching just as keen as all those riders had been. I saw the rifle laying there on top of the pack horse, and it wasn't no accident. The boss looked to be as careful as me and that Cat Foot.

We swung aboard out mounts and headed out. I noticed right off we were moving out in the opposite direction we had come in, but I didn't say a word until we got out of town.

"We ridin' somewhere else, Boss?"

He chuckled, then said, "Naw, I'm just thinkin' that we might be waited for up the trail." He reached inside his shirt and pulled out a big piece of paper. I could see a map was drawn on the one side of it and the other side was real important looking. He handed it over to me. I pretended to read at it, but all I did was look at the map, and that didn't make much sense to me either.

I handed it back and said, "That's real nice, Boss."

He grinned and said, "Won that little gold mine in a poker game while you were sawing logs last night."

Well, I was surprised at that. The boss didn't look like he was the kind to be interested in gold mining, and I knew I wasn't. I asked, "You plannin' on workin' that mine or sellin' it?"

"Think I'll just hang on to it awhile, Luke. Next trip into town I'll ride up and have a look see, maybe chip a little rock while I'm there. Could be what I need to restock my land. Those cowboys have been killing some of my sheep, and if it keeps up I'm going to be losing as many as I get natural. Can't grow like that.

That evening we found a little stream and camped near there. The Boss said he wanted to be up early, and we could make the ranch by afternoon the next day, in spite of the circle we were making.

It turned out that we got delayed just a little longer, and it was partly my fault. I was the guard for the first part of the night and I got real careless. It's not very often I get careless, but a man makes a mistake now and then. Trouble with making a mistake out here is that it only takes one little one to be your last.

I had been a couple of hours watching when I heard a noise that wasn't natural. I should have shook the boss right then, but I knew him not getting sleep last night had put him out real good and I figured he could use the rest. So, I moved real quiet over near to where I heard the noise. Everything was dead quiet, too quiet. The hairs on the back of my neck were raising, and I knew then there was something out there and that it was dangerous for me. That is a thing the good Lord gave me and I can't explain it. I just know when danger is near. I can feel it.

Soon as those hairs started raising, I went back to the camp. It wasn't that I was scared, but I figured I'd best raise the boss. I should have raised him when the feeling first hit me.

I hadn't got very far when the night lit up with short flashes of gun fire, sounding like a whole army was out there. I saw the boss come out of his blankets with his rifle. He always slept with a rifle snugged up against him. Only thing, that rifle was busted up some on account of a bullet that had hit it while the boss was in his blankets. He looked mighty funny running with that rifle stock dangling in a couple of pieces.

I went to ground right off and slid back into the woods. Those robbers sounded like they were bunched. They should have been spread out, because if they had been, it's pretty likely the boss wouldn't have been able to run for cover. A cross fire would have caught him. They'd have more of a chance to take me, too. Not much of one, but at least a chance.

I was raised in the woods and I can walk softer than anyone I ever met except an old *injun* I knew as a kid named Walking Twig. He was a friend to my pa and I always looked forward to when he'd come to the cabin. He taught me and Pa how to walk without first pressing down with the foot. I got to where I could feel a twig under foot before it snapped. That old *injun* had nary a soul left in his tribe, and I remember how he used to sit on our place, smoke this long skinny pipe and blow smoke at the East. I heard Pa say once that he was some big chief way back east a long time ago. We used to give him meat and things, and he'd hang around for weeks, then be gone for maybe a month and show up like he never left. One day he left and we never saw him again. Ma never missed him, but me and Pa did.

So, I got to using all the quiet I had in me. I felt like there were four out there, maybe more. I knew there was at least three because I heard three different guns shooting, and maybe a fourth. There was two rifles shooting, one revolver, and I think maybe there was another revolver.

Those robbers had missed their chance to take us out when they made too much noise crawling up on us, then opening up on the boss while they were too far off. Now, I figured they'd be content to rustle off the horses and try for the packs lying nearby. I wanted bad to hunt them there in the woods, but I was worried some about shooting the boss by accident, or him shooting me by mistake. When a body is hunting with another man, they both need to know where the other is hunting.

I rested near the horses, certain they'd make a try for the packs. Sure enough, I heard some whispering over in the bushes in a little while. They was arguing, of all things. Only a fool argues when a fight is going on. Time to argue is after the fight is over, not while it's going on. I just find it hard to believe some men have lived as long as they have out here.

It was plain from what little I could pick up, that they were arguing over who was going to sneak over and grab the pack. Since there seemed to be two of them, I figured I'd make up their minds for them. I slipped back aways to get a good line on the bushes they were behind. I could see the edge of a shoulder of one, and what looked to be the top of a head on the other.

I lined up my rifle on the shape that looked like a head and squeezed off a shot. The head disappeared and not even a peep was made out of them two, but that other shape leaped out of those bushes like he was scalded by a hot branding iron. Only thing, he moved the wrong way. If he'd done what a body ought to have done, which is drop flat and slide to cover, he'd like to have been alright. But, this fool ran like he'd eaten some loco weed, bleating like a branded calf. I slapped the rifle stock to my shoulder and let two shots his way. I missed him with the first one, but the second one clipped him in the shoulder and tumbled him.

He was a fool. But, I couldn't let him get to the tree he was running for or he'd have been in a good position to start shooting my way. With him gone, I had one less to worry about.

I figured that what was left of that bunch would be making for the horses now, so I yelled out, "Hey, Boss! Don't say nuthin'! I got two and I'm goin' huntin'. Don't be movin', cause I don't want to shoot you by mistake."

Then I crept away, heading in a long circle back to the rear of where I had first heard the sound. They'd be running for their horses and I wanted to get there first. In just a short time I spotted three horses standing over by some trees, just off the trail. I'd made it. I got in position and waited.

Pretty soon, a man came running likity-split, like there was a whole passel of *injuns* on his tail. His hat was gone and he had a revolver in his hand. The moon light made him real plain and I could have popped him easy, but I guess I'm soft-hearted like a woman sometimes. It was plain to me that the fight was over and that he wouldn't be troubling me no more. I let him get to his horse and as he was leaving I stepped out and sent a shot humming alongside his ear. He let out a yell like he was hit and I saw him dig the spurs in and beat that horse into a faster run.

I snagged the two horses and led them back to the camp. Before I got there though, I slipped over to where I'd shot at those two other robbers. I was pretty certain that they was both done for, but it was dark, even with the moon full out, and I had only seen a head shaped object. I knew I'd hit that object, but I wasn't sure what it was.

I came to the one I'd hit running for the tree. He was dead as a man can be. Then I went over to the bushes where I had shot at the other. This one was stretched out, and his bushwhacking days was over. It wasn't pretty, and I felt bad about having to shoot him like that, but I'd get over it.

I always feel bad over killing a man, even those who was trying to kill me. I always thought maybe those I killed, if they could come back to life would do things a mite different, and maybe not be so mean and all.

"Hey, Boss! Where you at?" I hadn't heard a peep out of him and I didn't want him fretting and getting impatient, and maybe shooting me accidentally.

"They all gone, Luke?"

"Yeah, Boss. Two gone to hell, I reckon, and one gone to Texas, probably."

He walked out of his hiding place, and I saw why he hadn't been stirring much. He wouldn't be riding real soon because it looked like, from the blood and leg dragging behind, that he'd been hit pretty hard and at least twice. There was a blotch of dark, almost black now, high on his right leg, and another dark mess on the side of his shirt. He stumbled into camp and sat down hard, stifling a groan. He was hurting bad, but the boss, he wasn't no man to cry about a thing like that. It made me think of poor Spoon. I still wished he had went out better than he did.

I tugged his shirt out of his pants and then opened it careful, peeling it back on the left side real easy. It was a mean one, but it wasn't one to finish a man like the boss. I got his pants off, then I dressed the wound as best I could. I made him a bed of some pine needles, and went back into the bushes for some rags. Those two men laying back there weren't going to be needing those clothes they were wearing.

After I washed those rags, I hung them all on a couple of rocks. They'd be dry sometime in the morning. I took one of the sacks of flour we had and dumped the flour in with the beans, because the bean sack had a lot of extra room. Those beans would taste a bit strange, but since neither one of us was used to having regular tasting meals, especially him, I figured it wouldn't bother us.

That sack made a fine bandage for both wounds, and I made a paste from some of that flour and put it on the bullet holes to help stop the bleeding. The bullet in the side pained him some on account of the ragged hole it made when it went out the other side. But, that hole in the leg was nice and neat, just a little black hole going in and another going out. I figured that nice hole coming out was because that part of his leg was against the ground for most any bullet hole I ever saw made a worse hole on the other side, except this one didn't.

The boss was nagging at me like I was his wife for the next three days. He was fevered some the first night, but the next day he was his normal ornery self, and he spent all that time trying to get me to help him onto a horse so we could move on. I just pretended I didn't hear him. I saw a cowboy once who had been shot by an arrow, and he made out like he wasn't hurt too bad and didn't rest himself, then he up and he died on us after a couple days.

The third day I broke camp. I would have broke camp whether he was well or not because the steady braying was getting on my nerves. I decided that if he wanted to kill himself, that was alright with me. But, he was fit, and except for a limp and his contrariness, you'd never know he had been laid up. We loped on out, worried some because we'd told his herder that we'd be back soon.

CHAPTER 7

We pulled into the ranch that afternoon, real late and the boss wanted to ride on out to the graze and see Miguel, but I told him to have a rest as he was getting some pale and that I'd have a look-see. He grumped some, but went on in, and I headed out for the pasture where we had gone by on the way to town.

It was still dusk, so when I rode up it was easy to see all those white and black-stained bodies laying scattered on the ground. But, I had smelled them long before I got there. I never smelled death like that before. I never counted the bodies, but there had to be more than a hundred dead sheep. I rode over to a tree where Miguel had made his camp and saw a note stuck to the tree. I was sure wishing I could read. I figured it must be from Miguel.

Back at the ranch house, I watched as the boss' face changed from pale to a dark red. If there had been one of them riders show up right then, I do believe the boss would have shot the man out of his saddle without any warning. I wasn't too sure I would have blamed him for it either.

He looked at me and said, "That tears it, Luke. They've put me out of business. I don't have the money to buy more sheep and they know it." He crumpled the note.

"Was that from Miguel?"

He looked at me kind of queer and I think it was then that it came to him that I couldn't read a lick. He said, "No, that was from a man named

Barnes. He rides for that big outfit north of here. The note told me that Miguel was leavin' and that I had three days to clear out."

I didn't say anything for this was something he had to decide. I knew what I would do, but it wasn't my place to tell him what to do. The boss looked at the window for a long space, then turned to me and surprised me by asking for my thoughts.

I said, "Boss, this is your thing here and whatever you decide on, outside of downright war, I'm with you."

He broke into a smile at that and said, "No, it ain't a war that I'm thinking about, Luke. But, I don't like those crooks to think they chased me off because I'm afraid of them. I fear no man, and if it was worth it to me, I'd start that war you're talking about. This place and those sheep just ain't worth maybe dying for or getting hanged for, and by the time I got done, I'd be a hunted man, wanted worse than you are."

I smiled, for that was my thinking exactly, but I was waiting for him to say one more thing and then I'd be pleased as apple pie. He just scratched his head though, looked at me and sighed.

I pressed him. "Boss, when are we leavin'?"

He walked over to the door and stood there, leaning forward some so he could look out. Without turning he said, "Well, I'm not too sure when they wrote this note, Luke, and I think I'll stay until they get here so I can find out when those three days are gone by. You head on down to town and I'll catch up with you there."

I grimaced and said, "Boss, is a bunch of stinking sheep worth it?" It wasn't that I was afraid. I just never put store by sheep and it seemed to me that staying and waiting for some men to come by and order me to leave on account of sheep wasn't smart.

He turned to me and said, "Luke, there is no reason for you to stay now. I can handle this. Besides, I can't afford to pay you anything, so I ain't your boss anymore."

I liked him for his straight talk. I always admire a man who will say right out what is on his mind and how he is thinking. I hitched up my pants some and said, "Well, I like 'boss' better'n John, so if you don't mind, I'll call you that. As for staying, I reckon if you're dumb enough to hang around them three days, I'll stick around and see what happens. Might be you'll need someone to drag your carcass over by them dead sheep of yours. You can all rot together in sheep heaven."

He chuckled at that and said, "I'm sure them riders will see things my way, especially when they know I'm moving on."

"They might not give you a chance to say much."

He shrugged, and I asked, "What are you goin' to do with this place?"

He said, "Luke, I don't own the range here. I took the sheep off the owner's hands after he give it up. We had a deal that I could run the sheep here and after three years we'd settle up any profits, fifty-fifty. I suppose he'll sell it to one of those ranches here."

We waited. I got bored, and if the wind came from the southwest, there was no staying around the shack. I rode off to get up-wind more than once. Sheep stink naturally, but dead sheep stink uncommonly bad.

It took a week for those riders to show. When they did, it was plain they came for trouble for there was seven of them, and they were armed to the teeth. Two rode up to the house and the rest hung back, all spread out, wary of a trap. They were careful and they weren't taking John Smith for granted. Big man like that puts respect in a person.

The two reined up and one spoke: "Well, them three days is come and gone, Smith. Our boss said we was to evict you if you was here."

Now, I don't know what 'evict' meant, but I knew it wasn't good. I figured it was a fancy way of saying 'kill.' I moved over to one side slow, not looking direct at either of them two, but keeping both in my looking eye, while I kept my other eye alert for any movements from those other riders. Any kind of sudden moves was going to send me into action.

That first rider looked over at me and said, "Don't go getting spooky, friend. There's five rifles back yonder, and there's Mac right here." He nodded in the other feller's direction. I had already took him in and didn't see anything special about him except he did look funny in the eyes, like maybe he was loony. He wore a rumpled old grey hat, a faded blue shirt patched in a couple dozen places, and wore boots that looked to be mostly tattered pieces of leather stuck together.

The boss spoke out real casual to me: "Luke, the little man on the mare is a real skin full of poison. His mama whored over near the border, and the customers kind of raised him. He's a little strange in the head, but he's good with that gun. Real good. But mostly, he's a back-shootin' little killer."

The boss shifted his rifle, then added, "If they start the ball, you take Barnes, and I'll take care of little Crazy Mac." He spoke so casual and matter-of-fact, you'd have thought he was giving out orders for the day to one of his riders to round up strays.

I took another look at that ugly little man on the mare. The more I looked at him, the more I could see some of what the boss was talking about. But, the more I looked, the more I kind of figured the boss wouldn't be fast enough, and I could tell from the gleam in his eyes that it wasn't the boss he'd be trying for first. He knew I was the one to take out. I had him figured to roll off to one side, out of line from the boss, and while he was rolling, he'd be slinging some lead my way.

I spoke real soft: "Boss, I ain't got time to argue, but I'll take care of Crazy here if it comes to a war."

The boss must have noticed the iron in my voice because he just nodded and said, "Any way you want it, Luke." I moved slowly to the side so that no matter which way that little killer rolled, I'd have a shot at him.

The man called Barnes said, "Smith, you can ride out peaceful or we can drag you out. Your choice. Don't make it hard, man."

The boss leaned against the porch post, give a little smile and said, "Barnes, I'm giving up sheep, mainly 'cause I ain't got none. You took care of that, and maybe one day I'll ride by and give a bill. But, I don't take orders easy, and I don't like being run. You ain't got some spineless sheepherder here. I ain't looking for war, but if you don't let me be, then I guess some of us are going to die here today."

I had to give my say, too. "Mister Barnes, I want you to know something. I reckon it ain't no lie if I tell you I can take the both of you, and likely a few of them, too." I nodded at the rest of his riders, then continued, "I ain't no sheepherder, and I growed up with a gun. Since I ride for Smith, his war is mine." Barnes ignored me, but the other man, the little crazy one, blinked like something got in his eye, and then he grinned at me. It was clear he was a bit touched in the head.

"Smith, I thought you had more sense than those sheep you run, but I guess I was wrong." Barnes shifted in the saddle and the leather creaked loudly, increasing the tension.

I got ready because Crazy Mac had a little yellow crawling into his eyes, like a hungry mountain lion cat just about to pounce. I figured I'd throw him off some. "Hey you, Barnes!" That Mac feller didn't waver in his steady gaze at me.

I kept my eyes on the one with the strange eyes, but I was talking to Barnes. " You brung this little killer thinking he'd be enough. But, I want to tell you, Barnes, the blood that's going to we the ground here today is going to be yours and your pet dog there. You got some riders back of you who might take us, but we'll get both of you and some of them. That's dead certain, Barnes. You better call this dog off quick. He's getting ready to bite and when he does, both of you are liable to end up dead. It ain't no bluff."

I think Barnes was fixing to tell that Crazy Mac feller to back off some. He put up his hand and said, "Mac..." when that killer went off like a stick of dynamite. Maybe he knew Barnes was going to back off and he wanted to try his hand. I don't know. I do know I wasn't surprised a bit.

He whipped out his gun and went rolling off his mare real slick. It was sure a pretty thing, graceful, real smooth and fast. Only thing, he never had a chance with me. At the first flicker from him, I'd crouched, and he just rolled right into my first two shots. He got off a shot, but it went into the belly of that mare of his, and she squealed, reared up, and then crashed into Barnes' horse. Barnes hollered some, because that mare hurt his leg, but soon he forgot his leg, because the boss had stuck the end of his rifle in that man's ear, and not too gentle, either.

"Call off your riders Barnes, or you'll be getting a bigger hole in your ear than God give you."

There was no mistaking the hard in the boss' voice. I could hear those riders coming, and Barnes looked over where the yeller-eyed killer of his was laying, all curled up like he was in his mama's belly, and then he looked back behind his shoulder.

"Hold up, boys!" he shouted.

I took the revolver out of his hand and the boss pulled him off his horse. That man was scared, but he wasn't begging. He was waiting to see which way the wind blew. We hustled him into the shack and the boss slammed him into a chair. I moved to the open door and waited there, watching to see if any of those riders tried to move in on us.

Smith stuck one big boot on the edge of that man's chair, leaned forward until his face was just inches away, then said, "Barnes, I'm leaving this place, but it's going to be when I'm good and ready. Might be tomorrow. Might be a week. Might be a month. I ain't made up my mind yet."

The boss took his foot off the chair, walked back a little ways, poured himself a cup of coffee, then continued, "If you or your men try and run me off, then I'm going hunting. I'll hunt you while you're branding and while you are sitting around a campfire. You'll be riding along, hear a couple of shots, and see two of your men fall out of the saddle. That'll be me, Barnes."

The boss paused, took a big gulp of that stuff he called coffee, but tasted more like axle grease, then went on: "It goes against my grain to leave this place, but I know you got the law bought, and I'd never make no money with you boys always shooting my sheep. Reckon I know what I'd have to pay for it, and it isn't worth it. But, there is a part of me that has no price, Barnes. You're touching on it now, you and your riders."

Suddenly he grabbed Barnes by the shirt front, raised the man up with a fist bunched into his shirt and shoved him to the door. "Take your boys and leave. I'll be pulling out one day, but until I do, if I find any of you on my property, I'm going hunting. Believe me, I ain't worth the grief I'll bring."

Barnes was silent during all of this. John Smith had made a believer out of that man. I know if that was me and he made the same talk at me, I'd have believed him. I'd have done just what that Barnes fellow did, too: shut my mouth, get on my horse, ride out and never look back.

Only a fool would want a war with a man like the boss. He'd play low down and mean, and for keeps. Them kind of fighters is hard to put a mark on. When you finally do put down somebody like that, you get to wondering who won the fight on account of all the hurting you got.

Those riders moved out real slow, and I guess one of them got to arguing with Barnes, but he wasn't one to argue long for I saw him knock that man out of his saddle. They all waited for him to climb back on his horse, then I saw Barnes lean forward in his saddle and say something to the man he'd knocked down.

I said to the boss, "You shore do have a convincin' way about you."

He gave me a funny look and said, "I meant every word of it, Luke."

"So, where you headed now?" For answer he pulled out that piece of paper and spread it on the table. After he'd looked at it a little while he looked back at me and said, "How'd you like to be partners with me in a gold mine, Luke?"

I thought it was funny and said, "Long as it don't cost me more'n a dollar."

"You're in! Fork over that dollar, partner." He held out that big paw of his.

"Boss, I though you was makin' some kind of joke! You ain't serious that you'd make me a partner in that gold mine for no dollar, are you?"

"Luke, if you don't hand over that dollar I'm gonna turn you upside down and shake you till it falls out."

Well, that beat all I ever heard of and I sure didn't want him grabbing hold of me, so I dug out the only dollar I had left and give it to him. He stuffed it into his pocket.

I felt there was something I ought to mention, so I spoke out, "Boss, there's one thing I reckon you ought to know about me. You might not be wantin' me to be your partner after you hear what I got to say."

He laughed and said, "Aw Luke, I know what you're going to tell me. You're going to tell me that you ain't partial to work!"

Well, he was making a joke about it, but that was what it amounted to. I said, "Boss, if that gold mine is down in a hole I reckon you can count me out. I ain't too taken with the idea of crawlin' down in a hole in the ground. It'll be hard enough to get down in that hole we all face one day. I just ain't partial to holes, Boss. They bother me."

That man laughed until the tears came down his face. I sure didn't see the funny and was almost getting riled, but he finally shut up and said, "Luke, I'm sorry I laughed at you, but it just seemed funny, you being afraid of a hole in the ground. I've met some tough men in my time, Luke, and you're probably the toughest man I ever met, and well, it just don't seem natural for a man like you to be afraid of a thing like that."

I sat down and puzzled over that some, then said, "I don't follow what you said, but if it's all the same to you I reckon I better take that dollar back."

"Luke, you're in and that's that! I'll do the digging, and if we hit something, I'll hire someone else to dig. You do all the chores, the riding into town for supplies, the camp guard, plus all the fighting off of the claim jumpers when they come rushing up here after we make our strike."

We shook on it, and there I was, part owner in a mine. I sure was grateful that I didn't have to crawl down there in it. I reckon I could have, if there was a good enough reason, but gold just ain't a good enough reason for me to crawl down a hole.

We packed up that night and left early the next morning. The boss said he'd proven his point and that he was satisfied that he was leaving of his own choosing and on his own schedule. We had four horses trailing behind and the clothes on our back. Oh, the boss had a piece of paper stuck in his shirt that said we was the owners of the Cortez Gold Mine. Well, it might have just said that he was the owner, but I wasn't worried none. The way I looked at it, if we never got a thing out of that mine, I wasn't out of a thing, except a dollar, and if we got rich, I was that much ahead.

If the boss was to cheat me out of my share, I was still out only a dollar. After all, he never had to give me half of that mine. I would have stayed around probably, and done the guarding and such without owning any of that mine. I just couldn't see any way of losing on this deal.

CHAPTER 8

We found that little gold mine stuck way off in the mountains, but we like to have never got the horses up to it. The boss decided right away to make a trail to it for the future. It was almost a mile off the regular trail, which wasn't much itself. We took to moving rocks, boulders, and chopping down a few scrub pines. I chopped trees and tossed rocks until my hands were raw. I never saw a man work like John Smith did, though. He'd see a rock that would take two men and a horse to roll, and he'd walk over to it, pick it up and give it a roll down the side of the mountain. It was hard to believe how powerful that man was.

After two days we finally got to the main trail, and I got to admit we did a tolerable good job. It wouldn't be much trouble getting to the mine at all, now. I told the boss that even old ladies could make it.

He chuckled, then got serious and said, "Yeah, and robbers too, Luke. Don't forget them."

"Boss, there shore ain't nuthin' here to rob. We ain't exactly pickin' gold nuggets off the ground, you know."

"No, but when we do, word will get around and you can bet the vultures will find their way up here."

The boss sweated down in that hole for weeks. Most of the time, I was resting in the shade. We weren't much in need of food, except some meat now and then. I'd shot a buck on the third day, smoked most of it, cooked some it, and ate a pile more of it. We made pigs out of ourselves the first night on that deer meat.

I admit, I was enjoying laying in the shade. It isn't that I'm lazy, but when there comes a time in my life like that, when I don't have to be up sweating and wearing out the seat of my pants in a saddle, why, I just take to it like a duck to water. I remember the first winter on the Slash-Bar when me and Spoon and another cowboy was in a line shack way up in the north part of the ranch. It got real cold and some good blows come by us that winter. We didn't work too hard, just making sure the cows had plenty feed, that they weren't drifting or hung in deep snow, and a few other little things. No brush popping for us, or branding.

I really enjoyed that time, but Spoon and that other rider nearly drove me crazy. They were constantly getting up and moving around, looking outside, walking the floor, talking to each other or themselves, and it wore me out just watching them. As for me, I could have stayed there a few winters all by myself and got along real well. It isn't so bad being alone when you know you're going to be seeing other people eventually. It would pain me though, to be where I wouldn't be seeing another soul for years. I don't crave that kind of lonesome.

One day the boss came stumbling out into the light, all excited and carrying on like a kid at a sugar cane field. He had a bunch of dirty rocks in his hands and he come rushing over to me talking about finding 'it.'

Over and over he said, "I did it! I did it! Luke, I found it! I did it!"

Real casual, I asked, "What did you find, Boss?"

He shoved that pile of rocks under my nose and said, "Right here, Luke. Gold!"

It might seem strange, but I didn't get excited. Right then, I know the sight of a platter of food from the eating place in town would have made me a whole lot more excited. I mean, it was good that the boss had found the gold, and maybe I would have been like him if I'd been down in that hole all them days and found what he did, but somehow I just couldn't get excited over that bunch of rocks there in his hands.

I looked it over and smiled to let him know I appreciated it. I felt guilty sitting there in the shade while he did all the work. But, it was his idea and I just went along with it. He walked back to the mine and disappeared for a few minutes. When he came back he was holding another bunch of rocks and they had more of that stringy gold in it. The boss talked about veins and lodes, but I never really knew what he was talking about. I never let on. I just nodded and smiled.

Inside I was laughing at him on account of him being so taken with this gold. I never saw a man get so excited over something. He just wouldn't shut up but kept on babbling and talking about all the things he was going to do, the places he was going to see and the house he was going to build and the ranch he was going to buy.

He stopped once, looked at me and asked, "What are you going to do with yours, Luke?"

I laughed out loud. He didn't take offense, but I could see he was put off a little, so I said, "Boss, I reckon I got to see real money in my hands and not a pile of rocks before I'll start thinking of spendin' anything. Anyways, I can't think of a single thing I want except maybe one of them new Colts and maybe one of those Remington long guns. I might even settle for a Sharps. You know, they shoot mighty long. I heard ..."

Smith gave a big sigh, looked at me and said, "Luke, you're just the medicine I need." He was talking easy now, not with that excited tremble. "Reckon I been like some kid, eh partner?"

I chuckled and said, "Well, you ain't exactly been a mountain of silence."

He went back and chipped some more and brought a lot of that gold out, along with rocks and stuff. We loaded up one of the horses with a couple of sacks of that rock the boss called ore samples, and the boss took off for town. I was to stay and guard the camp, and he promised to return in a day or so. I asked him to bring back some bacon and coffee on account of us running low on those items. I also asked him if he could bring back one of those pies. He said he'd look into it, then he took off down the trail.

I could see the excitement building back up in him.

That afternoon was slow and muggy, so I decided that my horse needed some exercising. I hadn't moved the horses at all in the time that we'd been here, but just let them graze pretty free with the hobbles. So, I threw a saddle on old Mash and rode out. That horse had a bad habit of trying to mash my foot anytime I was putting his saddle on, especially when I was cinching up. He tried twice, and once he mashed my foot real good, but I just kicked him back and shoved him hard. Probably didn't do much good, but it helped me feel better.

I rode down the mountain trail real slow, and near the bottom I took the fork that went the opposite direction that led to town. I'd never been that way and was a little curious to know where it went. For miles, there was a sea of green pine, with a splatter here and there of yellow. I could see a lot of aspen trees scattered around. A cool breeze made a soft hum in the tree tops, and it felt so good I unbuttoned my shirt and let the wind fill it up and rub my skin awhile. There's nothing to compare to the quiet of a mountain side. It's a gentle kind of quiet that makes the mind feel peaceful. I've always been partial to mountain breezes.

I frogged Mash up a small incline and walked him over to the edge of a clearing. The view was enough to make a Texas cowboy swear off of Texas for good. Way down into the valley there was smoke curling up out of the trees, likely from a cabin, and the trees made the whole valley a splash of blue-green. Over to the far end, I could make out Reata because there was more smoke there, and on account of less trees being around.

I got to thinking and my mind took me over my back trail. I've never much regretted things I've done in my life. If I do wrong, I remember it and try to do right next time. I think most of the regret I ever had come from losing my friends or family. I lost a good friend when Spoon died. We'd come to be good friends. I had even been teaching him how to shoot. It turned out that I didn't teach him fast enough.

Friends are something a body don't find often. I've only had four real friends in my life, but every one of them was true to me. They all helped me when I was down. I think a friend ought to help and he ought to do it without you asking for the help.

I had a partner once who called me friend, and I thought he was, but when I got bit by a rattler and was laid up for a spell, that friend turned out to be about as helpful to me as that snake. A new hand hired on and I was laying in my bunk, too weak to even get up, and half out of my head, and my partner sat by and watched this new hand drag my bunk away from the window and then drag his bunk over in my place.

My friend didn't say a word, but one cowboy I didn't even get along with too well told the new hand that when I got well, it was likely that he wouldn't be wanting that window any more. I recovered and that man had to sleep outside on the ground in his bed roll a couple of nights, until he fixed his bunk. It got broke when I bashed him with it. We had to replace the window, too, because when he went out, that window kind of followed him.

Me and that cowboy got along real good after that, and if he'd stayed around longer, we'd have probably got to be friends. He had a mean streak in him, but he'd get sorry, later. His problem was liquor. He'd drink and turn mean. He'd been drunk when he came in and moved my bunk that time.

I remember the time him and a bunch of us went to town together and I gave in and went into the saloon with them. They all knew I wasn't taken with liquor and didn't care for saloons, but I finally gave in and settled for some sweet water. They played cards mostly, and talked, trading gossip like a bunch of old women. There was a black rider, name of Brady—he's dead, now—and two *injun* cowboys, myself and a few others. I shouldn't have been there, or those *injuns* either, because they got awful when they got some of that jug in them, plus some of the men in there didn't like them in there with us. They'd tolerate the black riders, but them *injuns* were an irritation to some of them. They'd glare at them and make remarks.

There was a lot of men in the saloon by evening time, and most everyone I came with was drunk in an hour. There was a group of men near the center and they were playing cards and grumbling over the racket the *injuns* were making, particularly the one we called Gimpy Crow, on account of him being a Crow *injun* with a game leg.

Gimpy was sitting under one of the lanterns howling at it. Maybe he thought it was the moon. I don't know. At first, everyone had a good laugh at it, but eventually, it got to be irritating, like a cricket that crawled up close to your bedroll. It was bothering those men real bad, and it didn't set too good with me, either. Finally, one of them called over to us and told us to shove them two out into the street. Then, he told our partners they might as well clear out all the stink in here and throw the nigger out, too.

Well, there was five of us, plus the two *injuns*, but they never counted because they was so drunk they were hardly able to walk, let alone fight. Anyway, when that fool said that, this red-headed partner of ours, the one I'd tossed out the window, stood up and told him to mind his own business or he'd throw him out. Right about then, this crazy *injun*, Walking Stick is what they called him, staggers between the two and spits a whole mouthful of whiskey on this big mouth sitting there.

That tore it. That whole table, and a dozen others jumped up, and the fight started. Only man who pulled a gun was the fool that started the ruckus, and he was trying to shoot Walking Stick, but Red took that gun and beat him over the head with it. Then Red got hit with a chair. I wasn't going to mix in on that fight, but two of those boys at the table jumped over a couple chairs to get to me, so I was in. I suppose I would have mixed in anyway, because our side was losing bad. Someone had thrown Walking Stick through the little swinging doors, and those two that came after me was aiming to do the same for me.

I waited until the first one was near and was raring back to plow me under, then I laid one deep into that big belly of his, and it was like hitting a sack of flour. It wasn't as soft as it looked, though, and then I cracked him in the jaw once for good measure. He fell back into his friend, but that one shoved ole Flour Belly onto the floor and jumped at me.

I stepped up on a chair with one foot and pretended I was a mountain cat jumping on a calf. We crashed down together and his head slammed hard against a long shiny metal rail that ran along the bottom of the bar. He was out like a coal oil lantern in the middle of a Texas norther.

When I was getting up, someone like to have killed me with a chair. It smashed against my back. Only thing saved me was the man who had made that chair didn't make it too strong. It was good and heavy, but it busted all up. Even the bottom split. I still ache when I think about that chair. When that happened, I got riled. I don't recollect everything, but the boys told me later I was like a steer that had ate some crazy weed. I found out later that I pitched Gimpy Crow, one of our crew, and the bartender right out the door, and even kicked Red in the side of the head, besides breaking two tables.

I never went crazy like that since, and I hope I don't ever do it again. I did find out that I got a limit in a fight as to what I'll tolerate and call friendly. After that, it's no fight, but an all-out war. That's another reason I stay out of them places.

Liquor in a man is like hunger in a bear. Get a bear hungry enough and it'll do anything—crawl into a shack, a wagon, or even jump a horse and rider. Bears don't think clearly when they're hungry. They get bold and do things they'd never do with a half-full gut. Same way with a man and liquor. Pour him a skin-full, and he'll say things and do things a sober fool would never do. My pa always taught me that liquor was wrong, and Ma, she called it 'pisun' and said it'd rot a man's soul and make him a half-wit. I'm not so sure now she wasn't far from wrong because I seen it make a lot of my friends act like they didn't have a lick of sense, when I knew they did.

I've had two partners shot on account of liquor, and had another fall off his horse and break his shoulder; and once, I saw a cowboy shoot a sheriff, kind of accidental. He wasn't a mean cowboy and never meant no harm, but when a body is full of that stuff, he thinks he can do things he can't even do when he's sober, like shootin' a sheriff's hat off his head at thirty yards. Bored a hole right through that sheriff's back. Then too, there was that time when I was a kid and had to cut a man on account of him being drunk and foolish with me.

My ma never allowed liquor about. I remember an old trapper who lived about twenty miles from our place. He would come over a couple times a year and every time, he'd bring a jug. Now Pa wasn't one to tip the jug, on account of Ma making him swear off the stuff, and it used to rile that old man some when Pa would say no to his offer to tip it with him. He sip awhile, then hold it out to Pa. Finally, Ma couldn't take no more, and one evening he and Pa was setting there on the porch. The old man was holding out that jug to Pa, and Pa, as usual, he was holding up both hands, just saying, "Naw. I don't want none. I done told you that," like he'd done so many times before.

Ma walked out on the porch and asked if she could have some. That old man blinked a couple times, and me and Pa just looked at each other, and then at Ma. He handed her the jug and took to grinning like a fool. Now, right alongside Pap's chair there was this big old grindstone we used to sharpen axes and knives and such. Ma took the jug, made out like she was having a tough time hefting it, and then dropped it right on top of that grindstone. It looked like an accident, unless you knew Ma. She was as strong as most men, but more than that, she hated that liquor like it was snake poison.

She took to apologizing and all, but there was a hard look in her eye, and she wasn't smiling like most folks do when they're saying how sorry they are about something. That old trapper looked at his jug lying scattered in pieces beside the porch, and stared long at the wet stain on the wood, and looked back at my ma, then back to the stain, like he couldn't believe what he was seeing. Finally, he shook his head a time or two, muttered something to himself and walked off into the woods. He never did come back. Pa fussed with Ma some over it, because Pa missed his company, but my ma never missed that man once. In a way, Ma was as hard as Pa.

I put my thoughts aside, turned Mash's head about and went back to the trail. I'd have liked to spent the rest of the day there, but I didn't like leaving the camp for too long. Might be there would be visitors, and the boss wouldn't be too happy with me if I let somebody carry off all our stuff. Reckon I'd be upset too, but he had more to lose than me. Most of what I owned was on my horse.

I piddled around camp after that, waiting for the boss to come back. It was a good time to get in some practice with my pistol. I like to play with my gun about every day, if I can. The more you get to know something, the easier it gets to use it. My gun felt almost like a part of my hand and I didn't want that to ever change, at least not until this country I was in changed. I'd been in too many places with too many sudden men in my day.

First thing I did was work on my draw. Popping them rabbits for my pa was real good practice when I was a kid, and it kept my hand in good shape, especially since that old navy .44 my pa gave me to use weighed almost as much as I did, or so it seemed to me at the time. I'd gotten to where I could shuck my gun and hit a rabbit on the run most every time.

I adjusted the pistol so the butt rested just over my belly button, then hung my right hand down. Quickly, I snatched my pistol out and lined it on one of several pine cones I'd placed atop a rock. My hand was steady as that rock, but I could tell my aim was off just a hair. It's a strange thing how a body isn't quite able to do as good when it's not life or death. I know if that had been a man standing there with a gun and about to shoot me, I would have been right on target. But, I had to work some more. I wanted to be on target all the time, and not just when a man was facing me. I worked half an hour until I got that gun lined straight twenty times out of twenty.

Used to be that when I worked like that, I'd get a sore thumb from earing back the hammer, but now I had a callous on my thumb and never felt a thing. I kept on working with it, drawing, earing back the hammer as I drew, and lining on my target. It felt good, and the sweat was rolling down my back when I quit.

A body can draw a gun all day long, but the real test is when you put that little tug on the trigger and the explosion happens. I know a few men who can shuck a gun as quick as me, but when they pull that trigger they might as well be shooting the breeze because that's all they could hit. That pull on the trigger can throw off the best aim in the world.

I recollect a man by the name of Dale who could pull his gun faster than anything I've ever seen, but that man couldn't hit ten steers standing sideways. Another gentleman I knew by the name of Claymore wasn't no ball of fire getting out his gun, but when he did, there wasn't a thing standing or moving he couldn't hit. He used to be one of them Rangers down in Texas, but he got shot up one day in a fight with some Comanche and had to give up the Ranger life. He took to cooking. I used to like watching him roll empty peach cans, standing there, legs spread, leaning forward, with both of them hands of his wrapped around that big Walker Colt he had. I even saw that man shoot a horsefly right off the rump of a dun, once. Really, I did.

I have to admit, I was asked to do the same and I declined. I'm not saying I couldn't do it, because I did out-shoot that old man in some contests we used to hold now and then, although I couldn't beat him all the time. He had good days and bad ones, same as all of us. But, if I got a bad aim only once, I'd have been buying a piece of horseflesh I couldn't afford and couldn't even ride. Some things just aren't worth chancing.

I turned my back on my targets, settled my mind, then turned and drew, fired four shots fast as I could, then reloaded. Reloading was something I learned to do as a kid. Pa always said that a man with an empty gun is like a fool chasing a skunk. If he's lucky, he won't catch it, but chances are when he does, he's going to get more than he bargained for. Chances were, having an empty gun wasn't going to mean much most of the time. But, there would come a time when it did, and it only takes once.

I'd practiced for about an hour when I heard a noise behind me as I was reloading. I turned real slow, slipping the last load into my gun as I did, making like I never heard a thing. There, right smack in the middle of the trail was this big, bony 'jack' mule. He was maybe the biggest I'd ever seen, but what kind of took my breath was what was setting on him.

She was pretty as a picture, with a long, blue dress, and she had a big old straw hat perched on her head. What made her even prettier was the fact that her face was sun-kissed brown, like coffee with some sweet cream in it. She wore a white scarf tied on her head. It made me swallow a time or two, seeing something that strange and wonderful way up here where you don't hear anything but the moaning wind, and where a body don't see another soul except his partner. A body could stay in these mountains for years and not see another soul, if he was of a mind to do that.

She flashed me a big smile, waved, kicked that mule in the sides and he walked, stiff-legged, over near where I was standing. I must have looked like some kind of fool, standing there with my mouth hanging open, my eyes plumb full of that gal. I hadn't even had the sense to say howdy to her or even wave back at her.

She sat there on the back of her mule and just looked at me. Then, when she saw I wasn't going to say anything, she said, "I heard all that shooting and rode up the trail to see."

I got my voice back and said, "Well, suppose I had been a robber or something? Ain't that kind of foolish, riding up when you don't know what's going on?" I squinted up at her because she was framed by the sun, then added, "And suppose I was a bad man and I think you're just about the prettiest thing I ever did see and I don't let you leave."

I could see it stung her, and her face flushed deep red, but I didn't mean to be hard with her. I just have trouble talking to lady folks. It was the first thing that popped into my mind and it came right out. I always had trouble like that—speaking my mind when my mouth needed to stay shut.

She glared at me and said, "Well, I sneaked up, sort of. Besides, I could tell that it wasn't no gun fight by the way the shots sounded." She had her hands on her hips and was staring at me, daring me to argue with her. Then, with a sharp pitch to her voice she added, "And anyway, I could tell *you* ain't no outlaw."

I decided to drop that subject, because it wasn't too popular, and she looked to be ready to fuss with me. That little gal struck me as a mighty determined sort of female, one a man could tie to and would stick by him thick and thin. I wasn't thinking of making ties like that real soon, but a pearl like that don't come by often, and a man can't help thinking about it.

We talked for near two hours and the sun was beginning to sink when she jumped up on that mule and headed for home. Turned out home wasn't so far off. Her ma and pa had a small farm right at the bottom of the mountain just into the valley and a little to the east of the trail. It wasn't much from what she said, but it was theirs, and it was home. I promised that I'd visit one of these days, and she promised to have some sweet potatoes and onions for me when I got there.

Her pa was a dirt farmer out of Pennsylvania. They had tried farming in Texas, but the Comanche had pretty near got them, so they'd left. The *injuns* had been almost as bad here, too, but fortunately they were mostly on the run from the soldiers and they were doing most of their raiding to the south and west. After she left, I rubbed old Mash down, hobbled him and started a fire. I was getting hungry, and the boss ought to be trailing back soon. He'd likely be hungry. He might have decided to stay in town, so I figured that I'd cook and leave whatever I couldn't eat, and if he came in there would be something, and if not, then I'd have something to eat in the morning.

I turned in early, but I didn't sleep by the fire. In fact, I let the fire to go out. Light travels a mighty long way at night in the mountains and I didn't want to stir up the curiosity of any strangers. So, I carried my roll back out of sight, right near a clump of trees. Then, I led Mash over and tied a long piece of rawhide to his head. That horse would graze around and would waken me now and then, but if somebody came up, I knew Mash would raise his head quick and that jerk on the line would wake me pronto. I wrapped the line around my wrist and went to sleep fast as a lamp goes black when it runs out of oil.

Morning came, and I woke feeling good. Mash had lived up to his name and stepped on me once during the night, but I wasn't hurt, just mad. He did it on purpose, I know, for a horse isn't one to traipse about in the night, stumbling over people. A man might do something like that, but not a horse. I figured I'd have to trade him off or figure out some way to keep it from happening again. He might have stepped on the hand I shoot with instead of my leg, and then I would be in a terrible fix. I had to teach that horse some manners. I had an idea that maybe if I tied my rope on one of his legs and stretched it on the opposite side of me, then he couldn't get no closer than the rope would allow. He could still graze around hobbled, but he couldn't get close to me. I figured that was the thing to do.

The boss didn't show again the next day or evening, so I spent another night with Mash tugging me awake now and then, but nothing quick. That rope idea worked fine and I never had any more problems out of Mash. A man has to learn how to adapt. I've never had too much of a problem learning how to adapt, but I rode with some men who did. Me, I can get by anywhere and make my way. Had me a mule with a big stubborn when I was a kid, but I made do. The lessons that old mule handed out regular taught me how to handle Mash, so I didn't really come out short on the deal.

I'd rode with a lot of men, though, who just never seemed to learn a thing. Like the little dried up man we called Weasel, on account of his thin face, who never did seem to understand that in the morning, a horse just don't like a rider on his back. We took to watching him on account of it being almost a regular event. He'd get all saddled up and he'd get a bronc that had done some thinking. That bronc would pretend he was accepting the saddle and the ride, and just about the time Weasel would relax, that bronc would explode under him, and Weasel would sail off into the morning air. We'd howl, and the next day, Weasel would get a new bronc, would walk it around the corral, and just when he leaned down to unlift the gate, his horse would toss him over the gate posts.

I knew a lot of men that were dumb like him.

CHAPTER 9

Next morning I got to wondering if the boss had got himself into some trouble in town. If he didn't come in soon, I'd have to ride down and see what was holding him up. These were hard times and some hard men were in these parts. There were some gangs riding loose in these parts, and some bushwhackers around.

That afternoon I heard a noise on the trail. I'd just saddled Mash and was ready to swing into the saddle, when the boss rode in. He was pale and sickly looking, and had a kind of used-up look about him. He didn't step out of the saddle, but just leaned forward and kind of rolled off the back of his horse.

He spotted me and tried to grin, but it was hard coming, I could tell. Finally, he managed to say, "Luke, I'm sorry to be late. Got sick bad in town. I'm still weak. Got the runs and nothing stays down in my stomach" He stumbled away from his horse and fell on a pile of straw we'd made for beds.

I took the mare and hobbled her near Mash. By the time I got back, the boss was slack-jawed. He must have been pretty sick, since he's the strongest man I ever met, and that ride up the mountain plumb wore him out.

All night, he ranted and raved and tossed around like he was a live pig on a spit. There wasn't much I could do for him. He had a high fever, so

I piled some blankets on him to sweat it out. Then, he got to chilling, and I finally took my blanket and laid it over him, but that wasn't enough, either. It was a mighty cool night, and I was getting cold myself, so I took one of the horse blankets and laid it over him and took the other for myself. It didn't smell too good, but it seemed to be just what he needed. I knew that come morning, I smelled more like my horse than my horse did.

It took the big man nearly a week to recover. He was pretty weak after that. He tried his best to get me down in that hole working, but I just wouldn't do it. He even got mad a little, but I wouldn't give in. There wasn't a thing down in that hole worth me crawling in after.

Finally, he got better, enough so I didn't have to keep doing things for him. He was as grumpy as a she-bear with cubs in the Spring, and it was wearing thin on me. I decided to get out of camp for awhile.

I said, "Boss, I got an offer for some fresh vegetables. You don't mind, I'll go down and fetch some."

He was wiping some water off his face and spoke through the towel. "Good. You ain't worth nuthin' around here, anyway."

I got to the farm in just under a hour. There was a gate with a piece of wire looped over a post, so I leaned over, slid the wire off, swung open the gate, and rode on through. A nice little road with some pretty deep wagon ruts ran right up to the house.

I could see it wasn't much of a house. Likely, he'd been so busy raising his crops and clearing the land that he hadn't took the time to build his house yet, because this house had a dirt roof and part of it was dug into the side of a hill that ran behind it. That part that wasn't dug into the hill was half of a room and a porch. It looked to be cozy, but like I said, I'm not too partial to holes in the ground, even when they're made into a house.

I called out a hello, and a small woman in a faded gingham dress came out onto the porch. Her sun-darkened face broke into a smile and softened a lot of the wrinkles and worry put into her face by years of a hard life. She stepped off the porch, shaded her eyes with a hand and said, "You must be Luke."

I took off my hat and said, "Yes Ma'm, that's me."

"Mary said you'd ride by one day. You look just like she said." She smoothed her dress the way my ma used to do, then said, "She's out in the field with her daddy and her brothers. Just ride around that hill behind the house, and they'll all be back there a little ways."

I thanked her, swung Mash around and headed for the field. I spotted them about the same time I was seen. There was three young'uns, probably Mary's brothers, her pa, and Mary in this field. They all stopped work as I rode up, leaning on hoes and watching. Mary put down a little basket she had and ran over to where her pa was standing. Two of the brothers were older, one even close to my age, but the third one was young, maybe about like when I left home.

Mary waved as I got near, and hollered, "Luke!" She motioned me over, and I made sure Mash didn't trample nothing. I swung out of the saddle and Mary said, "Luke, this is my daddy, and this is Mather, my brother." She was pointing to the tallest one. He smiled at me and I smiled back. She introduced me to the other two. "This one is George, and that little runt over there is Lonnie."

"Mary, I ain't no runt and you better be takin' that back!" Lonnie was put out with his sister, I could tell.

Her pa stepped over some rows, came up to me and stuck out his hand. "Howdy, Luke. I'm Josiah Wilson. Mighty glad you came down. Mary here told me you'd be ridin' by. Hope you'll be stayin' for supper."

I took a liking to Josiah right off. He was close to the boss' age, with some white on his head near the ears. He wore a floppy brimmed hat and some old patched broadcloth pants with a blue shirt that looked like it had boiled a hundred times too many.

I grinned and said, "Well, I hadn't planned on it, but I'm persuaded since goin' back would mean eatin' my own cookin'."

They all got a good laugh at that, and Mary got her pa to let her loose from the fields. I rode back with Mary walking alongside. The rest stayed in the fields working. He apologized, but said he had to get some seed in the ground today, but I just waved a hand at him and told him there wasn't no call to stop working on my account.

Then that little brother of hers, the one called Lonnie had to mix in and say, "Aw, he ain't carin' if we stay out here. He come down to see Mary, not us."

That brought a roar of laughter out of them other two and a stern, hard look at Lonnie from me and his pa, and Mary was glaring at him, too. I could tell right there I was going to have to get that youngster alone and teach him a few things before too long. He just had that kind of look to his face, and them black eyes was grinning all the time. I figure he'd brought a peck of trouble to Mary in the short time he'd been in this world.

We went back to the house and I put my horse in the corral. That big boned 'jack' mule was in there, and I figured it was used to plow and pull the little buggy setting under a tree nearby. Mary told me that buggy had come all the way across Texas, and that her pa had taken it for wages from a man who owed him.

Mary wanted to put Mash away, but I stopped her. I wasn't used to a woman doing for me, and I sure wasn't wanting my horse to give that pretty gal a mashed foot. She'd hate me and my horse after that. I told her so, and she just laughed and told me that Mash wasn't nothing in his tricks. She said that mule of theirs, called Blackie, liked to try and brush off anyone on his back. When he got hooked into a plow, he tried to get it tangled in any brush that was handy, and when he got to pulling the buggy, he never wanted to do more than a slow walk.

I figured that mule had just had his way too long and hadn't had a man riding him, or he was getting the bit in his mouth, because I ain't ever rode anything on four legs I couldn't turn, except a loco steer I got tricked into riding one day. I've had a few horses run wild on me, but I turned them. One, I had to grab by the nose and pull to one side before he turned. The other two was easier. About all I did with them was throw the end of a rope in front of their face. They got to turning to avoid the rope, and I kept grabbing when they'd jerk their heads to shy from the rope until I grabbed the halter and fished up the reins.

That's one reason I started using a plain old hackamore. I got Mash trained so he moves at the slightest tug. But, if he ever did get moving on me and wouldn't turn or stop, I got me a strong arm and a strong rope. There isn't a horse's head made I can't pull to one side. I rode Fred, my old mule, with a rope, and he wasn't no gentle sort of mule, especially when I first started. He was mostly stubborn.

I drug up a chair and set down on the porch. Mary was inside helping her ma fix the food. I felt good setting there on that porch. It made me think of my old home, the good smells coming from the kitchen, the warm feeling, and that feeling of belonging. I missed that. It brought back old memories of my ma cooking in that little old log cabin we had back in the woods of Kentucky. The smell of baking bread, frying bacon, or hoe-cake, were things I'd grown up with and missed. I sat there for nearly an hour, enjoying the smells, and trading small talk with Mary now and then, when she'd step out on the porch from the kitchen.

I hadn't set there for more than an hour or so when I saw dust coming up the road. It looked to be near five or more riders coming. One of them stepped down and undid the gate which was set off a good piece from the house, and then they all came riding on through. I saw they didn't hook that gate back up, so I figured they weren't planning to stay too long.

I spoke out. "Mary, you folks got company coming."

Mary peeked out the door and ran back in. Her ma came to the door, a rag in her hands. Her eyes got big and she whispered to Mary, "Get your daddy, quick!"

I sensed the fear in her voice. I eased out of my chair, walked over to one of the porch posts and leaned up against it. I hooked a thumb into my belt. On the outside, I looked to be relaxed, but inside, I was primed, and my stomach got that old familiar empty feeling to it. I didn't know what kind of trouble these men were to the Wilsons, but I knew I was bound to make it mine, now.

All those rider came up real slow into the front yard, and all but two piled off their horses. That made four on the ground and two setting the saddle. Too many to fight all at once, but I learned something about fighting a long time ago. If you can get every man there thinking that he is probably the one you're going to take out first, or even second, you got a good chance of bluffing them. A mob is willing to fight, but when you get them one man at a time, they're not so willing and are afraid of dying.

One stepped up near the porch. He was a tall, lean rider, wearing a dirty shirt and greasy hair sticking out of his hat. He had a narrow face, with about a week's growth of beard on it. His nose had been broke at least once, and all that, together with a squinty-eyed look, made him appear uglier and meaner than he probably was. His pistol hung down in front of his pants where he'd moved it while he rode. He paid no mind to me at all.

"Where's your old man, woman!"

I've got a short fuse when it comes to men folk shoving themselves off hard to women folk. So, I walked over to that man, and before he even knew what was up, I took him by the shirt front and give him a shove backwards, making sure I had my foot right behind the one he was leaning on. He staggered back, lost his balance and fell hard on the ground. I wasn't watching him though. I was watching the others. Not a one made a move, most of them curious, I think. One of the riders still on his horse even gave me a grin and a wink.

The man on the ground came up fast, and while he was rising, I said, "If you come at me, I'm goin' to put you right back on the ground."

He knew I meant it, and he didn't have the sand in his craw I thought he had, because he backed off and said, "Who are you and what are you mixing in on this for?"

I smiled, but my eyes weren't smiling. "Mister, these people are friends of mine. Now, I ain't heard none of 'em invite you on their land, and for certain, not on this porch. So, you have your say, and then ride out of here." My voice had that hard in it that I'd learned to put in it during my days as a lawman. I found if I gave a certain low pitch to my voice, it took on a kind of gravely sound. One man told me once it sounded almost like I was growling.

He looked back at the rider who'd winked at me and said, "Take care of this trash, Bule."

The rider called Bule answered back, "Naw, I think I'll sit this one out, Lester." He grinned at me and give me another one of them winks, then added, "After all, Lester, he's only trash. Can't you handle trash, Lester?" He was grinning when he said that, and I could see he was enjoying the whole thing. I just stood loose, waiting.

Right then Mary's pa come running up, rifle in one hand and his hat throwed back. I could see he come for war so I held up my hand and said, "Hold up right there, Josiah!" I said it kind of hard so he wouldn't mistake what I was saying. I couldn't risk him starting a war and getting in my way, and them riders maybe shooting Mary or her Ma.

I give him credit. He wasn't like some men I knew who get mad or afraid and lose their ability to think. He kept his head about him and pulled up short, and stayed just to the side of the house. It gave him a good position in case something started. Then I said, "Mary, you stay back, and Mrs. Wilson, you stay in the house. Josiah, you keep the boys back there, too."

"We'll be alright, Luke." That was Mary. She moved back into the shadows of the house with her mother.

Lester looked hard at Bule, then over to me. Finally, he walked over to where he could see Josiah, but stopped when I told him that was far enough.

He said to Josiah, "You been selling your stuff in town again. You were told what would happen if you did that once more."

I cut in real quick. "If something is about to happen, you best cut me in on it."

Lester tried to put on a weary, patient air, and said to me, "This ain't no concern of yours, cowboy. I'm letting you get away with it now, because you don't know what's involved here."

"I'm involved, mister. You explain it to me."

He got his jaw a little tighter at that, gave a big sigh, then said, "Mister Johnson made a gentleman's agreement with Mr. Wilson to sell him all his produce. When he bought the land, that was the agreement, but Wilson broke his word, and he's been selling in town."

"And what's the promise you was just makin' to him? The one about something goin' to happen, you know?"

Josiah broke in while I was getting some hard stares from Lester and a couple of those men. "Luke, they was to beat on me. That was the promise they made last time. But, I had to sell in town. Mister Johnson, he's been dropping prices on me right along. In town, I can get four times what he gives me. Not only that, he took over my whole crop of beans the other day, sayin' that was payment for robbin' him."

The anger stirred deep down inside me. I don't know that I have ever understood greedy people. This Johnson man was getting all this good man grew, and getting it cheap enough, yet he wanted more. Fact is, I think Johnson wanted a slave. That's the way it panned to me.

I stared hard at Lester and said, "You ride out of here and tell your boss that Luke Adams will come and have a little chat with him one day. Meanwhile, I'll shoot any man I catch on this property. I'm ridin' for this spread, and if shootin' comes with the ridin', why that's all right, too."

Lester looked at me, then back to this Bule feller. He said, "Bule, you gonna just sit there?" That Bule feller just watched him, and Lester's face clouded up, then he raised his voice a mite and said, "You're just setting there?" He paused, waiting for a sign from Bule, who just sat there grinning. Finally, Lester threw up his arms and said, "You don't take this drifter now, you're through! You hear that?"

That grin wiped itself off Bule's face and he looked hard at the man for a long minute, then said, "Lester, I decided I was through this morning, long before we left for this place. I had made up my mind that if they put up a fight, I was gonna side them. I see I wasn't needed, though."

He put his grin back on his face and looked over to me. "It appears to me that you done bit the wrong leg, Lester." I could see those little devils dancing in this Bule's eyes. He was loving every minute of it.

Lester turned to the other men. "Well, what about you men? You just along for the ride, too?" Not a one of those men said a word, but just fiddled with their saddles or something, not looking at Lester. They were all cowboys, not gunfighters, and they weren't about to line up against a man like Bule and a proddy stranger like me who looked too anxious for a fight. I could see Bule's announcement had taken them all by surprise, and I could tell they feared him. None of them glared at him like a man might do to another man who'd gone over to the other side of a fight. It told me a lot about Bule. They liked him.

Lester glared at Bule, then me, then he stomped his way over to his horse and jumped into the saddle. I guess getting up on that horse made him feel kind of like God, on account of his being about 15 hands closer to heaven, because he leaned forward in the saddle, looked hard at me, and said, "When I come back, you better be gone. I ain't coming back with a bunch of cow nurses this time."

That man sure tempted me, he did. But, I let him have his say. If the women folks and the kid hadn't been there I'd have snatched him right off his horse, then. Turned out, Bule had some ideas of his own. I saw him undo his rope as Lester turned his horse to ride away. He shook out a loop, flicked it to the side and then dropped it over Lester's shoulders, slick as I ever seen a thing done. Lester hit the ground hard, then tried to get up, but Bule's horse had some real cow-sense, because it back away and kept that rope tight. Then, Bule moved his horse forward a step, gave a little flick and the rope came loose. He rode close to the man.

"Fall off your horse, Lester?" The devil was in them eyes again, and his grin was a mile wide. I was busting my buttons to keep from laughing right out loud. Me and Bule was going to hit it off fine. When Lester got on his horse and rode off I noticed he was leaning forward so a rope couldn't drop on him.

I stuck out my hand and said, "Bule, I'm Luke and glad to meet you."

He smiled and said, "Heard of you, Luke."

"What was it you heard, Bule?" It was curious to me that anyone around here had heard about me. I figured it probably had to do with that big feed I had down in the town restaurant that time.

He laughed. "Heard you was a bad man to tangle a loop with, and that you're wanted by one of the biggest ranchers in Texas for shootin' his son, and that you like to eat. That's all." He was grinning while he said all that.

I pushed back my hat and studied him. He was the friendliest man I ever met. I figured his age to be near mine. His skin was leather-brown and his grey eyes crinkled and were surrounded by a million wrinkles caused from squinting in the sun at a lot of cows. He had hair kind of like that stuff that comes out of the top of an ear of corn when it's ripe, and a flat-brimmed, dusty black hat that was cocked to one side of his head. He was wearing a faded blue shirt, with a big, red neckerchief knotted around his neck.

He didn't wear spurs, and his pants were wore slick on the insides and bottom. Only thing real difference about him from most cowboys I've known, as far as his duds and such, was that big, black-handled gun hanging down on his right side. It looked like it had been used often, and he had that look that told me he could use it tolerable well. But, what was really strange about Bule was his eyes and his grin. He was grinning from the time he rode into the yard until the time he swung down off his horse, and his eyes held a little fire in them, if you know what I mean. It was like there was mischief brewing there, like Mary's brother, Lonnie.

"Mind telling me where you heard that?" I was curious to know how the word had spread, since I didn't think Cat Foot had done any talking.

He flashed me a smile that was all teeth and said, "Well, that herd that was in here awhile back had a couple of riders with it from the ranch where you killed Briner's kid.. They told us about it. Way they tell it, Briner will likely come for you soon as he gets word. I remembered seeing you in town, and their description pretty much matched what I saw. Couple of the boys matched you, too. I reckon they might have said something. Don't know that for sure, but it's likely."

I had figured as much, so it didn't surprise me. I'd have to ride careful, now. But, I never was one to ride around without thinking about where I was at and who might be there waiting. No man could avoid an ambush completely, but staying alert had saved my hide more than once.

Josiah walked up and said, "Luke, you didn't have to take my part like that, but I'm thanking you for it. I'd have had to take a beating or kill somebody, and they'd have hung me if I did that. I think I'd have taken the beating because my family needs me."

He smiled at Bule then and said, "And you too, Mr. Bule. I thank you."

Bule shook his head and said, "No mister to it, sir. Just Bule. And, no thanks needed. Just doing what is right. It wasn't just you."

I only half listened because I was thinking hard on what Bule had told me. Trouble was on my trail and it would probably follow me right up to here. I had me some hard thinking to do. I had to decide whether to run or stay put. Hiding was out of the question.

I guess I was relieved in a way, now that I knew Briner would find me. It had come. It had been nice not fretting over that man, and now I'd be worrying again. If I stayed, I was going to be the cause, probably, of more men dying, because I'd not go easy. I'd take some of them with me. It was something I knew would trouble my mind for the next few days.

Josiah invited Bule to supper and he accepted, so we went to the porch to set. Josiah left and went back to the field because he wanted to get to them seeds down. We sat on the porch, me on the steps, leaning against one of the posts, and Bule leaned himself up against the house on the porch. There was a rocker on the porch, but I didn't feel proper taking it.

I asked Bule, "Who is this Johnson?"

"Aw, he's just about the biggest thing ever to hit the Territory. Ain't too much in these parts he ain't got a finger into. In fact, if he tells you that you can't settle in this part of the Territory, you ain't gonna settle."

"He's that powerful?" I could feel something rising in me.

Bule's eyes crinkled with his grin and he said, "He's got the law, the troops over at the fort, two ranches full of riders, some of 'em slick with a gun, some slick with a hot iron. Besides all that, he's got most of Reata owned, except for the bank, a saloon and the blacksmith shop. Ain't much bought or sold in these parts that don't involve that man one way or another."

Well, that did set me back some. I never knew a man could have so much or be so powerful. I always thought that was the way those kings lived that my ma used to read to me about from the Good Book. I never knew there was kings out here, too.

I asked, "Where does this Johnson live?" Bule took a piece of grass from his mouth and poked back his hat. For a short second that smile left his face. "If you're thinking of paying him a visit, forget it."

"Why?" I asked.

Bule leaned forward and said, "First of all, he's always got two men with him and those two men are *hardcases*. Bad news, friend. One is Billy Horran, and the other don't have a name we know about. We just called him Sandy, and it stuck. He's the real bad one. He never says a word, just watches with them green eyes of his and chews on a little bitty cigar, but never smokes it. I've seen him in action, and he's a real bad 'un."

I wanted to find out something so I asked, "Could you take either one of 'em, Bule?"

He grinned wide at that. That devil was playing in his eyes again and he said, "Straight up, I could take Horran easy. Sandy, I dunno. I could get one in him maybe, but he's like a rattlesnake without his rattles. He's fast and he don't give a warning. He's good."

"Every man gives a warnin', Bule."

"Well, I thought that too, 'til I met Sandy and watched him in action a time or two. I tell you, Luke, he is a snake without rattles."

"Well, how about answerin' me. Where does this Johnson make his home, or can I see him in town?"

Bule didn't want to tell me. But, I suppose he could see that I was determined to find out because he answered me.

"You got to get to the other side of the valley near the town. Strike east there at the road. You'll come to a house about a mile down that road. It's bigger'n two barns drug together and has a fancy little road winding up to it. There will likely be a man at the gate, although the boss...I mean Johnson, has taken to leaving it without a man there most of the time."

"How come he has a man there in the first place?"

Bule laughed at that. "Well, Johnson didn't make too many friends at first, and he rode over the tops of a lot of folk. So, he took to making sure that only people that he knew wasn't any kind of enemy, or ones that had business with him, got through. But lately, he's been getting it in his head that it is a sign of weakness. He wants protection, but he don't want to advertise it none.

"It's kind of funny. You can tell when he's put over a rough deal on someone, because the guard goes back out on the front gate. Then, after a few days, Johnson will call him off."

Johnson sure was a strange man. It sounded more to me like he was one of those gentlemen crooks. One thing my pa always taught me about men was to look on them all the same. I don't mean to say that one man is not bigger or stronger, or even smarter than another, but I mean that when you boil him down, he's just like any other man. He draws his pants on same as me, drinks water from what's handy if he's thirsty, has needs and wants, and makes mistakes now and then. There's not a soul living that isn't built that way. So, I just looked at this man same as any other man, except he had a lot of money. That isn't so special to my way of thinking.

I said, "I'm ridin' over there, soon."

"You are loco." His grin faded when he looked at my face.

I shook my head and said, "No, but my pa told me a long time ago that if I had me a problem with a man, I should take it to him personal and break it out in the open. Longer a problem sits on a man's head, the heavier it gets. I like knowing where things lay between me and another man. See, this Briner feller who's after me, I understand him. I know what he wants, and there ain't a need to ask him any questions, though I would like to tell him a couple things."

"Luke, I can see that it's no use telling you not to go, so let me go with you. Might be I can get you in easier."

I wasn't too sure about that idea, for I had seen what Bule had done to Lester, but he talked like it wasn't real dangerous with him along and that there wouldn't be trouble for him. He convinced me and I agreed to let him ride with me–not that I could have stopped him anyway. He said he had some things to pick up at the bunk house, plus some wages. We agreed to go there in three more days. I figured the boss would be strong by then and wouldn't be needing me for a day. I planned on stopping by that eating place in town too, as long as I was that close. I made up my mind from the first time I ate there, that when I got close to that place, I would stop in again. If I was broke, I'd offer to wash all the dishes, paint the room, chop wood, anything they might need. I sure liked the food in that place.

We had a great feed there at the Wilsons. It wasn't fancy, but it was the kind of food I had many times before. My ma used to cook beans like Mrs. Wilson did, full and juicy, with hot hoe cake underneath them and a pile of greens stacked on the side. A big cup of sweet buttermilk to wash it down made that a great feed. Then, she trotted out a big, blackberry pie, and honestly, I could have ate the whole thing, but I held back, even though she had two more setting over on the window.

After I ate the first slice Mary said, "Like that pie, Luke?"

I smiled and said, "Sweetest blackberry pie I ever sunk my teeth into, girl."

She kind of looked down at her plate then and her ma piped up and said, "Mary baked those pies."

I could see she was mighty proud of it, and I didn't want her thinking I was lying, so I asked for another piece, and so did Bule.

Lonnie was watching all that pie disappear and it must have grieved him tolerable, because he said, "Can I have another, too, 'fore it's all gone?"

His ma give him a hard look, and me and Bule pretended to be too busy with our pie to notice. I kind of felt bad, because I knew we were being treated special, and I wasn't used to it.

Soon after supper, I saddled Mash and got ready to leave. Bule stood beside his horse jerking the cinch tight. I looked over at him and said, "You want to see a real gold mine?"

I wasn't too sure how the boss would react to me bringing home a stranger, but since I was a partner, I figured it was my right. The boss could run that gold mine any way he wanted, but no man could tell me who I couldn't make a friend, or who I couldn't ride with. I had already decided Bule was a man to tie to and that he'd make a good friend. I figured I might as well start right off finding out if I could trust him. No better way, to my way of thinking, than to show him that gold mine. If he tried to steal it, then all I'd lose was some gold, because I'd never fight for that hole in the ground, at least not against a man I called friend.

He grinned and said, "Suits me. Never saw one before."

As we was saying goodbye, Mary came prancing out of the house and she was carrying something with a rag laid over it. I guessed at what it was before she even got to me. She was giving me one of those pies. I hated to take it on account of that boy and the other men folks wanting some more pie, but she must have read my mind because she told me right out that they would be getting more pie the very next day and that I wasn't to worry about taking food from them. She called Lonnie fat and he bristled some at that, but the look on his ma's face made him keep his trap shut, for which I was thankful.

We rode out, and it was a good feeling I had for this day. True, I'd made some enemies, but I had made up for that and gained me a whole family of friends, and a friend riding with me. I would have made a lot more enemies for that.

CHAPTER 10

When we rode into camp, it was dark. As we rode up to the edge, I heard the hammer of a rifle being eared back and I knew the boss was up and stirring.

He called out, "That you, Luke?"

"Me and a friend, Boss."

Smith stepped out from behind some rocks and leaned the rifle against a log by the fire. I could see some color had come back into his face.

"Boss, your face has got its ugly back and a little color besides. When I left, you was all white and puny in the jaws."

He growled and said, "Luke, if you was as sick as I was, you'd have swore off on food, likely."

We traded some more insults and I introduced Bule. The boss didn't ask me nary a question about him, and I appreciated that. It told me that my friend John Smith was trusting me and anyone I chose to call friend. That made me respect the big man a whole lot more. Him and Bule hit it off right away, and they got to discussing cows and gold, and all kinds of things, so I put away both the horses while they were getting acquainted.

After both horses were hobbled, I went back to the fire, and they were already talking about the gold mine, and then the boss surprised me all of a sudden. "Luke, how would you like to make Bule here a partner? He can help me in the mine. You ain't good for anything but laying in the shade and watching the clouds roll by, anyhow."

He was smiling when he said it, and I didn't take offense. Besides, it really was the truth. I reckon if he wanted to trade me for Bule as a partner, that would have been alright, too.

"Hey Boss, you know I don't care much for this here gold mining. It's really yours, but you done took me in as a partner. I only went along with it to keep you from standin' me on my head and shakin' that dollar out of my pocket. Why should I care if you want Bule, too?"

"You got a say in it, Luke, as a partner. You'd have asked me if you wanted another partner in."

I laughed at that and said, "Boss, I wouldn't wish this hole off on an enemy. Poor Bule here ain't quite right in the head and he don't know he's goin' down into Hell with the devil leadin' him. Reckon every fool has to learn, though. If that's what he wants, why go ahead. I'll stay up here and make sure no clouds gets your gear wet."

We had a good time after that, swapping tales and such talk. I broke out that pie and the boss' eyes got wide. He used to tell me he wasn't too keen on sweet things, so I figured I'd have a little fun. I took that pie, held it up to my nose and made a big display of it smelling so good, and talked a little with Bule about how good it was, then I cut out a couple big pieces for me and Bule. I cut the other piece in half, and when the boss reached for one of the pieces, I grabbed the pan and handed it to Bule.

"Bule, you want a second piece of this pie? The boss, he don't eat sweet things, you know."

Bule picked up on it right off and said, "That so? Now Boss, how come you don't like pie, especially this here blackberry pie that is the sweetest, tastiest pie I ever did eat?" Bule was a born actor, because he stuck a big piece of that pie in his mouth and took to yummin' and ummin', and it was all I could do to keep from busting out laughing.

The boss glared at him, then at me, then threatened to bash us, but we didn't give in. Finally, he said, "Look, I'm asking real nice for that pie.

I ain't riled up to the point of knocking your heads together yet, but I'm getting close to it."

Bule looked at me and said, "Luke, I'm awful full. You want this piece?"

I grinned over the fire and said, "Naw, I've had plenty." We both looked at the boss sitting there with his eyes glued on that pie. I said, "Say, you reckon he might want some?" I nodded my head at the boss

He looked at me like I was crazy, then leaned over and grabbed the pan out of my hands. He took a big bite and we sat there grinning.

I said, "You know, the boss was tellin' me the other day that he didn't take to sweet things too much. Said it made a man weak, like a kid. You reckon the boss will be too weak to work in that mine tomorrow?"

Bule said, "I don't know, Luke. He looks like he's growin' stronger by the minute. Could be he was angling to get your piece of pie when he told you that. He shore don't believe that now."

In between bites, the boss glared at me, then with a mouthful, said, "Aw, go stick your fool head under your horse's feet awhile, will you!"

We laughed, then he started laughing, too and choked like he did that time I met him and I got the idea about his Half 'n Half Stew in my mind so I said, "Hey Boss!"

He stopped laughing and said, "What?"

"Boss, I think you ought to make us up some of your special Half 'n Half Stew tomorrow. Bule here, never had any, and I'm developin' a powerful hunger for some." The boss smiled real innocent, glad to get on the other side, and he mumbled about being too tired, but after I coaxed him he gave in. I looked forward to tomorrow's evening meal, only I sure was going to make sure I had me something else handy to eat.

Bule and the boss went into that hole the next morning early and stayed for most of the day, coming up now and then for some air and some beans. They sweated like I never seen a body sweat, and both of them had their shirts off. John Smith was a might powerful looking man, with muscles running down his arms and back like big chunks of rope. I noticed Bule had a few scars on him that wasn't put there by his mama. Looked like a couple of bullets had made some of them, and one was a knife cut, for certain, or something equally as sharp. He wasn't nearly as strong as the boss, but he was a stayer, and he worked right along without complaining or asking for mercy. But, I could tell he was near the end of his rope the last time he came up. He fell against a rock in the shade and drank deep from a jug of water, closed his eyes and trembled some.

Finally, he said, "You were right on the mark, partner."

"You mean about that mine?"

He swallowed some more water, opened his eyes and said, "That hole is Hell in disguise and the boss is the devil for certain!"

I didn't laugh because I did feel sorry for him, and I knew that trying to stay even with a man like John Smith was impossible to do for most any man. Even just off his sick bed, he was hard to keep up with.

After awhile, Bule went back down, and in a couple hours they both come stumbling out, the boss dragging a sack full of rocks. He said they had six more sack loads to bring up, but they'd wait until morning. Then, they both went to their bed rolls and flopped down. I could see the boss's Half 'n Half Stew was going to have to wait for another time.

I cared for the horses, gave them a little grain, and cooked up some terrible tasting beans. They was all crunchy inside, and Bule spit his out and went to bed hungry. The boss just mixed in about a bushel of peppers with his and didn't say nothing about how bad they were. That man could eat anything, long as it had some peppers in it. I sat around the fire thinking after they had gone to sleep, wondering how I was going to handle that rancher from Texas. It troubled me, because I didn't want to kill that man. I had already killed his son and it would pain me to have to kill him, too. But, if he was determined to hunt me, I wasn't one to stand still and let him take his shot.

Finally, I decided that no matter what, I would not kill that man. It gave me a good feeling, but I wasn't too sure how I was going to avoid it. I knew if the man drew a gun on me that I'd have to shoot him, but I'd not shoot to kill him. Now, that might sound easy, but when you're shooting at another man real sudden, it's not like shooting a pine cone because the man is shooting back and he's moving some. I remembered this kid down in Texas who shot next to a *greenhorn's* foot. He tried it again, and that poor *greenhorn* was so scared he jumped right in front of the bullet and it blew his foot off. So, although I was bound to try, I wasn't certain I'd hit what I aimed at.

Next morning, I got the job of setting on the ground and busting up all that rock they carried up. The boss had turned over a big rock nearby, and it was kind of flat on the bottom. I laid some of them rocks on that big one and broke them with a hammer. Ever little bit of rock was saved. I wasn't too sure of what I was doing, but I followed orders and saved it all into a couple of wood buckets. Later, the boss showed me how to wash all that rock and what to look for.

I hadn't ever seen gold in rocks, other than the stuff the boss had brought up that one time, but I knew it was yellow. It was a whole lot of work for some little pieces of rock, and we did get us a little gold, but I could tell that boss wasn't too happy and had expected a whole lot more. After that second day, he said it looked like we maybe had fifty dollars in gold. That sounded like a whole lot to me, but the boss felt like it ought to have been richer on account of those pieces he'd found earlier.

That night, I told the boss that I had some business to take care of in town and that I'd be gone most of the day. I told him about the meeting with those riders and that I aimed to set things straight for this Johnson gent. I also told him Bule was going to draw his pay and pick up his gear there. He wasn't too happy to have his only rock-pounder and his human donkey leave him that way, but there wasn't too much he could do about it. I got him to give me some money and told him I was planning on eating in that place again. He asked me to bring him back some of that chicken and I promised to do that. I was fond of it, myself. I asked him if he wanted me to bring him any pie and he just glared at me.

Next morning early, Bule and me headed out. I was feeling good, especially with getting away from breaking that rock. It just wasn't my line of work. We took it slow, and when we got to the bottom, I thought about riding by and seeing Mary, but I decided not to. I'd stop by on the way back.

We rode by the town and came to the road Bule was talking about. A couple of riders passed us once, and I could see they were cowboys on account of their outfits. They were friendly and they knew Bule, and one of them warned him to stay away until things had cooled down. Johnson was said to be pretty upset at Bule for not bracing me that day at the Wilsons.

We got to the gate and a guard was standing there. He smiled at Bule, but he acted like he didn't even see me.

"Howdy, Bule. Didn't figure you was comin' back." He rubbed the end of his carbine alongside his neck to scratch it with the sight. I thought it would be pretty funny if it went off, accidental. He'd have a time explaining to his boss how he blowed off his ear. He'd say, "Well, I had this here itch ..." and they'd be telling that tale around every campfire from here to Californy.

Bule smiled at him and said, "Just comin' to collect my things, Clyde. Got some wages, too."

All the friendly went off that Clyde's face and he said, "I don't reckon I better let you in Bule, unless you're comin' to stay. Boss might not like it."

"I'm riding through, Clyde. Around you or over you, however you choose to make it." Then, because he knew I'd be having trouble with Clyde, he said, "My friend is ridin' with me."

Clyde wasn't wanting any part of Bule, I could see. He started whining and said, "Bule, you are gonna get me in hot water. If I let you go in there and you start some trouble, I'm gonna have to answer for it—you know that. I'm asking you not to try, Bule."

"You're in the wrong business, Clyde. Better go back to chasing cows." Bule sat there with his hands crossed on the horn of his saddle, looking down on Clyde with them devils dancing in his eyes. It was clear that he was going to ride right over this Clyde if he had to.

Clyde was making up his mind. I wasn't too sure which way he was going to jump, so I moved to one side, staying ready. Finally, he looks back at Bule and said, "Bule, will you say you pulled your gun on me and took my rifle?"

Bule reached down and took the gun out of Clyde's hands. "Give me your pistol, too." We rode through and when we got away from Clyde he said, "I would have taken them anyway."

We rode up slow to the house. It was something right out of a picture book and put me in mind of a book my ma once showed me. Two big trees stood right smack in front of it, and a garden ran along the whole side of the house. It was all white, with red windows, and had four big posts holding up the front of it. This was the biggest house I ever saw in my life. Off to one side, just a little ways from it, was this other house, not near as big and plain as my face. There wasn't a lick of paint on it and it was long. Bule pointed it out to me and said it was the bunk house for all the men who stay on the place, including guards, drivers, a man who tended the garden and stuff, and the cook, plus all the hands. There was a little house way off, and that was where he said an old couple live. They were some kind of servants.

We tied up out front next to a fine looking buggy. Bule leaned over to me as we were tying up and said, "Now, let me do the talking at first, *amigo*. It might pan out that you won't get a chance to have your say, but if you waltz in there and spout off, I can almost guarantee neither of us is gonna have a say."

I gave him my promise, but in my mind I made myself a promise that I was going to have my say, no matter what. We took them steps two at a time and walked right on in without knocking. Bule went in first, and when I followed, he raised his finger to his lips for me to be quiet.

That first room we walked into was bigger than the whole house I grew up in. I reckon my pa would have been stumped for words at describing it. There were pictures hanging all over the walls, some real fancy rifles crossed over each other, hanging on a wall, and a whole bunch of *injun* gear stashed on a table, and some more on the wall at the far end. I've never seen the like of that room.

We crossed over and went up to a big set of doors. Real gentle, Bule turned the knob and eased one of them open. He motioned me in and I followed him close. I could hear some talking going on somewhere near, but didn't see a thing until we got inside. Just to the right was this little wall that jutted out from the main wall, with shelves on it. On the other side of that little wall with shelves, I could see four men. One was standing with his back to us and his hands were clasped in back. He was looking out a big window. I could tell two of the men I spotted were *hardcases*, for they were wearing guns like no cowboy did, and they had that the look to them of men who'd rode some trails in the dark. One of those two had his arms folded on his chest, and the other was standing there with both hands in his back pockets. That sure wasn't a good position for a gun fighting man to be in at any time. The fourth man just stood quietly in the shadows near a corner, watching the others.

The man looking out the window was older, maybe fifty or so, and he spotted us or heard us. He glanced quickly over his shoulder and said something in a low voice to one of the other men. That man looked over his shoulder at us and his hand moved down toward his gun. The man who'd been standing in the shadows moved toward us.

"Hold it, Sandy!" Johnson wasn't caring for a gun fight right here with him as a possible target. He had one of those voices that boomed, and you could tell it was used to being obeyed. That Sandy feller just quivered a little, but didn't make a move for his gun, and stopped. The others just stood still, waiting for orders.

"We're friendly, Boss. Just don't do nuthin' sudden, Sandy, or you either, Bill. I just want to get my gear and my pay, and Luke here wants to talk at you some, Boss."

Johnson smiled. I could see he wasn't worried at all, and if he was even surprised, I couldn't tell it. He acted like the whole thing was all normal and that there wasn't a thing to get disturbed over. I even found myself liking him some, until I got to thinking of my friends, the Wilsons. But, he was a mighty friendly soul.

He smiled big at us and said, "Bule, there is no need for you to quit. I like you, boy, and you've a place here with me as long as you want it. I would have a difficult time replacing you." He talked to Bule more like he was a son than a rider of his who'd taken the other side from his boss.

Bule looked over at Sandy, then said, "Sandy here can take up the slack, Boss. I took the other side and I can't climb back on this side now. Besides, if I came back, I'd have to shoot Barnes, and he just ain't worth a bullet." Bule was grinning as he finished talking.

Johnson didn't say a word in response to that. He just smiled, then he turned to me and said, "And what can I do for you? You looking for work, maybe?"

I smiled at him and said, "No sir, but if I was, this looks like it would be the place to come. You got a right nice place here, Mister Johnson."

"Well then, what can I do for you?" He raised up a glass of something, it looked like maybe it was wine, and drained it. His eyes never left mine and they stayed friendly and warm. It was hard to believe that this man was what I knew him to be. You'd never have guessed him to be a hard man, unless you got to looking in his eyes. It showed there deep down inside, and in the steady fix they held onto a body. You could see power and confidence in the man. It radiated from his whole being.

I kept my smile on and said, "You can leave the Wilsons alone. They are friends, kind of like family."

He didn't act like that surprised him either, and that surprised me. I had figured he'd act innocent, then maybe rant and rave about how they were cheating him, or ask me what I was talking about, only he didn't.

He just said, "I see."

I didn't think he did see, so I figured I'd best make sure. My pa always taught me to speak right out and show a man what was on my mind. That way, there could never be no doubts or him saying later that he didn't know that you was upset or that you meant something else.

"Mr. Johnson, I don't make threats, so don't take this as one. It ain't a threat, but I do want you to know what them friends mean to me. I reckon if anyone was to trouble them, I'd take it like I would if someone was to have troubled my ma or my pa, 'fore they died. I'd die for family, sir, kill for 'em, and even steal for 'em." I waited a little, then added, "The Wilsons are like family, sir."

He took all that in, smiled, then said, "I assure you, there is no cause to fear. The Wilsons and I have always been on the best of terms."

I saw then that he was fooling with me and thinking to drift some smoke my way. I said, "I don't think you understand yet. The Wilsons are goin' to sell their stuff in town from now on. If any of your riders give 'em a hard time in any way, you ain't goin' to have a dirt farmer to deal with, but you're goin' to have a cowboy who grew up slingin' a gun first and a rope second."

I shifted my gaze to that Sandy feller and went on, "You might think all you got to do when I leave is turn your pet dog here loose and I'm cared for, or maybe you think I can be arrested. I got to tell you, sir, that the first sign I get of this man on my trail, or the law, I ain't even stoppin' to fight. I'll be huntin'."

I fixed my eye on Sandy and my voice got kind of low and soft like it always does when I'm facing trouble, and I said, "I'll hunt you like I used to hunt cougars for the families back home."

I moved back some, because that Sandy feller was getting edgy and I wanted to to be where I could see everyone in the room. Then, I continued, "Look at it all this way, Mr. Johnson. You got a nice place here and you got all you need. One thing you don't need is grief, and sir, I'd be bringing you a lot of it. Some things just ain't worth messin' with, sir."

He never said a word, just watched me with them hard, shiny black eyes of his. I went on. "Now, I ain't wantin' none of that kind of trouble, for I've troubles enough, but you don't want none of the kind of trouble I would bring to you, either. So, don't be settin' your dogs on my friends, or me, even if they're called the law. You do that, and I'll come for you. I give you my word on that. And, this man and a dozen like them won't stop me from gettin' to you." I nodded my head at Sandy as I spoke.

I looked Johnson hard in the eyes while I spoke. I wasn't smiling, and I know there was as many devils dancing in my eyes as there always was in Bule's. He swallowed hard, then turned back to the window and studied on what I said. I gave him credit for that. He didn't make a sudden decision, or let his temper run him, and maybe that was why he got to where he was. I think he was a careful man in his way, knowing who he could ride over and who he could not ride over.

Finally, he turned to me and said, "What's your name?"

"I'm called Luke Adams, late of Texas."

He smiled at me, but it was one of those smiles like a wolf gives, if you know what I mean. He said, "Luke, you are a most convincing man. You have a way about you. Not many men do I take serious, but now and then, I take a man for what he says. I think you really would do what you say. I have to confess, I really do not wish to have to worry about a man like yourself hunting me." He paused a long minute, pulled a long cigar out of his inner pocket, bit the end off, and gave me a faint little smile as he spit the end into the palm of his hand. He put me in mind of that gunfighter I'd met in town. They had some of the same qualities.

He walked over to his desk, dropped the small end of the cigar into a little dish, pointed to Sandy and said, "Only thing, I really can't guarantee your personal safety from this man. He makes his own way, pretty much. I won't send him after you, but I can't stop him. Sandy is his own man, though he draws my pay."

He lit his cigar, blew smoke at the ceiling and continued, "When he hired on, he let me know that he'd do whatever I needed him to do, but laid down the law to me that he wouldn't be told how to run his personal life. So, I reckon he hunts his own trouble, and if you and Sandy have trouble, please don't hold that to my account, and if you run afoul of the law, don't hold that to my account. I wont *sic* them on you, but I can't guarantee they wont come after you if you give them an excuse."

He paused for a moment, took a long drag on his cigar, then added, "And, from what I hear, the law in Texas already has an interest in you."

It didn't surprise me that he knew, and I was glad he said it. He was letting me know that the law could come for me, and even Sandy might, and so, he didn't need to get involved. He was a smart man, I could see.

"Fair enough, sir. Just don't take me for a fool." Sandy stood near one corner looking at me like a hungry wolf looks at a baby calf.

Johnson nodded, gave another little smile and said, "Good. I think we understand one another." He rubbed his hands together, poured himself another glass of that red drink, but didn't offer us any. I understood. He just wanted us gone.

Then he said, "As for the Wilsons, well, I guess I will have to write that off as a bad investment."

"Mr. Johnson, I think you had yourself a fine investment there until you got greedy. That poor man wasn't makin' hardly enough to feed his family."

He blinked a couple of times, gave me a hard look, then put that smile back on, but I saw the flicker of anger in his eyes. "You've got a point there. An excellent point. I will take it as a lesson for the future, Mr. Adams."

Bule looked at me and grinned, and I grinned back. He said, "Boss, I'm sorry it had to come to this, but you know how it is with me. I got itchy feet and I'm off to see some more of this here country." I had to grin at that, because I knew all he had seen and was likely to see for a long time was the black innards of that hole we were calling a gold mine.

Bule turned to leave, but I had some more to say, so I held up my hand. "Mr. Johnson, I appreciate your understandin' this matter, but there's just one more thing here."

I turned my look back to Sandy. He was beginning to irritate me with that cold, steady hate pouring out at me from his eyes. "Mister, you got it in your craw to try me, I can tell. Well, I ain't never been one to leave a skin full of hate behind my back for long, so I reckon you and me can walk outside and settle it now. I don't want to bother with you later and wonder when you might come crawling along my trail. So, if it's all the same with you, I'll be outside waiting for you."

That skin full of poison and mean straightened up some and his eyes squinted a little. Johnson didn't say a word and I knew he wouldn't, because he'd be hoping I'd catch a bullet. But, I was plumb out of sorts with that Sandy on account of the way he had been staring at me. I needed to settle with him now, before my Texas trouble got here.

Bule followed me and closed the door. He was holding his sides, trying to keep from busting out laughing. He clapped me on the back and said, "Luke, you're the hardest steppin' man I ever run across. If I hadn't been there and heard it all, I'd never have believed it. You even got that snake Sandy doubting himself!"

We walked outside and I moved over to a shady place. Bule stood to one side and was quiet, because he could see I was settling my mind for this thing with Sandy. We'd only been there a couple minutes when the door opened and a man came out. He was carrying a little envelope and he came over to Bule and stuck it in his hand. Then, he turned to me, and with a slight grin on his face, said, "Mr. Johnson said to give you Sandy's regrets, but that gentlemen has decided he will join you at another time."

Well, I was so primed that I was minded to go in, call him out, and make him fight, because I knew next time we met would probably be on grounds he chose and at a time when I might be occupied, like when that rancher came up here.

But, I just shrugged and gave it up. Bule got his gear and we rode out. Clyde was still there, but we noticed he had got himself some more guns. He was real happy to see us riding out peaceful.

"Everything alright, Bule?"

Bule grinned at me, then flashed him a smile. "Yeah, real good Clyde. You keep scratchin' those itches, now, hear? Maybe we'll all get lucky." We rode off laughing and poor Clyde frowning and wondering what the joke was.

CHAPTER 11

Spring wore into summer, and it was more hot than usual to me, maybe because I was spending so much of my time beating on them rocks. I was getting more and more weary of that work and was taking off more than I should. Every time I could, I'd sneak off and see Mary, or ride into town. We were getting close, there was no denying that, and it was making me uncomfortable some, but not enough to run away from it.

I saw Sandy once in town and I gave him his chance, but he passed on it. I got to thinking maybe I was wrong about him, so I gave up on my plan to make him fight. I had it in my mind to crowd him every chance I got, on account of the hate for me I had seen in that man. I'm not a man to look for trouble, but I learned a long time ago that when a body is bound to do you harm, there's no point in walking around it. They're going to follow after you, so you might as well bring it to them and be done with it. But, since he passed again, I figured maybe I was wrong, and maybe he was willing to leave things lay.

I took off work one day, leaving the boss yelling about me being lazy and good for nothing, and even Bule calling me worthless, but I paid them no mind. I was headed to see my girl, then I was going to town and get some things I needed. I loped on out and got near the bottom of the mountain when all the hairs on my neck raised and I got a funny feeling. Mash jerked his head a little and that was all I needed. I dove out of the saddle.

I felt kind of foolish, because it could have been some kind of animal in the rocks, but I learned long time ago that it's paying attention to such things and doing what your instincts tell you that can mean the difference between living or dying. I rolled as I hit, but I guess I wasn't rolling fast enough. Whoever was in them rocks caught me on the roll, and I guess he was smiling, because I got to admit, it was a tolerable good shot. That bullet smashed into my shoulder and rolled me a couple turns more than I'd planned. I dug one leg into the ground, then jerked myself behind a rock with a little shrub growing out of it. A second bullet burnt the back of my neck as I disappeared behind the rock. That man could shoot. He'd gone for my head and nearly got it, even with me moving.

I knew it had to be Sandy, or else that Texas trouble had finally lit. They sure had time enough to get here by now. I'd looked for them for weeks. Whoever it was up there wasn't green, because I never saw anything move or heard a sound after that second shot.

I was breathing hard, the shock was wearing off, and the pain was beginning to slice into my shoulder like a hot knife. It felt like a fire was lit there, but there wasn't too much blood, yet. I ripped off my neckerchief and plugged the hole where the bullet went in. I tried to reach where it came out, but couldn't make it, so I just bit off some of the neckerchief and stuffed it down the back of my shirt. My shirt was a soggy mess in front. I was grateful that it wasn't my gun arm that was shot. I could still use my gun, but only if the bushwhacker made his move pretty soon. I knew that if I shot a man like me, I wouldn't be coming down to see if he was dead, especially if he was a dangerous kind of man, unless of course I had to make sure he was dead. It just doesn't pay to take chances with some men.

After an hour, I knew I had to move or die. It was getting hotter, and if that man was still there, then he was going to have to shoot my horse, because I planned using Mash as a shield. I give a low whistle and Mash looked over at me, his ears pricked. He walked over and sniffed into my hand. I sure hated to play a trick like that on him, but I had to get out of that place. If I stayed too much longer, I was a goner for certain.

I put my gun away and grabbed the saddle horn with my good hand. I stuck my right leg into the stirrup, drew myself up and just hung there, my teeth set hard against the ragged pain that shot through my body. I made a couple of kisses to Mash and he moved out slow, not liking my new way of riding at all. He kept stopping and giving me a curious look, as if to say he thought I chomped on some loco weed.

No shots came, so I stopped Mash, struggled into the saddle, then headed the short distance down the trail into the valley and towards the Wilsons. I knew I'd never be able to ride up to the mountain camp, and besides, I knew Mary would care for me a whole lot better than the boss or Bule could. I wasn't sure how bad hit I was, but I knew it was the worst I'd ever been shot. I got shot down near the Pecos by a 'Pache buck, but it was in the leg, and it hadn't hurt as bad as this one did.

By the time I got to the Wilsons, I was in a fog. I don't remember even coming to the gate, but Mary told me later that her ma was washing some clothes outside when Mash just walked up to the gate and stood. She thought it was me on account of recognizing Mash, but they couldn't tell for sure until they got closer and saw me laying on my horse's neck. When they tried to get me off, they had to pry open my legs and jerk my hand off the saddle horn.

I laid up there at the Wilsons, eating soup, soft eggs, and lots of different kinds of herb teas that Mrs. Wilson made for me. She was better than any doctor. Her and Mary dug out the bullet. Reason I hadn't been able to find the hole in back was because it hadn't made it all the way through, but was lodged just under the skin, about a half an inch, they said. They said I lost a lot of blood, and told me my saddle was covered with it. They threw away my pants and shirt on account of them being so stained with blood.

The boss and Bule showed up every now and then, until I told them to get back to that hole of theirs and quit worrying about me. They laughed and said they had got a kid off a farm from the valley to help out. Bule had taken over my job, and the kid was down in the hole with the boss. I found out later that they had tried to give Mrs. Wilson some money, but she wouldn't take it, and then they tried to give it to Mary, but she wouldn't either. Finally they tried Mr. Wilson, but he just told them to talk with Lucy, his wife, and that he didn't want nothing. I should have told them to see Lonnie. Reckon he'd have taken it and snuck it into his ma's dress pocket.

I finally got embarrassed over Mary doing so much for me. She fussed over me like a hen with her chicks, and once, she even tried to give me a bath, but I flat refused. She said all she'd do was raise the covers up at the bottom and wash my legs, and then she'd take the top down and wash my chest, but I told her I never had a bath from a female, except when I was a *yonker* when my ma gave them to me.

She got a little huffy and told me I could go on and stink up the place if I wanted to. I didn't give in, though, and instead, I bathed myself like she would have done. We got pretty close, and got to liking each other a lot more in those days. She fussed with me some on my being so handy with a gun. That bothered her a lot, and she let me know how much one evening when I was on the porch sitting in Josiah's rocker.

She was sitting on the porch step, chin in her hand and looking up at me kind of funny. She said, "Luke, are you going to look this Sandy fellow up?"

Well, that surprised me, for I had never said a word about who I thought shot me. I figured maybe the boss or Bule had been talking. I knew it wasn't that rancher from Texas because Bule told me that there were no new riders who'd come to town, and none was seen before I got shot.

I said, "I got no choice, Mary."

She said, "You could ride off. Go somewhere else, Luke." She was pleading with her eyes, and fidgeting with her fingers. She looked down at her hands and added, real soft, "I'd go with you, Luke."

I felt like I did the first time I got kicked in the belly by a horse. I swallowed until my mouth got dry, and finally I managed to talk. "Mary, I guess it's pretty plain that I'm plumb in love with you. I been thinking about asking you to marry me soon as I get some money laid up, but Mary...Mary,

I can't do what you ask. I can't ride away from this thing. I got to take care of this problem, then I got to take care of my Texas trouble. I ain't runnin' no more, Mary. Reckon they'll bury me here before I run again."

She was upset at that, but I couldn't change the way I was. She tried to argue some, but when she saw how set I was, she gave up and ran into the house. She did bring something up which I never thought about before and couldn't answer when she threw it at me. She said she'd always live in fear that someone would one day ride out of my past and gun me down in front of her and the kids.

She shut me up good with that one, for there are some men, some Texas men, who'd do just that, if they ever found me, and it was certain they'd find me one day. She also said she'd worry that if we had a boy, he'd grow up wanting to be handy with a gun, like their pa. I give her a good argument on that one, because it was my pa's teaching me to use a gun when I was a young'un that kept me alive. I would always be grateful for my pa teaching me things a man ought to know, like shooting and some other things. I remember Ma used to fuss some over Pa letting me play with a gun, but he never budged on that one. I'd never budge, either.

In about a month, I was feeling good, although my shoulder was stiff, like when you been branding all day after being laid up during the winter. I always hated that first day of branding, because everything hurt the day after. Just getting out of bed the morning after first branding was agony. That's the way my shoulder was aching. I figured it was time to move, so I packed my gear, thanked the Wilsons and rode out.

When I left, I knew I wouldn't be coming back quite as often, for I had made up my mind that until I got that Texas trouble off my trail, and this Sandy was cared for, that I was going to try and put Mary out of my mind and my life. I knew I'd think about her most every day, but I just couldn't bring that girl grief like I had on my trail. She was right on that. So, I threw myself into the work at the mine, and in another month my shoulder was giving me no trouble at all, except in the morning it was usually stiff.

I was busting rock with Bule, while a kid by the name of Charlie Jones worked with the boss down in that hole. Me and Charlie was hauling some rocks over to the water one day when Bule came riding in hard, his horse near winded. He'd been into town for supplies.

He slid off his horse and flipped the reins to Charlie. He took me by the arm and steered me to one side. "Luke, they're here. I saw them in town, and Luke, they're both *hardcases*. They got the look and they're packin' the iron. They been askin' around about you, pard."

I let my breath out real slow. It was finally here, and not too soon. True, I wasn't long off my sick bed, but I felt strong as ever, and kept my practice up with my gun. I was even getting fat.

I said, "They're are goin' to have to wait in line."

"How's that?"

"Well, Sandy maybe thinks I'm a pile of bones at the foot of the mountain. Or, maybe he thinks I got scairt and have left. But, whatever that little weasel thinks, I got to care for him. I can't be bothered with him while these men are sniffin' my heels. Besides, next time I might not be so lucky."

I saddled Mash, and when I was done, I jumped into the saddle and headed down the trail. In a couple of minutes I heard a horse running on my trail and Bule came up riding the boss's mare.

"Where you headed now, Bule?"

"With you." Those eyes of his was dancing with devils again.

"Ain't no need, Bule. I fight my own fights. I don't need no help with that little snake."

He grinned, then said, "Why don't you shut up and get on. You're blocking the trail, Luke."

There was no arguing with him, and inside, I was glad, because if those other two were in town, Bule could hold them off until I got to them. We headed on down the trail. I knew the boss would be upset at me running out on him again, and worse, on account of this time taking Bule with me. I wasn't coming back, though, until this business with Sandy was cared for.

I'd make up for it later. Maybe I'd even work three days straight at them rocks. Or, maybe at least two.

We didn't talk much on the way down, although Bule did try and ask me some about what I had in mind. I just told him I was going to lay up in the hotel until Sandy come to town. I'd know more what to do when it came to do it. I'm not much on planning far ahead. Bule's that way, himself. He likes to do his planning on the run, same as me. Seems like all the planning I ever did that was more'n a day ahead, came apart somehow. Besides, when you got a plan and something comes up that don't fit in your plan, you're liable to get planted while you're making the change in your plan. I leave making plans to men like the boss. He's got the kind of mind that'll make a good plan, and if something comes along to spoil it, he's got a plan already figured to take its place.

We got to town late, for it was afternoon when Bule had come back to camp. The sun had set, and we put our horses away, then took a room at the hotel. I wasn't hungry, so I didn't go to that place and eat like I usually did when I came to town. I wasn't up to a big feed just before trouble, because after I ate like that, I never felt like fighting, only sleeping.

I didn't want to go into the two saloons looking for Sandy, so I got Bule to go for me. I figured if I got to nosing about, word would get around and Sandy might dodge me, or I might run into those two Texans, and I didn't want to deal with any of them just yet. Bule grinned and said he wouldn't mind that job at all.

I laid up on the bed with my shirt off because the night was still warm. I kept the window open for air and the noises from the street came through. I heard some real loud laughing from somewhere, then a lot of cussing. I got up and looked out and saw a man come flying out of the doors of the saloon across the street. Just as he was getting up another man came out the door in the same way he did, like they were pitched.

He landed on the one trying to get up, and they both went down. They took to fighting, and one went down without even being hit, and the other feller started going through the other man's pockets. He didn't seem to find anything, so he walked back into the saloon. He wasn't in the place a half a minute when he came flying out again and fell on top of the one he'd come out with in the first place. He tried once to get up, flopped over, and laid still beside the other man. They were out for the night.

About an hour later, I saw a rider come into sight at the end of the street. He was walking his horse slow. The closer he got, the more I was sure it was Sandy, on account of the way he sat his saddle. Men got different ways of setting a saddle, and I can tell some men even if all I can see is him sky-lined from way off. It's just something you get to know.

The rider rode right under my window and through a splash of light from the hotel. It was Sandy, and he was all fancied up, wearing a flat, black hat that had never seen a drop of sweat, I'd guess. He was wearing one of those long-tailed black coats, like the gamblers wear. A skinny cigar jutted out of the side of his mouth, and I noticed he was wearing iron, because it peeked out from under those coat tails. He was planning to howl tonight.

So was I.

I didn't know which saloon Bule was in, but I saw Sandy go into the one Johnson owned, the Golden Bell. I laid back on the bed and waited. I wanted to give him a chance to pour himself some courage, because I didn't want a repeat of what had happened twice before. I couldn't shoot him if he refused to fight, like he did before, so maybe if he had some liquor in him, he'd have some courage. I didn't want him drunk, because I didn't want anyone calling it unfair, but I didn't want a dodge put to me again, either.

I couldn't afford to let this man run around loose on me. I'd end up dry-gulched again, only this time for keeps. I wondered if he didn't fight me, whether I could just shoot him out of the saddle like he did me. I gave it some careful thought, then decided I couldn't do that. But, I knew if he didn't fight me, I'd have to meet him somewhere out of town, and I'd have to hurt him bad enough that he couldn't bushwhack me or anyone else again. I'd shoot him in the hands and cripple him bad. Those were evil thoughts, I know, and a mighty poor thing to do to someone, but it was either that or end up dead, because this man was too good at bushwhacking.

In a minute Bule rapped on the door and whispered, "It's me, Luke." I opened the door and I smelled him same time as I saw him. He had a flush to his face and a shine to his eye. I was sorry to see that, because Bule had him too mean a temper to be messing with liquor. It was liable to get him killed one day.

He said, "He's over in the Golden Bell, Luke."

"I saw him ride past the window. Looks like he's plannin' to howl."

"Luke, this is your fight, but there are men in there who might take Sandy's side. I'll be in there backin' your play, partner."

I clapped him on the back. It felt good to have a friend like Bule. I asked, "What about them Texas riders?"

He shook his head and said, "Don't know, Luke. They rode out of town this afternoon according to Bill, the clerk downstairs. Didn't announce their destination."

I had some ideas where they was headed, but I kept them to myself. Probably they had learned enough to look for me at the Wilsons. If I was lucky, they'd heard I was dead, only I didn't count on that.

After awhile, I stood up and began to adjust my gear. I checked my loads, made a few practice draws, checked my hideout gun tucked inside my vest, then went to the door. Bule was already in place, probably somewhere near the back. I wasn't looking forward to this, but it had to be done.

I went in quick and quiet, and no one even noticed me at first. Then, I went up to the bar and I could see a few heads turning my way, and some whispers made. I ordered a glass of water and the barkeep asked me to repeat it. I think he just want everyone to hear it. I glared at him, and he said something under his breath, then went to fetch my water. I had given a good look-see when I came in and had spotted Sandy right away. He didn't notice me because he was so busy talking to some female who looked like she forgot to dress herself before she came in the place.

My ma had always warned me about painted women and liquor. If she was beside me now, she'd have took me by my ear, I'm sure, and marched me to the outside. But, not without some words to a couple of those women. There was a pretty fair sized crowd in the saloon, and more smoke than fourteen steers branded at once would make. It choked me some and stung my eyes, but I'd not be long in there.

I saw the woman he was with lean over and whisper something in his ear, and he turned and looked back my way. I could see the surprise wash over his face, but he didn't show any scare. I reckon he had his nerve poured tonight. I left the water setting there and made my way back to his table. When I got there I smiled, but he didn't smile back, because he wasn't a smiling sort of man, if you know what I mean.

"Howdy Bushwhacker," I said.

He nodded and said,, "Adams." He had a little cigar in his mouth and didn't take it out to talk.

I said, "Did you figure I was dead?"

He took the cigar and said, "Knew you were alive. I went back next day and followed your trail. Almost went on in and finished you while you stayed with the Wilsons, but it ain't my style to involve women in my fights."

"Yeah, I know your style. From behind a rock."

He laughed at that, tossed off a drink and said, "Funny thing about blood. When it runs out of a man, it don't matter much what he was. Good men bleed the same blood as bad men. In the end, it don't matter one whit what a man was in life." He leaned back, enjoying the attention.

He continued. "Take you, for instance. You're a piece of trash with some notions of being one of those kind-hearted souls who thinks everyone's business is his business. When you're dead, it won't matter that you were a fool. Won't matter you're trash. When you're dead, things like that just don't matter." He smirked and added, "Won't matter to you that Mary Wilson don't ride with you no more, either."

I knew then what all that hate was that he had for me. This man had his eye on Mary. I'd messed up his game. I was standing in his way. He wanted Mary Wilson and he'd kill any man who got in his way.

I stepped closer and said, "Well, I got me an idea your blood ain't red at all, but yellar, kind of like that stripe on your back." Then, I leaned down and got near his fact and said loudly, "And Mary Wilson wouldn't ride the same saddle you sat on, Bushwhacker." I spoke loud so most everyone could hear.

He got red in the face and slid his glass to the center of the table. He stood and said, "I'm going to kill you for that."

I smiled and said, "You going to sit there and talk all night about it, or do it? You one of them talkers, Sandy? Got to talk up your nerve? Bet you was talking to your horse all the way out, the day you bushwhacked me. It had to gall you that I was laying up there in that bed being tended by Mary every day." I wanted his emotions to take over. A man in a rage didn't think clear.

The barkeep ran up then with a shotgun, waved it at us and shouted, "You two ain't shootin' up my place and killin' my customers. You want to kill each other, that's fine, but you do it outside!"

I was never one to argue with a shotgun, so I edged through the crowd toward the front door. As I neared the door I paused and said, "I'll be waitin' for you outside, like last time. You remember that time, don't you? The time you didn't show on account of being too scared" I knew he'd come for me now. There just wasn't any way he'd take abuse like that in front of so many folks.

I walked over to the edge of the street. It was dark, but there was light from the moon, which was full and bright, plus lamps from the saloon gave us pretty good light. I waited. There was already a pile of people running about, trying to get a good look, shoving each other to get outside, but also trying to get the safest place to watch from.

He came out quick, and I expected him to at least step off the porch and then go at me face to face, but he must have been so mad he couldn't wait. As soon as he reached the door and stepped through it, he drew his gun. But, I was ready from the time I walked in that place, and he didn't catch me off guard. He was plenty fast. I probably have seen a faster draw, but not in a long time. He got his gun out and boomed off a shot, but that shot was at the moon because my two shots slammed him up against the saloon wall. He coughed once, stepped back inside the saloon, then sat down hard in a chair. I could see his legs in the chair.

I kept my gun out, but I moved quick out of the light. Inside, I could see a mess of people bending over him, so I stepped onto the porch and went in. I hoped Bule was still looking out for me. I saw Sandy slumped in a chair. He'd never trouble my trail, again.

I called out, loud enough for all to hear: "This man bushwhacked me on the trail awhile back. I settled the matter tonight. Now, you all seen it and know it to have been a fair fight. If there's anyone here who wants to take Sandy's side of the matter, then let him step out now. Don't you be waiting and talking of it later, because I'll have to make another trip into town. I'd as soon settle it now."

There wasn't even a whisper from anyone. I knew my little talk would help stop a lot of idle talk that some fool might have been tempted to make. Get some fools to talking and they'll get you and themselves talked into an early grave. It was a fair fight, and that's the way I wanted it to lay.

I moved back outside and went for the hotel. Soon as I got there, Bule showed and we went up together without saying a word. I had kind of lost my taste for staying in town and knew I wouldn't be able to sleep in that room, so I took my roll and told Bule he could have the room to himself and that I'd see him at the mine tomorrow. He understood how I felt, because he never said a word, but only nodded.

I spent the night in the valley. I found a little spot near the river, but I had to move back into the open after awhile on account of the *skeeters*. They got so bad even Mash was complaining. I smeared my face with some mud from the river and it helped. I laid on my back late into the night watching the stars and thinking, settling my nerves.

Killing Sandy was a kind of comfort to me because that kind of man is too good with a gun and too cold blooded to have running around. Sooner or later, he'd have killed me. I was still angry at myself for not pushing things with the man in the first place. Everything in me had warned me about him and I'd ignored it. I wouldn't ignore that feeling again, not ever. Sometimes, you can't afford to let another man live. He'll bring grief to you or those you love.

CHAPTER 12

Next morning, I went back to the mine, but I was real careful. I figured these two Texans were nearby somewhere, so I stayed off the trail much as I could. I passed on by the Wilsons, for if those men were there, I didn't want to meet up with them and have a shootout right in Mary's front yard. I reckon that would have been the end of us for certain, if that happened.

It took me longer to make the trip, but I got back in time for dinner. And, I took a pass. The boss had gone and made his Half 'n Half Stew. When I rode up, he was standing there stirring with a little smile on his face like he was somebody's sweet mother slaving over a hot stove. That poor kid was letting himself in for some grief, for I caught some of the conversation as I was putting away Mash.

Charlie said, "Boss, you don't have to worry about me getting offended over your cooking. My pa used to cook for us when Mama was laid up sick and I ate his cooking. It wasn't good, but when you're hungry it don't matter what it is. I like your cookin' Boss, and if this is a special meal, I'm sure I'll like it, too."

The boss looked over to poor dumb Charlie talking himself into a hole, smiled real polite and said, "Boy, I appreciate your kindness to me. I suppose I've been mighty self conscious over my cooking ever since that lazy, worthless cowboy over there told me my cooking was terrible. It hurt me awful, especially since I really tried hard to make it tasty. But, I reckon he's used to them cowboy cooks that use all that flour and bacon and such."

Charlie looked over at me and said, "Aw, Luke probably didn't mean anything, Boss."

I figured I might as well help out, so I said, "Naw, I was just funnin' you, Boss. You ain't such a bad cook, and I'm real sorry I hurt your feelin's thataway."

The boss smiled that big innocent smile of his and said, "Long as you didn't mean it, Luke."

He slopped his stew out on the plates, but I pretended that I wasn't hungry on account of eating in town. The boss slopped my stew back into the pot and muttered something about that being all the more for him and Charlie.

He gave the kid a smile and said, "Eat up, Charlie." Then, the boss took a big bite out of that hell on a spoon and acted like it was honey on a stick.

The kid gave a quick little smile to show that he really was thankful and to show the boss he wasn't no complainer like me. Then he dug in. Two swallows later, Charlie turned red as my shirt, and I saw tears spring into his eyes. But, he was a stayer, I give him that. He choked that stuff down, put some more on a spoon, studied it some, then bowed his head. I ducked down quick to give a little peek, and sure enough his eyes was shut tight. I reckon poor Charlie was praying that God would take the fire out of that spoon, but this wasn't no hell God had made. It was pure, man-made.

After another bite, the kid mumbled something and excused himself. He wanted to run so bad he had to stop himself twice on the way to the water jug. I saw him start to walk fast, hesitate, slow down and walk a little faster. But the kid was no quitter. I figured he'd stay away or come back and give some excuse about not being hungry, but instead, he brought a water jug with him. His face was red as my neckerchief. He certainly had determination.

The boss looked at him real polite like and said, "Pretty good, huh,

Charlie?" The boss took a big bite and chewed on it like it was apple pie.

Charlie nodded and gave the boss a weak smile. Then, to show he wasn't ready to give up, he put another bite in his mouth. I reckon I couldn't hold it in no more because when he popped that jug up to his mouth, I busted out laughing. The boss took to grinning, then he started laughing too, and the kid realized that he'd been roped in, and he got to laughing, too. We were all sitting around laughing like that when Bule rode up.

I could see he wasn't feeling as chipper as he usually was. It looked like he had raised the 'pisun' too many times. That grieved me some, for he was a fine man, and strong. Too strong to let himself get ruined by the jug. He swung off his horse and asked us what we were laughing at. I winked at Charlie, and I knew the boss would follow right along, for we'd wanted to catch Bule right from the first.

"Aw, it ain't nuthin', Bule. The boss here was just tellin' us how he knew this cowboy who had a drinkin' problem." Bule looked kind of hard at me, but I went on. "He didn't have a normal drinkin' problem, but a strange one like no one ever did see before."

I could see Bule was interested in the story, but he was interested more in that stew. He peeked over at the pot and smelled. I got a little worried, but it did smell good. A body would never know that was brimstone bubblin' in that pot just from smellin' it. No brimstones ever smelled so good.

He dug up a plate and slopped some on. "I'm so hungry I could eat my horse with the saddle still on it."

"Hey you ornery cuss!" I said, "You got to hear my story before you get to eatin'. It ain't polite to eat while I'm talkin' to you."

He gave me a funny look, but I guess he was too tired to argue. He put the spoon down and said, "Well, get on with it, Luke. I'm powerful hungry and I sure don't know why you can't talk while I'm eating, but tell that story. I'll wait."

"Well, as I said,, this gent had a drinkin' problem. Everytime he set down to eat, he had to get up and run get a drink of water. He'd set down, eat a little, then jump up and get a drink of water. He used to drink a gallon of water with his meals."

Bule give me a shake of his head and said, "And that's what you were laughing at? That's what you held me up for? I think you're going daft, Luke."

He lit into that stew, and in a flash he had himself two bites down and was digging for the third when it hit him. Bule's eyes got big, and he looked over to me, but I looked away, then he looked over to the boss, but the boss pretended to be looking at Charlie. Then he exploded from the table we had set up, knocking it over in his hurry to get to the water jug.

We were hugging our sides, but when he got through drinking a half jug of water he came back, and we was still and quiet. He was looking hard at both of us, and then I looked up at him and said, "Looks like you done gone and caught that cowboy's drinkin' problem, Bule." The boss couldn't hold it in no more and he started laughing, and Charlie started in, but I was holding back as long as I could. Bule, he just stood there holding that jug and staring at me, then I seen a grin break out, and we both busted up at the same time.

I was kidding poor Bule for a long time about his 'drinking problem.' We had us a tussle a time or two over me kidding him, but he always took it good enough. We told him about Charlie, and he got to laughing over that, and then we all got to laughing again at Bule, then we took off on Charlie again, then the boss told about the first time I met him at his ranch, and how I had run outside and almost fell into his well trying to get some water, and we all had a good laugh over that. It was real enjoyable time and it put my mind out of worry for awhile.

We worked the mines a couple of days, then the boss gathered us one day and pulled out some little sacks. He said, "Boys, this is what we been working for. I've divided it all up into three parts. Charlie, you ain't a partner, so you ain't gettin' a full share, but just the same I got a sack for you, too." He handed it to each of us.

The boss said, "Luke, you, me and Bule each got about $200.00

worth of gold. That ain't much, considerin' all the work we put in." He looked at me and frowned, and with a pretended look of pain on his face, added, "Well, all the work *some* of us put in."

He looked at Charlie and said, "I give you $75.00, kid. Figured you earned at least that much."

The kid tried to give it back and said he didn't care if it was only a dollar, long as he could stay on, but the boss wouldn't let him talk.

I held up my hand and interrupted. "Say, Boss. I reckon I got to have a say on this deal." I tossed my sack at him and said, "You three been doin' most all of the work, and it don't seem right I should get the same as you and Bule. I reckon you ought to trade my sack for Charlie's."

The boss bent down and picked up that sack from the ground. I could tell he was peeved. He stomped over to me and shoved the sack down the front of my shirt and said, "Luke, I'm running this gold mine and don't be giving me no orders on how to pay. You take what I give you and quit your belly aching. It ain't enough I got to do most of the work around here, but I got to put up with your whining too."

I opened my mouth, but shut it. I wanted to argue, but I just wasn't too sure how serious he was. Might be if I pressed him, I'd have to fight him, and there just wasn't no chance I'd be mixing up with the likes of him. Not with bare hands. Well, maybe if I could hold a tree in my hands. I held up my hands and told him I surrendered. Didn't seem right, but some folks you just don't argue with.

I asked if those two riders had been by and they said no one had seen them since they left town. I figured they'd come by and had a look see already. I knew I'd sleep light and away from the fire for a few nights. I was learning to live careful.

On the third night, those two came in quiet as a couple of wolves sneaking up on a baby calf. Only thing, Mash has got ears keen as an *injun's*, and his head come bobbing up, so when he jerked his head up, the rawhide on my wrist raised up my hand faster'n my mama's hand used to go up in church. I came rolling out of my blankets easy and quiet, my gun drawn and ready. I slipped off the piece of rawhide and slid into the night.

I got to hand it to them. They weren't fools, and they weren't green. They found my blankets and Mash standing there beside them. A fool would have walked over and got to discussing with the other fool about why the roll was empty, and where I was. Those too knew why it was empty and both knew they had bought some serious trouble.

I watched them whirl and disappear into the night as silent as they'd come. I was already ahead of them, and I headed down where I figured they'd have left their horses. I'd scouted around the first few days I was here, and I knew there was only two likely places. Judging from the direction they'd run, that narrowed it down to one. In another couple minutes, I spotted the horses. Two long-legged Texas *broncs* stood hobbled, one done up with some fancy *injun* gear, and the other dressed plain, but sturdy.

I moved to a nearby rock and waited. Pretty soon, they came into sight, moving slow and quiet. When they got to the horses, one of them said softly, "Think he spotted us, Webb?"

That Webb feller answered, "Dunno, Ed. All I know for sure is the hair on my neck raised when I saw that empty roll, and it ain't gone down yet. I figured there we'd done bought the ticket home."

"Yeah, I know what you mean. I had the same feeling. Think we should go back later?"

That Webb feller was quiet for a long spell, then he said, "No. If he ain't in his bed, then it means he's walkin' about, or waitin' for us."

Ed laughed low and said, "Yeah, we might walk onto him real sudden."

"Webb said, "Way I hear, it ain't healthy to come on that man sudden."

I rose quietly from behind the rock, eared back the hammer of my gun and said, "If there ain't no sudden moves, you boys will live to see the sun rise in the morning."

I heard the one called Ed let go with a low moan and a slow whoosh of air. He'd sucked in his belly and had been primed to move. I reckon if I hadn't spoke out same time I eared back the hammer, he'd have gone into action. The other never moved a button, but just stood there by his horse.

I said, "Boys, I'm movin' up close now, so don't go gettin' spooked on me and makin' any kind of moves. Just raise your hands so I can see 'em pointin' at the moon. If you even shiver at the cold, I'll shoot you where you stand."

I eased over the top of the rock I was behind, taking care not to trip. I stuck their guns down the front of my pants. It was the way I'd carried a gun when I was a kid, until I found an old tattered leather pocket made for carrying a gun. I remember my ma used to hate for me to carry my gun shoved down the front of my pants. She was always worried about it going off.

I herded them two back to the camp. Everyone was still asleep, so I got some rope and tied them up against a small tree. Then, I laid down a few feet away.

I looked over to those two *hardcases* and said, "I sleep awful light. If there's whisperin' or moving goin' on, I'll come alive, and sometimes when I wake sudden, I shoot before I know what's the matter. Don't be wakin' me before sunup, boys. Good night." Then, I laid down and went right to sleep.

When I woke, Bule was squatting over the fire making coffee. The boss and Charlie were still sleeping, and one of those Texans was asleep. The other, a lean gent with cool grey eyes, was watching both of us careful.

I sat up and pointed a finger to the Texan. "This here is a Texas visitor, Bule." Then I asked, "You the one called Ed or Webb?"

He said, "Ed."

I said, "Bule, Ed and his friend here rode all the way from Texas just to see me. Ain't that nice?"

Bule grinned, poured me a cup of that steaming coffee and one for himself. I got up and loosened the rope off both of them, and got Bule to bring them a cup of coffee. That Webb feller muttered a thanks, but the other was quiet.

I figured it was as good a time as any to make my speech, so I said, "I'm givin' you boys a cup of coffee, and even something to eat if you want it, which is more'n you was set to give me. Then, I'm turnin' you loose. If you ride back to Texas, that's fine. If you don't, then I reckon I'll take it that you mean to do me harm."

I took a long swallow of coffee, and it was strong, but bitter. Then I went on: "If I see you around, I ain't goin' to ask no questions from you. I'll just open up on you wherever I see you.

Ed nodded, and with a funny little smile, said, "That's real polite."

I smiled at that, but let it pass. "If either of you, or both of you want to try and earn the money that sent you on this little trip, I'll give you your chance this mornin'. We can take a little walk over there and have it out, one at a time." I took a big swallow of coffee and said, "It ain't my idea of how to start a day, but I reckon if I stick in your craw, or you figure you got to earn your pay, then we might as well settle the matter now."

I had an idea that Webb was a decent sort of feller. He proved me right when he said, "Adams, I've took some bad jobs before, but this is the worst I ever tied to. Everyone knows Ben Briner was no good and beggin' for it. I reckon if you was what old man Briner had made you out to be, we'd be layin' beside our horses. You had us cold."

I just nodded at him, took a long sip at my coffee, and watched Ed. He was different. He wasn't doing any talking, for he wasn't too sure which way the wind was going to blow. The more I looked at him, the more I figured he'd not be taking any rides out of the territory without making his try at me. He kept his trap shut, but he was studying me. I've seen that look before. It's the same kind of look a dog will give another when they meet up. They may get to the sniffing stage, or they may just have it out. Either way, they're both looking the other over real close.

That dog was content to look at me now, but I knew that once loose and with a gun, he'd not be content with looking or sniffing. He'd want a piece of me. I made up my mind right then to make sure he got all he could handle of me. I'd backed off on Sandy and it nearly cost me my life. I had known all along that he'd try to bushwhack me one day, but I'd backed off and fooled myself. I should have trusted that feeling that comes from looking another man in the eye. I had looked deep into Sandy's eyes and saw an awful lot of poison and grief there. I looked into this man's eyes and saw plain murder. No hate, but only a kind of look a man has who is patient, who knows his business, and who intends to do murder.

Ed was interested in my proposition, I could see, only he let it pass because he figured he could do it another way, easier. That other didn't look interested in me any more, front or back.

I asked Webb, "What'd Briner pay you for my head?"

"We got a hundred..."

"Shut up, Webb!" Red spotches appeared on the man's face as he glared at the other. His eyes were flat and hard, and his voice was barely above a whisper. "You've gone soft and your days of riding with me are done. I'll settle with you, later."

Webb didn't back off from him one whit. He took a long swallow of his coffee, and his eyes tightened as he said matter-of-factly: "I got a feeling you won't be getting that chance, amigo." He was looking at me when he spoke. I think he had guessed what I was thinking.

I finished my coffee and got up with a small groan. Cold ground has a way of making a body ache in places he didn't know existed. I tossed my cup to the ground and strolled over to where Ed was sitting.

"When you're done with your coffee, take a little walk yonder." I nodded my head over to the little clearing that stands in front of our mine. I backed off and added, "I'll be waiting."

He raised his eyebrows at me in surprise, then a little smile came over his face as he replied. "I suppose it might be the best way after all. Quicker for certain. Easier, in the long run."

I went over to the clearing, and he took his time with his coffee. Finally, he stood, hitched up his belt, gave Webb a long stare and a sneer, and then sauntered over my way. He was cool as they come, and it didn't appear to me that a nerve in him was tingling. I got a deep empty feeling inside.

I tossed him his gun and said, "Load it." Immediately, he flipped the chamber open and began plunking shells in as calmly as if he was getting ready for target practice. It was plain to me that this was a man who'd growed up with a gun in his hands. That easy, familiar way was sign enough for me.

He dropped it in his holster, then looked up at me and said casually, "Mind if I work it a little? I'm a mite stiff from the night air. Turn my back if it makes you feel better."

I said, "Back sounds fine, only I got to tell you that if you try something fancy, my two partners there wont have no qualms about shootin' you down."

He smiled, turned and began workin' that gun in and out of the black leather holster at his side. I got a little nervous, for I saw that he was one of those true, natural men with a gun. He moved like him and the gun was one, like it growed onto his hand. It came to me suddenly, that I was about to face a man who could well be the killing of Luke Adams. I swallowed hard, but it was either this or wait for him to catch me when the time was of his own choosing. That could be a time when my back was turned to him, and he wasn't the kind of man to let a chance like that go by. This man was a professional killer, and I had the feeling that he could kill from the front or back, it was all the same to him.

I needed something in this fight. I reckon I'm better than most with a handgun, but in this fight I needed to better than I ever was. I needed to be mad at this man, but I wasn't. I needed to hate him, but I didn't. Those fellers who make their living with a gun don't need a mad or a hate to help out in a fight. They are mostly like this Ed, cool, quiet, all business, and as good when they are mad as when they're not. But, I'm not built like that. When I fight, it helps me a good deal to be mad or hate. I reckon a good scare will do in a pinch. The big trouble with being good with a gun, like I am, is you get to where you're not afraid of another man with a gun, because you know that you are going to get your gun out no matter how good he is.

It makes for over-confidence, and that can bring a man to an early grave.

I figured if I was going to keep from getting tagged, I was going to have to get mad at this man. So, when he turned to face me I said, "You don't look like you've nursed too many cows in your time. Did you always shoot down other folks for a livin', or what?"

I wasn't too sure where that little dig would lead, but I was hoping he'd cuss me some. He was cool and calm, just like before and just gave me a little smile.

I tried again. "When you die, do I write Gunfighter, Killer, Slow, or what on your marker?"

He gave a little shake of his head like he was being patient with a fool, then said, "You talk too much."

I said, "Your friend, Webb, he don't have much regard for you. Maybe he seen the bushwhacker in you, like I did." His face got tight and his eyes narrowed. I'd hit a nerve.

I was finding my anger as I thought about how this man would have murdered me in cold blood. "You was all set to bushwhack me, weren't you? You'd have shot me in the back while I was asleep, wouldn't you?"

His face lost that calm, relaxed look and flushed red. The time had come. No one made a sound. The boss was sitting on his blankets by the fire and Charlie was standing nearby with Bule and Webb.

I turned a little to the side to give him a smaller target, and it placed me right for throwing out my gun. I have almost always worn my gun at my belly, so standing sideways gives me even more of an edge. He faced me square, his hat tugged down to shade his eyes. He'd stuck a piece of grass in his mouth, and had been chewing on it like he was at a social gathering, but when he got mad he spit it out and moved his hand so it hung loose near his gun.

I drew first. Giving that man first draw was same as giving him first shot. Turned out, he got first shot anyhow, because that man showed me something about getting a gun shucked clear of a holster and firing that I never knew before. He had his gun cleared and two shots gone my way by the time I was squeezing off my first shot. One shot tugged at my neckerchief and the other raked across right under my arm pit, humming like a big angry bee on its way to sting the fool who got him mad. I didn't even feel the pain.

My first shot took him off his feet and piled him on the ground. It was a clean hit and would have taken most any man out of a fight, but that feller must have growed up kind of like me, because he rolled on the ground and got off another shot at me. It went humming past my left ear. I suddenly got sense enough to put two more shots into him.

He didn't move after that. I got to thinking of what he'd done. I never believed a man could get two shots off at me, and two good shots at that, before I got one off at him. He would have hit me, except when I shoot, I always drop into a crouch. That, plus the fact that I was sort of sideways was the only thing that saved me, I know, because that man was shooting for my head, and the first shot would have took it clean off. The second shot, the one that come near to taking off my left shoulder but passed under, was his correcting shot, and if he'd just took a bit more time with it, I'd have took it in the brisket. The good Lord was sure looking after Luke Adams that day.

The way he throwed his gun was different. It's strange how a man will think of things like that when he's likely to die. All I could think of when I saw him drawing and firing was that it was the most amazing and fastest way of handling a six-gun I ever did see.

When he drew his gun, he was pulling it backwards, instead of throwing it to the front like everyone else I ever seen draw. While he was jerking it back, he was lining up his left hand, and a couple of slaps on the hammer with that hand got off two of the quickest shots I ever saw. It was quick as a man can blink. I've seen some men in action who could probably get a shot in me straight up, but I'd take them down with me. It bothered me, but I had to admit now that there used to be one man who could get two shots in me straight up, and me never getting one in him. It didn't happen that way, but it could have. If that gunfighter had taken a bit more time on his shots, I'd have gone down permanent. It gave me a chill as the thought came to me.

I went over to him and turned him over. He was still holding his gun, and I took it from him. I'd maybe work with that gun some day and see if I couldn't get as good as he was. One thing I knew for certain was that this kind of shooting was for a gent with a feel for his gun and his aim. You don't aim, but you just bring up the gun and the rest was feel. When you felt like you were on target, you fired. It wasn't something you think about, either. It's just something you do.

I put his gun in my holster, and it felt pretty good. I liked the feel and the balance. There wasn't too much special about his holster, except he'd whacked most of the front away. I reckon I could do that with my own holster. I took his holster off and handed it to Charlie. He took it, give me a funny look, and then laid it on the body. I just shrugged. I'd give it to Bule if he wanted it or I'd take it and see if I could adapt it. The boss wouldn't want it because he preferred a rifle.

I spoke to Webb. "Drag him out of here and take him to Reata. Use whatever money he has on him to bury him and keep the rest. Put on his marker that he tried to kill Luke Adams."

Webb stood looking at the body awhile, then said, "I always knew he'd meet up with someone good as he was. I backed off from that man more than once. He was the best I ever saw."

I asked, "How long you known him?"

"I reckon I've known Ed a dozen years. He took a liking to me because I helped him in a fight once. Asked for me special when Briner sent him on this job."

"You think Briner will send any more riders after me?"

Webb nodded. "As certain as death, mister. It might take him awhile, because we been having some rustler problems, but soon as that's cared for he'll show. Especially now. Ed was the best he could hire."

I hoped Mr. Briner had a lot of rustlers to catch because I wasn't too anxious to try any more of his killers out, especially if they were anything like the last one. It did give me some satisfaction to know that this was costing Briner a lot more than he figured on. I just hope it didn't cost him the one thing he couldn't afford: *his own life.*

CHAPTER 13

We kept on working the mine all summer, then winter came along and it got too cold, then the snow started to fall. We decided that we'd best stay in town. The boss was all for building a little shack and him staying up there all winter busting rock, but we talked him out of it. He'd have loved it, no doubt, but I know such a life is not for this cowboy, and the snow can get pretty deep up there. He'd have had to lay in a lot of grub for the winter, and it just didn't seem to be a good idea to any of us but him.

The boss divvied up the gold again and still insisted on giving me a full share. I tried everything to get him to just give me a little of it because of me taking off so much and being laid up that time, but he got mad again, and I had to take it. I snuck into his room one night in town while he was snoring and loaded about half my gold into his two small bags.

Life in town was pretty good. I ate until I was fat as a hog. Bule enjoyed the easy life too, but the boss suffered terrible. He wasn't a man given to setting and had to be busy at something all the time. He made himself some snowshoes, something I had never seen before. He put them on and went loping across the snow looking like a bear when it tries to walk like a man. We all had a try at them, but Bule was so bowlegged he couldn't walk a straight line. He was a sight.

Charlie was the best at them. They got a good laugh out of me because when I was stumbling around on those things a dog got after me, latched onto my pants leg and got to tugging with all his might. I fell backwards, but the dog just kept on chewing on my pant leg. I had trouble reaching him because of those snow shoes, so finally, I took one off and whacked him a good one. Bule was sitting on the porch laughing so hard he had tears, and the boss was choking as usual when he laughs too hard.

Once, we saw some kids in town with a sled. They were using it on a small hill on the edge of town. We got with them and I offered to pull the sled behind my horse. They really took to that idea, so I drug them around for awhile. Finally, I asked Charlie if he'd care for a ride. I gave him a couple good fast rides, and then I got Bule on. He wasn't too keen at first, but the kids got to hollering for him to ride, so he gave in. Bule sat down, I booted Mash in the ribs, let out a Texas yell, and we took off down the middle of the street. Bule was yelling for me to slow down, but I just kept Mash on a dead run. Finally, I stopped, and Bule was about to tell me something when I kicked Mash in the ribs and we came tearing back down the street again. Time we got back, Bule looked like one of the snowmen the kids were building.

Then, Bule insisted I had to ride, and those kids wouldn't hear nothing of me getting out of it. I knew I was in for a terrible ride, because Bule was going to try and outdo me and pay me back for that ride I gave him. I got on, and immediately, he gave out a yell like a Comanche coming for my hair, then we were moving faster'n a lizard over hard ground. I turned over once when we came to a little hill and he had to stop while I climbed back on.

He finally headed back to town and I was thinking maybe it wasn't going to be so bad after all. He was slapping Mash on the rump and hooting, and we got to flying so fast that my hat flew off. Then, just as we were nearing the corral by the blacksmith shop, Bule steered straight for it. I yelled at him to watch out where he was going, but he didn't pay me no mind. Then, just as he came up on that corral he yanked back on the reins, put Mash on his haunches, and then moved him out of my way with a little step to the side. I come sliding likkity-split into that corral, right in among them horses.

They got spooked, got to squealing, snorting and stomping around, and mud and manure was flying all over. I got stuff in my ears, my nose, and even my mouth, on account of yelling at Bule. Then, before I could get off, Bule booted Mash into a dead run back the other way and snaked that sled back out of the corral slick as if he was taking a calf away from its mother. I almost got my head taken off, and the bottom of the corral pole scrapped the top of my head enough to give me a lump.

I could tell he had thought this out real good, and by the time we got back, I was covered with mud and manure and nursing a sore noggin, but we had fun and those kids had a lot of laughs out of it. Fact is, half the town got a good laugh at it because most everyone came out to see about the commotion. I was a sight to behold. But then, every kid wanted Bule to pull them like he did me, so he make himself a lot of work, only he didn't pull them as hard as he did me.

It was a good winter. I saw Mr. Johnson a couple times, and he smiled at me, but never spoke. He had a new man to take Sandy's place. He was a short, ugly runt of a man, with bad teeth and a dirty beard that was as black as my hair. He had muddy-brown eyes, and I took him to be another skin-full of poison and steered clear of him. He'd never look at me, but always to one side. My pa always told me that a man who won't look you in the eye is hiding something and never to trust him. I don't think this one's own mother would have trusted him.

Mary and me was getting friendly again, although she fussed with me some about hanging around and waiting for those Texans to come. I never told her about the two who'd come already, but someone did because she brought it up to me once. We still differed fierce on that matter. I also learned she was seeing a miner now and then, and I learned that he had asked her to marry her, but she had turned him down. I had seen him around town now and then, but he never would speak with me. I always went out of my way to be friendly to him, but this man never would talk to me. He wouldn't even look my way, but avoided me like I had a bad sickness.

Spring came early, and the boss got to getting nervous and anxious to get back to the mine. I wasn't looking forward to breaking that rock. But, finally, we packed our gear, took a couple loads of food with us, and headed out for the mine. The air had that fresh, wet smell to it, and the breezes were cool enough to make us wear our coats. I didn't mind getting out of town because it was wearing on me, but I wasn't looking forward to that pile of rocks, either.

At the camp, the stream was swollen with all the melting snow. I stuck my hand down into it and slurped at the water. It was cold as ice and clear as glass. There just wasn't any better tasting drink than cold water out of a mountain stream. I knelt, took a couple gulps, and splashed some onto my face.

All day was spent making camp and figuring out where to build our cabin. I got the job of sawing down the trees, along with Charlie. The boss and Bule were to do all the notching and making up of the cabin. I never built a cabin and hadn't much of an idea how, but the boss had built three, and he said he built a house once out of plank wood. Bule said he had built a cabin for use as a line shack once. Charlie had never built a cabin, but he had help build a barn with his daddy, once. Only thing I ever built was a lean-to out of pine branches for hunting back in Kentucky.

We had us a long, double-handled saw, and it took me some time before I got the hang of it. The kid just took to it like he was brought up doing it, which, from the way he talked, was just about what had happened. He had cleared trees with his daddy and took out stumps since he was a little tyke. In fact, it turned out that the reason he had run off was because his daddy was fixing to have him clear out a stand of aspen for use as another field. I didn't blame the kid at all after I put in the first day on the saw. It was plain murder.

Then, Charlie had to put me to shame by telling me he used to use the saw all by himself. He took it up once while I was laying down groaning and proceeded to show me by sawing all the way through a tree by himself. That kid could handle a saw like I could handle a gun.

We had all the wood cut for the cabin in a week. The boss and Bule notched and put it together in no time. I didn't like their floor at all, though. They should have put down some planks from town as there was a saw mill just south of town, and no real trouble to haul up here. Instead, they put down a whole bunch of little tree trunks all scrunched up tight. It beat any floor I ever was on for staying clean, for the cracks between them little trees let the dirt fall down and the round tops kept it from collecting there. The boss said he had gotten the idea from an old trapper he had met once in some woods somewhere far from here. It suited him, but it wasn't the kind of floor a cowboy would take to, I can say for certain. It just didn't feel solid like a real floor or the earth itself.

We made up some beds for inside, and since the cabin was big and roomy, we even made a long bench from a log. Me and Charlie hauled up buckets of mud and clay, and Bule slopped it onto the outside and in the cracks. It hardened, and made a wind tight cabin. We figured we could haul up a stove and put it in some time later. I even got to thinking maybe I would stay on here through the winter, but I came to my senses later and forgot that idea. The boss said he'd be spending the next winter here. I told him he'd be all by himself unless the kid was crazy enough to stay with him. I knew Bule wouldn't.

One day about two weeks after we got the cabin finished, I was down at the stream washing some of the busted up rock we had, when my eye caught something laying right there in the bottom of the stream. I reached over and plucked it out of the stream, and the nice yellow shine it gave told me I had found gold. I ran up to the camp and hollered for the rest.

The boss looked at it and said, "Luke, you have to be the luckiest man I ever knew. I been digging in that mine now for months, learning what it's like to go to hell, and here you are playing in the water and you find gold." He shook his head and muttered to no one in particular, "It just ain't fair, somehow."

We got down to where I found it, and he walked right into the stream and began scooping up big handfuls off the bottom. There was a lot of rocks and some sand. He dug another handful and came up with a little nugget. We got to whooping and carrying on, and pretty soon we were all soaked, digging up gravel and turning over rocks, and throwing them on the side of the creek.

The vein the boss had been looking for in that mine of ours hadn't showed, and we had been getting less and less gold out of the rock. But, here was something even I could do and enjoy. I didn't have to bust up any rocks, just pick it out of the water. That suited me fine

The boss dug out some tin pans that we had been using to wash our rocks with and gave us each one. He showed us how to scoop, and then sift for the gold, kind of like we had done with our crushed rock, only now we were looking for sandy pieces of gold as well as nuggets. We all took to scooping and sifting and forgot all about the hole in the ground up there. It wasn't but a couple of hours later that we had us a small pile of gold laid on the blanket on the side of the stream. We took more in one day that we'd taken from the mine in all those months. It made me feel good that I had been the one to discover it.

They all got to talking about how rich we were going to be, and the boss was talking of owning more than even Johnson. I didn't say too much. Somehow, I just never could get excited about it all too much. I figured I'd give much of my share to Mary's parents, save enough to get married on, and buy a ranch somewhere far away from Texas, maybe even Mexico.

All next week we sifted through the stream. We took less and less out, and we never did find half as much as we did on the first day, but we did take out more every day than we had taken out of the mine in a month. This made the building of the cabin useless, in my opinion. Sure, we could sleep in it when the weather got bad, or in cold snaps, but mostly, I liked sleeping outdoors.

The stream would be frozen in winter, and there wouldn't be no reason for busting rocks from the mine. Of course, I didn't reckon on the boss's stubborn. He had set himself to work up there next winter, and he said he would be there, no matter what.

I had nearly eight hundred dollars in gold, and it was enough money to get a small place. I gave some thought to settling in this area, but I gave up on that idea because I knew me and Johnson would tangle our loops if I did. So, I figured I would wait a little longer and get a little more saved. I was sure in love with this New Mexico Territory, and I figured I would mosey south one day and see how it was down there, because I really wasn't taken with all the snow up here. I might head all the way to Mexico.

Josiah had got back with Mr. Johnson and was selling all his crops to him, but at a fair price, so I was glad to be shut of that worry. A new mine had opened up just south of the Colorado line, and they were hiring miners, so Reata was filling up with all kinds of critters. Those miners would work all day, and then come into town to whoop and holler, wearing the same dirty, smelly clothes, and smelling worse then six wet dogs. I steered clear of most of them, although I did meet a few I liked.

I did finally get the man who was courting Mary to speak to me. He was a big man, wide in the shoulders, and with a face full of white teeth. He didn't strike me as being too smart, but he was awful big, had a better looking face that I did, and looked as strong as the Wilson's mule.

We bumped into each other in the store one day. I was buying some pants, and he came stomping in. Loud as it was, I looked up to see if a steer had come in by accident. He went up to the counter and slapped some money down on the counter. I heard him ask the clerk for some kind of cloth. I watched the clerk get it, and then, as he was cutting on it, I walked over.

"You're Mosley, ain't you?"

He grunted, then I guess he changed his mind about wanting to talk to me because he turned and said, "What do you want, Adams?"

I smiled and said, "Just to say howdy. Since we are chasing the same filly, I figured we ought to at least get ourselves introduced."

"Adams, you got a 'rep' around here, but you go to bothering Mary, I'll take you apart! You hear me, don't you?"

Well, I didn't have a bit of trouble hearing him. I reckon the whole town could have heard him, he was so loud. He had one of those booming kind of voices. I kept my smile on and said, "Friend, I don't want no trouble with you. A man would be a fool to tangle with someone as wide as a barn door, and you shore got that, hoss. Besides, if you and me tangled, I reckon it'd shame Mary, us brawling over her here in front of everyone." He glared at me, took his package and stomped out. On my way back to camp I stopped off at Mary's house.

She was sitting in the rocker on the porch. Her ma was inside and I could hear her singing softly. She had a good voice, like my ma. I nodded at Mary and said, "Howdy, Mary. Thought I'd stop by on the way back."

She flashed me a smile and said, "I'm glad you came by, Luke. We need to talk."

It sounded serious. I slipped off my horse and walked to the porch, then sat down on the steps, the reins hanging from my hands. A splinter found its way into my backside, so I shifted slightly and the prick of the splinter went away. Mush nuzzled my hands for some sugar, so I dug out a piece of candy and gave it to him.

She said, "Luke, it's about us." She got to fooling with her hands in her lap, looked down at them, then looked back to me. "Luke, I think I'm going to marry John Mosley."

I didn't move, but inside, I felt like someone had hit me solid in the belly. I wanted to jump up and shake her and ask her if she was joking. But, I knew she was dead serious. I reckon it was then that I realized I was plumb sick in love with that little gal. I never been hit so hard since my ma died. It was kind of like being kicked in the chest by your horse, or catching a hoof in the belly when you are trying to wrestle with an onery steer that don't care for the smell of a hot branding iron. I couldn't move or speak for nearly a minute.

Finally, Mary said, "Luke I'm sorry. Really I am." She had tears in her eyes.

I looked at her and said, "Mary, don't be sorry. I reckon I know how you feel, and anyway, you shouldn't get yourself tied to no gun-throwin' cowboy with a price on his head and bounty hunters on his trail."

She gave me a strange look, then said, "Luke, I love you, and I guess I'd marry you even now, if only you'd leave this place and put up your gun. I can't live wondering if you're going to get shot every day of my life. That's something I won't have to worry about with John."

I stood up, moved over to the side of my horse, gave a little jump and rolled into the saddle. Then, I leaned down, smiled at Mary and said, "You done the right thing, Mary. I was raised on guns and fightin' and it ain't something that comes natural to a woman. I don't reckon I'd change, and I'll probably die with my boots on."

I gave the reins a tug to the side and said, "Be seein' you, Mary."

I wasn't much good for a long time after that. I quit looking for gold, and even quit riding into town. I wasn't up to anything but sitting by the stream and tossing rocks in. Then, one cool summer day Bule brought me some news that snapped me out of it.

He came in with some grub and walked down to the stream where I was sitting. "Luke. There's three new horses in town. They got the look of Texas on 'em, partner."

I asked, "You see any faces with those horses?"

"No, but word is they got the hard look. One of them is said to be older. Might be Briner. Nobody knows."

I thanked him and laid back on the grass to do some thinking. It was good to get my mind off my hurt and onto something like this. Staying alive has a way of making you perk up and pay attention.

I asked, "Bule, what would those three do if I refused to fight?"

Bule laughed. "Luke, they won't be asking you to fight. They'll be telling you to die."

Well, I had give it some thought before, and I figured maybe it was worth a try. It might be the thing to get me loose of those men and back with Mary. Maybe if she saw I was trying not to be shooting all my enemies, then maybe she'd forget that Mosley. I knew the town wouldn't stand for those men riding in and just shooting me down. I was liked in town. I did a lot of things to help out, including helping with putting up a new church, and once, I even filled in for a few days when the marshal went out of town. I figured if I wasn't wearing a gun, they couldn't kill me, at least not as long as I stayed in town and out in the open. It went against the grain, but I was bound to make my try. I didn't think they'd be gunning me in town, if I chose not to fight them. Outside town was different. They could pop me there and be gone before anyone could do a thing.

"Bule, get the boss up here, will you?" I walked over to my stuff on the ground and began making my roll up. I'd made up my mind that town was a safe place to be and I'd just wait those men out. If I had to, I'd stay in town for a year.

Bule came back with the boss and I told him that I was giving up my share in the mine and that he could take it or give it to Bule or Charlie. He tried to talk me into staying, arguing that it was safer here, but I just wouldn't hear any of it. Besides, I figured there wasn't much left down in that hole, and the stream looked to me to be playing out. Oh, we were getting some gold out, but not much more than I used to make as a cowboy, which was thirty and found. Maybe one man on that claim could do all right, but four of us busted up the take too much. And, I was real tired of the place. I had a hankering for some good food and a soft bed.

I rode off, but not before I threatened to whip Bule if he didn't stay in camp for a day or two, until things settled down. I headed Mash down off the mountain, feeling lonesome and nervous. Suppose I was wrong and those hard cases just jumped me in the street without warning? I had to think they wouldn't be that foolish. Besides, Briner didn't strike me as that kind of man. I didn't doubt he might bushwhack me, but he wouldn't shoot me down in front of a whole town. Not unless it was in a fight and I didn't plan on fighting. I counted on him not shooting down an unarmed man.

It was late when I pulled in and I was glad because I didn't want to be noticed yet. I swung into the stable and gave up my horse to the kid I woke up on the cot next to the door. He wasn't too happy about getting a customer at that hour, but he didn't give me any trouble, just some grump.

Next day, I went out late, not wanting to have trouble right away. I was worried about leaving my room without a gun, too. I knew I had to shuck my gun, though. That got to bothering me more than I thought it would. I haven't walked around without a gun on me since I was a tyke, on account of it being the surest way I knew to die. My gun had saved my life more times than a few, and it just felt unnatural. There are lots of men I know who don't carry a gun, but they are usually the kind of men who don't get bothered, who bother no one else, and who just go through life never getting into trouble. I never have been that way. Trouble has dogged my trail since I was a *yonker*.

I finally compromised and stuck the gun I took from that gunman named Ed down the back of my pants, in the small of my back. I had bought me a dress-up coat, and it hid the gun well enough. As far as anyone could tell, I wasn't armed, and I planned to tell those men quick that I wasn't armed. But, just in case I was wrong about them, I would have some chance.

I went down and had something to eat, then went over to the store and bought some candy. I stuffed my pockets full. The kids always knew I was good for a stick of candy when I was in town. A couple of the little ones even called me the 'candy man.' One little runt came by with his mama, grabbed her by the skirt and hauled her up short, like a cowboy jerking a critter up short. He squalled out that the 'candy man' was across the street and could he come and get some. She cuffed him, but he hollered until she gave in.

I found a spot to sit and had been there in the shade most of the day when I spotted two of those Texans. They came riding in slow, looking tired. They must have been out all night, and it was probably me that was the cause of it. They walked their horses over to where I was sitting and I saw one speak to the other. I smiled as they pulled up, but they didn't smile back.

"Howdy." I was full of polite and I had opened my coat wide to show I wasn't packing iron.

The one with the crooked nose and the green eyes said, "We're looking for a man and we figure you might be him."

I answered, "If it's Luke Adams, that's me."

They looked quick at each other, then one looked down the street. I could see he was calculating the chances on just shooting me and riding out.

I spoke up quick. "Don't try it. You might get five miles into the valley before they caught up with you. Folks around here don't take kindly to murder. You can see I ain't armed. Shoot me down and you'll hang. Briner pay you enough to hang?"

I could see I had put the notion to rest. The eyes of the one man softened just a little as the fire in him died down. I leaned forward some and continued, "Everyone in this valley knows who you are and why you've come. Likely, if we was to get into a fight and you put me down, they'd not bother you none, but if you shoot me while I'm unarmed, which I am, then you're headed for a tree out yonder."

I leaned back and smiled, then added, "You boys better get the lay of the land before you move sudden."

They were surprised, and it showed. Finally, Crooked Nose said, "We'll take what you said into consideration. Briner will have to make the decision, but if he decides you're fresh meat, then it's open season, cowboy. You can bet your bedroll on it."

They pulled away and went to the livery. I watched them walk into the hotel. Probably that third man was in there, and they were going to tell him about what I said and then make their plans. I figured I had me a few hours of peace.

I guessed wrong on that, though.

Shortly after those two left, a couple kids come by and got some candy off me, then a couple ranchers came by and we got to talking cows. Then, big John Mosley came to town. It was curious, him raising so much dust and running his horse like that in the heat.

He pulled his horse to a stop right near me and came up the steps to me without tying the reins. I could see he was real agitated, and I figured he had gotten it into his head somehow that I had bothered Mary. I stood up and moved back a bit.

He looked at me and said, "I told you to ride clear of my girl, told you what I'd do if you didn't. I came to her today and caught her crying. She wouldn't tell me why, only I found out you had been there, and she ain't stopped crying since." Then, without warning he swung the biggest fist I ever saw, except for the one the boss has. It caught me on my cheek and I felt the skin split and my whole face was on fire with pain. I slammed against the wall and the sun got real dim.

I have been in some fights in my time, and I've lost a few of them, won some more. Every fight I lost started just like this one, with me taking a hit that let me be able to stare at the sun and still not see light. I never wanted a single one of them fights I lost, wasn't mad when they started, and by the time my mad got itself ready to fight, I was laying on the ground asleep. I sure didn't want to tangle with Mosley, because I wasn't mad, and I knew he was a mighty powerful man, plus I had nothing against him.

I knew he would hurt me bad unless I got my mad up. Not only that, I understood how he felt, loving a gal like Mary and not wanting some outlaw around her. Reckon I'd feel the same as he did. But, I was in it, like it or not. Trouble just seemed to come to me natural.

I ducked under his second punch and slammed two fast ones right into his belly. It was like punching the sides of a horse. There wasn't a lot of give, but there was a lot of bounce. I've whomped a horse in the belly most every day of my life and never did find one with a soft belly. That Mosley didn't even take a breath, but just stepped in and let me have one right alongside the head. It knocked me flat on my face in the street and liked to have been the end of the fight.

Then he did something he oughtn't have done, because I had already made up my mind to take a licking. If he'd just been content to bat me around some, I'd have never fought him hard enough to hurt him bad, and would have taken the punishment he handed out, plus I'd have let it go at that. I ain't one of those fellers who has to win every fight and nurses a grudge against them that whip me fair.

I hit the dirt hard and he gave me a kick to the head that like to have clean tore it off. Only thing that saved me was that his heel snagged my coat as it whistled by and took a lot of the power from the kick. I rolled a few feet, took another kick to the side, but I wasn't feeling no pain then. I had got that old red look in front of my eyes, and suddenly, I was plumb outside of myself. It was like I wasn't me. I've been that way before, and it scares me because I'm not in control.

I reckon it's kind of like them folks my Uncle Joe, who was a book reading man, used to tell me about called Vikings. He said they used to go crazy like a frothy dog in battle. I had always figured it was something they drunk, but I knew it wasn't. I knew how they felt. It was just something a body can't explain, but suddenly, blows don't hurt like they did, and you have strength in you that you didn't have before. And too, the only thing on your mind is killing someone.

He must have seen the change because I saw his jaw go slack a second, and then I was all over him. I know he hit me some good ones, but I never felt any of those blows until after the fight, and then I felt them for weeks. I think he could have hit me with a tree and I wouldn't have felt it. I was plumb taken up with the need to tear that man up, to destroy him.

I hit him on the run for the second time, and I got to hand it to him, he was fast and strong, but he just wasn't up to handling what I was giving to him. As he came off the ground I made my hands into a giant fist and crashed them right into the side of his head. Most any man I know, except maybe the boss, would have went down for keeps, but he just fell over, then came up at me, blood streaming out of his ear and snarling like a dog. I ran to him and we met toe to toe, there in the middle of the street, fists hammering, knees driving, grunting, and snarling.

Then, I dropped down, and when he leaned to get me I fell on my back and drove my boots smack into his face. That jacked him up straight as a board and he let out a scream that was mostly pain, but part rage. As for me, I was still seeing red across my eyes and I picked that big man up right off the street, big as he was, and threw him against the hitching rail. It cracked into pieces, and Mosely staggered to his feet and came at me with a piece of that rail. But, I was already running at him and I jumped at him like a kid would jump off a river bank into a river, feet first. I hit him square in his chest and we both went down. I got up first and slammed him twice on the jaw as he was trying to get up. Then, before he could move, I picked up that piece of hitching rail he dropped and clobbered him with it. He slumped over with a little moan and fell into the dirt.

I staggered over to a horse trough and stuck my head all the way in. Blood was streaming down my face, and when I came up, I didn't know if it was blood or water on my face. My clothes were in tatters and I ripped the rest of my coat off and used it to wipe my face. Most of what I was wiping looked to be blood. One eye couldn't open, and my whole face was numb and throbbing. My nose felt like Mash had stepped on it. One thing I knew for certain was that I'd be eating soft foods for a few weeks. My tongue was sore and bloody, and my teeth hurt. One whole side of my face was raw meat, and the jaw bone was tender to the touch. My knuckles were bloody and my whole left hand was swollen. I prayed to God that John Mosley would never come around wanting another tussle.

CHAPTER 14

I was laid up in bed for three whole days from that fight. It really took something out of me. I had both my hands swollen so bad that I couldn't have pulled a gun if I had wanted to, not even to hand it over to someone else. I soaked them in hot water for two days, and I was afraid after the first day that I had done something permanent to my hands. They were swollen and purple in some places, but after the first day I was eased somewhat in my worry for I couldn't feel any kind of sharp pain like a broken bone might make.

My back was bruised real bad, too, where I'd fallen on the gun I'd stuck back there. Some kid had picked it up from the street and handed it to me when I staggered back inside the hotel. I know the soreness in my back was almost as bad as the side of my head where Mosley had whacked me.

The third day I came out of my hotel room. I had some food that was good and hot, and that made me feel new again, for all I had taken them first two days was some broth on the first day that I had sent up, then some cold beans left over from the restaurant on the next day. I had a steak and felt real good the third day. My hands had stopped throbbing, and I could move them real good without real pain. The swelling was going down, even though they were still sore, kind of like a hand will feel after a solid day of roping, after you been off the rope a spell.

The fourth day, while I was eating, I had a visitor. He was sitting over against the wall, and I noticed him staring my way. I could see he was a man of some importance for he was dressed real fine, and his boots must have been worth a half a year of cowboy wages. Finally, he got up from his table and walked over to me. He had a big cigar in his mouth and a soft, grey Stetson on his head. He was a fine picture of a man, and he had steel in his eyes for me.

"You Adams?" That voice was low and mellow, not at all the hard in his eyes. Inside, I knew who it was.

I nodded, and he said, "I'm Briner." He twirled his cigar in his mouth with his fingers some, then added, "I'm going to kill you."

There are some men who will make a threat, and you know they are just being windy. Others, they can make a threat and you know they'll try, but they don't have what it takes to carry through with it. Then a man like Briner comes along who looked to me like he'd sell his soul if it meant he could keep that promise he made to me.

His eyes were grey, and there was a hard, bitter cast to his face. It was a face used to looking at scorched ground, and it was a face that had been used up on the hot, dry Texas plains, for it was wiped clean of any expression except one of always looking, always squinting at the horizon, and it was a face burnt brown like a piece of paper that's been scorched. Up close, his look was one that made it look like he was seeing right though you. He was the most unsettling man I ever met.

"Your boy tried to gun me without warnin' or cause, sir." I knew it wasn't going to do any good, but I had to say it.

He took that cigar out of his mouth, examined the end of it and said, "No matter. It's done and when you shot him, you signed your own death warrant. I've had to spend a pile of money on you, Adams, and I finally had to take off from the ranch and see to the job myself. I will see you dead when I ride out of this town."

I didn't say a word and I made no moves. I had the feeling that if I pressed things with him, that he would just pull out his gun and do the job himself. I just folded my hands on top of the table and waited.

"Adams, if you won't fight, as my men have told me, then we will just shoot you down. Be better if you made a show of it."

I smiled at that. "Better for you, Briner? Better so you wouldn't be hunted as a murderer?" I laughed out load. "No, I won't fight any of you, sir. Especially you. I reackon that if I got it in my head, I could kill you, sir, but I have no desire to do that. I'm askin' you to go on home and forget it all. I lost me a good friend in that fracus, and you lost a son. I am willin' to forget that it was your son who started the whole thing."

"Aren't you forgetting something, Adams?"

"What's that," I asked.

"Aren't you forgetting that if you hadn't been rusting my cattle none of this would have started?" He took a long pull on his cigar and blew the smoke at me.

I said, "That was a story your son made up, sir, in order to hang two rag-tag cowboys . One of your own riders admitted that."

I saw the blood rise up in his face and for a second I got ready to dive under the table for he looked like I had touched on a raw spot.

He said, "I'll settle that one day with Mahew."

Then, he turned and left. I stayed and finished eating, and I thought carefully about what had just happened. He was bound and determined to have my scalp, no matter what. I think that if his son had come out of the grave to him and admitted he had started the fight and that it was his fault, that man Briner would still want my hide.

I didn't see the man for a couple of days. Then, I was sitting on a rail at the corral near the livery one day and I heard some horses pull up behind me. I turned, and there they were, three of them. One had a rope and he dropped a loop around me quick as a snake striking. No way I could have dodged it.

That rider's horse was raised right, because it started backing off real quick, just like if it had a calf on the end of that rope, and I fell right on my back. In a second, that man had turned his horse and was riding at top speed right straight through the middle of town. I rolled and tried to get free, but there wasn't any use trying. I could smell my skin burning, and it was like being drug through fire. He kept going outside of town and headed through some rough, hard ground that had more than a few shrubs. He didn't dodge a thing, then when he'd dragged me through what seemed to be half of the Territory, he stopped near the edge of town and shook loose his rope.

I wasn't hurt too bad, except a lot of skin was missing, and a lot of me was bruised, and some of the hurt I was getting over from the fight with Mosley started hurting again. I'd knew I'd hurt for another month now, but I was alive and not damaged permanent. If they were willing to leave it at that, then I was too. I knew they were hoping I'd get mad enough to fight. I walked back to the hotel, went in my room, stripped down to see what I could, then began wiping blood off, tearing a few pieces of hanging skin off and trying to make do as I could.

Mary had heard about my fight with Mosley and sent word by Lonnie that she wanted to see me, but I told him I was laid up awhile. Then, Lonnie told her what the riders had done, and she was in town the next day. She brought some kind of grease her ma made up and rubbed it all over my back, my right leg, and both my arms. It was cool at first, then it got awful hot, but it did something because I felt better.

I had a bad fever the first couple days, and was out of my head a time or two, so I was told. Mary said I called out for Ma a few times, but mostly I kept saying, "Where are you, Pa?" over and over. It was a bother to me that I seemed to be spending a whole lot of my life getting well from trouble other folks had brought me. But, at least my trouble seemed to come in spurts. I would have troubles, and then a dry spell. I felt my dry spell was just about due.

Turned out my dry spell would be a long time coming.

Two weeks went by, and I was as fit as ever. I stayed careful so that those men didn't catch me like that again. I only ate when they were sleeping, and I stayed off the streets. Once, late at night I took a chance and rode out of town and went up to our mine. They were all glad to see me and Bule decided to come back with me. They hadn't heard about the riders roping me, and I didn't tell them.

I stopped on the way back to see Mary because we were getting friendly again. After the fight, her and Mosley had a big fuss over me, and he left saying he was through with her and all women. I think I know how he felt. Bule and me pulled in at the crack of dawn, just in time for breakfast. We had big slabs of ham, with four eggs all golden in the middle, laid on top of some yellow biscuits dripping with sweet butter, and about a gallon of coffee sweetened with honey and mixed with some cream. I forgot all my troubles for awhile. Mary sure could cook.

We talked some, and I chatted with her pa, too. The boys left for chores, and then Josiah had to leave for the field. Me and Mary talked, and Bule spent his time talking with Mary's mother, and then she went to her chores and Bule began teaching Lonnie how to throw a knife. Mary didn't have too much to say, but she did say something that sure made me feel powerful good.

She said, "Luke, I have been wrong, and my pa said if I didn't tell you about it I deserved a good whippin'."

"What on earth have you done that your pa would want to whip you over, Mary?"

She looked over at Bule and Lonnie and said, "I was wrong about you running from those men. Pa said that if you did what I wanted, that you'd never be worth a corn of husk after, and that men like you was what this kind of land needs. He said that I could...could, uh..."

"Could what, Mary?"

"That I could get you killed!" The words were practically whispered, and now she was crying and I just didn't know what to say.

I said, "Mary, your pa has a pretty good idea of the man I am and I reckon he is right, for I've been dodging a fight, and it almost got me hurt real bad. It sure would have been a whole lot safer and easier on me if I had just gone ahead and fought those men"

I stood up and stretched, then continued, "Only thing, Mary, I ain't dodgin' this fight just on your account. I reckon when you told me it was all over for us, I had some idea that maybe if you heard I was trying to stay out of trouble, that you'd come around, but actually, I want to dodge that fight too, Mary. See, this kind of fight is goin' to end with some dead men, and I am tired of havin' to kill my troubles. I don't want to have to kill Briner. I killed his son, even if it was a fair fight and one he started, but I don't want to be the cause of a whole family dyin' off. That ain't right, Mary."

Well, she took to crying in earnest, got up suddenly and ran into the house. I got up and started after her, but stopped. I never would understand a woman. I looked at Bule, but he was looking out at the trees and pretending he didn't hear anything. We left.

In town, things were awake, and I knew trouble was coming soon as we rode in because those men were on the porch of the hotel and they saw me coming. I had taken my gun with me, just in case, and had forgotten to hide it back of me. I knew they saw it, and I knew I was going to have to fight. There would be no way around it.

I told Bule, "There's going to be a little war startin' in a minute, Bule. Stay away from me and don't interfere." He didn't answer and I didn't look at him. My whole attention was on those men.

We put away the horses and walked over past the hotel. The one with the crooked nose called out, "Hey, Adams! You got a gun. Use it or die."

Crooked Nose stood there primed and ready. I just looked past him and kept on walking. Bule looked at me strange, then stopped. I told him to keep walking, but trying to stop Bule from doing something once he's got his mind set is like trying to stop a runaway herd of cows.

Bule stopped dead in the street and said, "My friend don't have time to waste on you, drifter. Besides, he lets me handle all the tramps and such."

Well, there it was, and there wasn't anything I could do but step aside and make sure it came out in Bule's favor, and to keep anyone who didn't belong from mixing in. That man might take Bule down, but he'd be falling right along with him, and he wouldn't have a chance for I didn't plan on giving a warning.

There wasn't time for any more talking because that Texan just went for his gun. You could tell he spent a lot of time with his gun by the way he pulled it smooth and fast, and it was like he was doing something he was supposed to do. Everything was perfect. Only thing, Bule had grown up like me, throwing a gun since he was out of diapers.

Not only that, Bule was a bundle of springs in skin. He had stepped aside and drawn his gun as quick as a man could, and it looked more like the way a big mountain cat would move, for it was graceful and light, and full of quickness. He laid two shots into that man and the gunman from Texas pulled off one shot into the dust, sank down on his knees and fell right smack on his face right there in the street.

The other gunman didn't move a muscle, for I had a gun out and lined his way. Briner, he just leaned there on the post, cigar twirling in his mouth, nothing showing in his face. Bule gave them both a hard look, dropped his gun in the holster and turned away. We walked, me mostly backwards, to the hotel, and he checked in right next to my room.

Later, the old man that served part time as a sheriff came in and talked to us. It wasn't anything special and he knew both of us well, so we knew it was just something he had to do. I did tell him that those other two were spoiling for a fight and I had tried to avoid it. He knew all about it, even though he had been away at his ranch when I got dragged through the street. He heard about that later and told me that if I had shot that man down later in cold blood from cover, that he'd have done nothing about it. It was good to know where the sheriff stood in this matter, but I told him that I didn't fight that way, and if I could, I was going to try to get out of this without a fight.

Things were quiet for awhile after that. I saw Briner now and then, and I could see that his patience was wearing thin. He quit dressing so well, and went now and then without shaving for a few days. Then one day I saw him in his range-riding clothes. Somehow, he looked completely different. If I didn't know him close up I would have swore they were two different people. He wore chaps and pants that was shiny on the bottom and sun faded all over, except on the insides and the front.

He come up to me and said, "I'm leavin' you for awhile, Adams. I got some troubles on my range, and I'm needin' every man I got. You can't stay in town forever, and when I come back I'll get you to fight, one way or another, and if I fail to do that, I'll just shoot you down and take my chances on a hanging."

He tugged on his hat, then added, "When I come back, it won't be with a few like this time. I'll be riding back here strong, boy." I thought over what he said and the more I thought about it, the way he talked to me and all, the more I felt like he was hoping I wouldn't be here when he came back. I kind of got the feeling that old Briner had talked himself into killing me, but that time had wore out his madness, and now he just wanted to be shut of the whole thing. For the first time, I felt like maybe this thing was going to end.

It was a relief to me, for it meant I could get on with living a normal life again. I wanted to see about getting on with one of the ranches in the valley, maybe even with that Johnson. One thing I knew was that me and that gold mine was done. I sat there soaking up the sun for the rest of the day and long about sunset I got a notion that took me plumb out of my chair. I ran to the saloon where Bule was at to give him my idea.

He was near the back, and was sitting with his back to the wall, chair propped up, and his boots on the top of the table. I ran past one table and nearly upset it, getting a cussing for being clumsy. I was too full of my idea to care, though.

"Bule! Bule! Partner, I got it!"

He was napping and glared at me some, then said, "What, the plague?"

I jabbed him in the chest and blurted out my idea to him. "Bule, you and me, the boss and Charlie are goin' to buy us a ranch!"

Bule was bright and quick to take up something. He saw it right off, same as I did when it hit me. He jerked his feet off the table and sat up straight. "Luke, that shines! How come none of us thought of that before?"

We were both grinning, and when we went for the door we was in such a hurry that we tried to go through at the same time. I finally shoved him on through and we ran for our horses. We left town on a dead run, both wanting to be the first to the mine with the news.

By the time we got there, we had cooled on the idea some, but not enough to keep from grinning. We talked it out, and I mentioned that rustlers were bad in these parts. Bule laughed and said me and him was bad in these parts, too. We both figured that any rustling that came up could be cared for by the two of us. We had enough mean in us to make rustling plumb unhealthy for those who tried it.

None of us had the money by himself, but between us all, we could maybe buy a small spread. We were all known in town, and I figured the boss could get a deal worked out if anyone could. We'd eat beans and hardtack, but I'd been eating so good lately that I could eat bad for a year. Besides, I could always go to Mary for a feed now and then when I got some time off.

We gave the idea to the boss and he wiped off his surprise, then slapped his knee hard and told us it was the grandest idea he ever heard of. Charlie was excited about the idea too, and we got our stake and started to count it out. But the boss reached over and grabbed my leather bag out of my hand then took Bule's and asked Charlie to get his.

I couldn't figure what was up. He got all the bags together, and I could see that the boss had a whole lot more gold than we did. Bule had two bags and Charlie and I had one. The boss had at least four, but he dropped them all into one sack and clapped his hands together.

"There! Now we are all equal in this here land investment program!"

I said, "Boss, I kind of figured we'd all get whatever shares we could afford. You put up most, so you ought to get the biggest share." He made a fist and glared at me.

The boss was one man I never argued with, so I just nodded. He was the most generous man I ever met and there wasn't a small thing about that man. We talked late that night about the ranch, divided up the chores, figured out how many cows we should have right off, figured how long it would take us to get rich, how we would deal with rustlers, and how we would expand. We talked that dream right on into the early morning.

The boss said he'd do some dealing at the bank, and since he had more experience and knew numbers and reading and such, we were more than glad to let him. Besides, he was still the boss to us, and we all knew he'd be the real boss on the ranch. We'd all be sort of foremen in our specialty, and boss each other. If it came to fencing or clearing land, why Charlie would boss it, because the kid grew up doing nothing else; but, when it came to chasing cows, why I took over. Bule would be boss on any drives we made and he'd care for the horses, but the 'boss' of us all would be John Smith.

It took us about a month to find a place. When we heard about it, I was ready to buy it without even looking at it, but the boss wouldn't have none of that. He wanted to see it first. This little spread turned out to be better than any of us hoped for. A family owned it who'd worked it for four years, fighting *injuns*, rustlers, and doing all the hard things you got to do on a ranch. But, the man of the house was stove up, and the rustlers had pretty much cleaned them out. He didn't have any sons, but a daughter, and she was doing a lot of things a man ought to do. They were flat busted, and when they heard about us, the daughter came to talk with us.

She told us that Johnson had been after them to sell out to him, but the price had been so miserly that her pa had held on. They were just about to give up and take his offer when they heard we were looking for a place. We discussed the price, and Bule thought it was too high because it was without cows, but I voted to pay what they asked, and Charlie sided me. We left it up to the boss, and he said it was a good deal for us because it had some of the best water around. She told us one of our borders was a small river and there were a couple of creeks besides.

We drove the family into town in the Wilson buggy, because their wagon was busted, and they were down to one horse. The girl rode the horse, and I noticed she stayed right alongside Bule most of the way. The man and his wife rode in the buggy with the boss, while Charlie and me trailed along. The man talked pretty free and easy with us on the ride.

He told us we were buying some awful sweet land, but that we were buying a peck of trouble as well. I told him, "If you mean them rustlers, me and Bule can handle them, I reckon."

He said, "Boys, I can't hide it from you, and I got to tell you that Johnson will try to drive you out of here, same as he did me. Only reason we lasted as long as we did was on account of Nellie here." He nodded towards his daughter.

The boss asked, "What's she got to do with it?"

He snorted and said, "That man has tried everything to get Nellie's hand in marriage. Nellie ain't wanting no part of that man. Said he was too old, and everyone knows he makes regular visits to the whore house in town."

His wife jabbed him in the ribs at that and said, "Josh, don't be talking so bad. Ladies are present, you know!"

He grimaced, then went on: "I wouldn't let her marry him even if she wanted to. He's a crook, and I know he's the one behind the rustling in these parts. Couple fellers got caught rustling over at Chosen Butte a year ago and one of them told a tale on Johnson before he swung. Nobody believed him, but when I heard it, I believed. He said that Johnson was the one who bought all the herds they stole. I brung the tale to Johnson and asked him personal about it. He just laughed at me and denied it."

Well, it didn't surprise me none, and I reckon I felt like between the boss, myself and Bule, we could handle those rustlers, no matter who was behind them. We didn't talk much more after that. The family was likely thinking of having to give up their place, and we were thinking of what we were going to do with it.

We got to town and finished making the sale. I signed a couple of papers that I didn't know much about, except it had some numbers on it with some writing, and all of us had to sign it. The boss took to explaining it to me, but I just waved him off and told him if it was alright with him, then it was alright with me. We were all as quiet and mannerly as if we was all standing in front of a judge.

We came out of the bank the owners of a ranch, and the boss told us he had some more good news. We had got it without having to give up hardly any of our gold. The banker said we could deposit that and draw on it for improvements, and to stock the ranch. He figured we'd make good on the ranch, and make it a valuable piece of property some day. We figured same as he did.

We bought a wagon and loaded supplies to take back. It was liable to be a long time before we got back into town. It had taken most of a day to get from the ranch to town, and it took us a day and a half to get back with the wagon. It was slow going because that wagon was loaded down, and sometimes we had to rope the wagon and help pull it up some of the steep parts of the trail.

When we finally got to the ranch and settled in, the boss sprung another surprise on us. He told us he was going back, and he was taking Charlie with him to buy some cattle. Charlie and him would drive them back to the ranch. He figured on going to a couple of ranches and trying to buy some. It was a good time for buying, because winter was coming on, and if a rancher was overstocked, he would not be wanting them cows to winter with him. So, they took off, Charlie grinning all over himself because the boss was taking him instead of me or Bule.

That kid just wasn't smart at all. He'd soon get tired of chasing those critters through rocks and brush that cut a man like a razor. We'd be laying in the shade and enjoying life for a change.

CHAPTER 15

We worked that little ranch hard all summer and late into the fall. The boss got nearly two hundred head of cattle, and we also picked up a good deal on a string of horses. A trader, coming back from near Sante Fe where he had sold a bunch of horses to the Army, had about seventeen horses the Army didn't take, and we got them pretty cheap. They had flaws, but they'd do us real fine, so we took them and was grateful.

I took off one day to get the lay of the land and told the rest I'd be back in a day or two and not to worry none. I climbed my horse into the hills nearby and was out of sight in no time at all. I skirted a string of boulders, leaned over in my saddle when I came to a stand of trees so the branches wouldn't rake me, and headed for some of the loneliest parts of the western part of the ranch.

We had been told that there was a small branch of a river that made our western boundary, and near that was some mighty fine pasture. The old man we'd bought the ranch from had told us he used to have over four hundred head grazing there, but his daughter had told him there wasn't more than twenty head left. They had all been rustled. I figured I'd have a look-see, and if it was as good a spot as he said, we'd build us a cabin near by and just winter up here with them cows to make sure someone was about all the time.

I rode for nearly two hours, picking my way careful around boulders, some scrub pine, big slashes in the earth that looked like God was doing some plowing there, and gullies that seemed to cut me off every time I got to moving pretty good. It was a walk all the way, and a careful walk at that. Not much of what you could call open ground, and for certain not much where you could run a horse.

Once I made it back into the deepest part, the sight nearly took my breath away. It was the prettiest piece of ground I ever laid eyes on. It hit me that what I was looking at belonged to me. That pasture the old man had told us about was more than he let on. It rolled for nearly a mile in one direction, and I could only guess that there was maybe five miles of pasture going the other way. Then, way to the west about a mile, I could see a thin line of dark green. That would be the river his daughter had told us about. It was a perfect boundary.

I booted Mash in the side and headed for the river. I was excited, and was already planning a house. I guess I was planning even more than that, because I got to admit I could see Mary standing there, right smack in the middle of that house. I had the house pictured right close to some trees and at least a mile from the river. I never have liked being too close to a river, except for swimming, because of the *skeeters*. I have been with men who never had a *skeeter* bite in their lives, and I seen them critters practically lift me off the ground while them fellers who never had got a bite sat next to me grinning. I never understood that.

One time I thought I had the answer. I used to ride with a man who was able to sit around and never get bit. One day, I got close to him as I reached across the fire to grab the coffee pot. I caught me a whiff of him, as he was up-wind, and it like to have knocked me over. I figured I had the answer then. If I was a *skeeter* I'd steer clear of that body, for one bite and I'd drop dead for sure.

I told all the other fellers about it, and most of them had been down wind of him a time or two. They agreed with my idea. We all reckoned as how it wasn't fair that we got bit and he never got bit. Besides, we figured there would come other times when he'd get upwind of us, and all in all, it just wasn't fair. So, we threw him in the river, and when he came out, we piled on him with some lye soap that the cook had give us, and we proceeded to give that man a terrible bath. I say terrible, because it was terrible the way he carried on. I got bit, and two others got gouged, and everyone of us got hit or kicked. But, it was mostly terrible for him, because some of us hit back, and we weren't too gentle about the scrubbing we gave him. He was awful red by the time we threw him back in, and some of his skin came off from that brush.

When he came back out, we threw him in again. The cook hid that man's gun, and when he went to find it, he went into a rage and tried to get one of ours, but we told him we would give him another scrubbing if he didn't settle down.

That night we all watched keen when we sat down to eat. I was close to him, and the whole time I swatted and moaned at the way them *skeeters* was attacking me, but that cowboy never even had to brush one away. We all knew then that it didn't have nothing to do with his clothes or his smell, so we never did find out why some men don't get bit. I know I do, and I got the holes in me to prove it.

Suddenly, I snapped out of my daydreaming. A bunch of riders were sitting right in front of me, quiet, and definitely interested in me. They were all *injuns*, but not like any I'd ever seen. They weren't lean and fancy like the Comanche. They were short, most of them, real dark, some almost as dark as as that black cowboy I used to ride with, named Spoon. They looked as tough as "whang" leather.

One had a derby hat perched on his head, and it looked awful uncommon, especially on him. I saw a few with soldier clothes on, and I knew those weren't clothes that was give away, neither. One had him an officer's coat, and there was still a big splotch right over where a man's heart would be in that coat. My belly took a feeling all empty, and I got to thinking about how many I could take with me.

I sat real still, nodded once and smiled. One of them trotted his horse up. He was carrying a U.S. Army rifle and a Colt revolver stuck in a holster, but instead of being belted across his middle, he had it slung across his chest. I had seen some Mexicans carry a gun like that, but mostly they just slung their ammo belts that way.

This *injun* was the ugliest one I ever laid eyes on. He stared a hole right through me with eyes that were as black as the insides of that gold mine of ours. He stopped just in front of me ,and then surprised me by talking right out in American.

"You cow man?"

I smiled at him and said, "No cows yet, but later." I wasn't sure what he was after, maybe a couple free cows, maybe just some talk. Whatever he wanted I was sure going to try and oblige him.

He said, "We take this many. You give." He held up three short, grubby fingers.

I held onto my smile and said, "Partner, I ain't even got one cow right now, but if you will hang in these parts for a few days I reckon I can chase three your way."

He whirled his pony around and ran it back to that group. They jabbered for a few minutes, looking over at me now and then. Finally, I saw him shake his fist at another, shout something, then he rode back to me.

"You bring. We wait." He paused then looked back to his companions then back to me and said, "You bring soldier we hide. Come back and kill you dead man."

I had to admit there wasn't any mistaking what he meant. He was a plain talking man, that was for sure. I nodded, and they all moved away at once, riding slow, not looking back. I decided that I would have my look at the river some other time.

I went back to the ranch house instead of staying out like I had planned, for I wanted to get this chore done with. I hoped that it didn't encourage more requests, but my experience has been that if a body was fair with the *injun*, he left you in peace, at least until some fool stirred him up. When they got stirred, it was like being around hornets, because there wasn't no such thing as friends and everyone was liable to get stung. I figured this bunch was on the run and needed food. They'd hang around and rest up on the beef I gave them. Then, they'd leave, and maybe if I was lucky, I wouldn't see them again, or at least not for a good long while.

Time I got back it was dark, and a light showed me someone was still up, probably the boss reading. He could read more than any man I knew. It was amazing how he could take a big old book that was thicker than two steer steaks laid together and have that writing put into his head in just a night or two.

I gave out a hello and as I came up the boss stuck his head out the door. He saw it was me and give me a howdy. I put away Mash and went in. Charlie was laying over on the floor snoring, and I guess he had a hard day because he never twitched when I came in. Bule was sitting on the edge of his bunk whittling as he was prone to do at night, and the boss had a big book dangling from his hand with a finger stuck in it to mark his place. He sat down and stared at me, waiting for my report.

I sat down at the table and gave them a quick story on what happened, and I told them what a grand place that pasture was. The boss said he'd help me drive three steers or maybe even more, up there. I told him it might be best if he waited until we had us a cabin up there, or we'd lose all our cattle like that family before us did. He agreed with me and we decided to leave first thing in the morning.

Neither of those two said a word against me for agreeing to send up those cows. Bule had driven cows to market before, and he knew what I was up against, and that it was best not to make a fight unless they got greedy, or unless the whole tribe moved in on us. The boss knew that too, but I think it struck him more like they was kin or something, on account of him living with the *injuns* for those years when he was a kid. Probably, if I'd suggested ten steers, he'd have agreed.

Next morning, we set out with three steers. Bule and Charlie wanted to go, but we figured if there was trouble, two more wouldn't make no difference, and besides we needed someone to stay with the ranch who was handy with a gun. If all of us went, we might come back to find every cow missing. Things were mighty uncertain those days. Man could be rich with cows one day and wake up the next day and be poor as a *Mex'* sheep herder.

It took us most of the day, because the steers kept finding their own trails instead of the ones we wanted them to follow. It was hard to stay alongside on account of the rocks and such. Finally, I got one by the horns with my rope, and after I drug him some, it got the idea and moved along behind me. The other two followed right along, and we moved faster after that.

That band of *injuns* watched us from way off. I could see them sitting on top of a ridge. When we came out into the open, they moved off the ridge and towards us. We met in the pasture, and I shook my loop off that one steer and it ambled off kind of tired, looking for some place I wasn't, and for grass to munch. The others followed right along.

The same *injun* with the derby hat look at my companion and said, "Boss cow man?"

I laughed at that, but I reckon John Smith just looked like a boss to anyone. He was a leader, and anyone could tell it. I said, "Yeah, he is that. He's big boss and got many little fellers like me ridin' for him."

The boss raised his hand and said, "He's boss, like me. We stand together."

The *injun* grunted at that and said, "Mebbe so, but you big boss."

Smith surprised me then, and surprised that *injun* more, because he started talking the same lingo as the *injuns* talked. I'd never heard him do it before, and that's why it surprised me. It wasn't fast, and it didn't sound like it was coming from his nose like it did when they talked, but they knew what he was jabbering, because they were grinning and talking back. He was treated real special after that.

They talked for most of an hour. Then, without goodby or nothing, they got the cows and left. I had a feeling it wasn't the last we would see of them.

I asked the boss, "What did you jabber so long with them about?"

He laughed and said, "Mostly about his family. He offered me a place in his camp as a chief, and even offered me a wife."

"What did you tell him?"

"Told him to bring her by some day and we'd see about it."

I nearly fell off my horse. Here was the boss, educated, and a white man, talking serious of marrying an *injun*. It beat all I ever did see. Now, I've heard of some men marrying *injuns*, but never heard of one like the boss doing it. They was all a cut under the boss, if you know what I mean. It isn't that I am against it, but that it was just so strange thinking of a man like him marrying an *injun*. I might do such a thing and it'd be all right, but not the boss.

I could imagine him saying some dark night to his squaw, "Bring me that book about them Round Table riders," and she'd come back and spit out some *injun* at him, and finally he'd have to get up and show her the book he wanted. It just struck me awful strange. I took to grinning as I thought about it.

We headed over to the river because I hadn't got to see it before and we were both interested in it. It was a fast moving stream and there was a pile of boulders all down the middle of that stream. We followed it for a few miles until the banks got steep, and we moved off a little ways. I saw a lot of places where a body could build himself a fine house, but like I said, pretty as it was, I didn't want to live near water like that. The boss got to talking of moving the whole operation up here and leaving the ranch house we had as a lower pasture. I felt like that was a fine idea, and we scouted for a good place to locate.

He settled on a spot that was far enough from the river to not have a skeeter war, yet near enough so water would be easy to fetch until we got us a well sunk. I liked it, for it was sort of snuggled by a cluster of huge boulders and some sweet pine. The winds wouldn't blow us away in the winter, and we'd have shade in the summer. Also, there was lots of room for a bunk house, and not too far off there was a spot that I wanted to look over closer whenever I decided to build a house for myself.

We left that spot and looked around some more. When the sun was setting, we pulled up in the hills and made a short camp, eating some hard biscuits I had brought, with a couple of pieces of beef. I wished I had brought a coffee pot and some grounds along, but I settled for some of the river water we had filled our jugs with and drank deep.

As we were sitting there, me leaning on a rock, the boss sitting on top of a big rock, I said, "How come you to want an *injun* for a wife, Boss?"

He gave me a curious glance, but saw I was really interested and said, "Luke, I was married once, nearly twenty years back. She died on me, but before she died I reckon she made me one of the most miserable men on the face of this earth. I can't say I was sorry when she passed on, for she had to be the sharpest tongued woman I ever run into."

He took out his pipe, stuffed it with tobacco, then went on: "I swore then that I'd never marry a civilized woman again as long as I lived. I was some years as a kid with the Indians, and I never once saw a wife treat her man like that woman treated me."

I said, "You reckon all civilized women are like that, Boss?"

He sucked on his pipe and gave a real thoughtful look at the sky, then said, "Well, I suppose not, but I never could get up the nerve to find out. I know an Indian woman ain't like that, and so I figure it's best to stick with what you know than to grab onto what you don't know about."

I said, "Well...what about a man who, uh, well, a woman who is, you know ..."

"Who is what, Luke? What are you trying to say, boy. Spit it out."

I dug my toe in the ground, then my heel, and was real uncomfortable, for I am not able to express myself clear in some matters, and this was one where I was shy like a horse is to a bridle in the morning. Finally, I managed, "Well, Boss, suppose that woman was really in love with a man. Don't you think she'd pull her load without trying to run away with the pack? I mean, if she really liked him, she'd try and do for him, wouldn't she?"

The boss chuckled and said, "Well, this love is a funny thing. I thought I had me a true love, but when I opened the package, I found out I had a pile of grief. The wrapping was fine, but the inside was a mess. I don't know that I'm the one to talk to about love, boy. I never seen it, never heard it, never tasted it, never drank it, never touched it, and never felt it, least ways not with a woman. If I was ever in love, I didn't know it."

That got me real upset, for a man like the boss ought to know such things. If he could read and write, had been married, had been on this world almost twice as long as I had, and if he didn't know about love, then who did? I just shook my head and figured that maybe I could find out about it some day.

I thought of Bule and how we had gotten close. We were like brothers, and it was plain that he and I were close. We wrestled, talked, played jokes on each other, and gave each other a hard time as much as we could, but it was all just our way of saying we cared. I reckon if I had gotten a brother, I would have wanted him to be like Bule in most ways, except for his love for the jug. Not that he tipped it more than anyone else, or was even bad off about it, but I have seen too much of what the jug has done to a lot of men in this land, and I just think a body is better off without it, especially a man that's good inside, like Bule.

Charlie and me would never be close, I knew. Something would always keep us from being close. I didn't really know what it was, for the kid was always friendly with me, and I with him, but we never did strike a spark. I think maybe it had to do with the time he saw me shoot that man up at the mine. I had noticed then how he looked at me different after that and acted different with me. I guess maybe he might have gotten scared of me, but I don't know.

The boss and I were close, but not like Bule and me. I guess I felt more like the boss was a father to me and a friend, but not the kind of friend you fool around with and play jokes on all the time, although I did play jokes on the boss now and then. It was just different with the boss. I respected him like no other man I know, except my pa, and I'd stand up against the wall for him if need be, but he still wasn't close as me and Bule.

With Bule and me, it was like we had the same blood, even though he was light-haired, blue-eyed, and a mite wooly, while I was quiet, mostly, with black hair and dark eyes. I wasn't given to drink, and mostly kept to myself. Bule, he would talk to most anyone. When we were chasing cows, he'd be talking to the cows, to his horse, and to himself. I even heard him give a cussing to a cactus, once.

I gave some thought to my Texas trouble, too. I figured maybe that Texan might just choose to forget it, but I couldn't count on it. I knew that if he came back again, I wouldn't be able to stay in town like I did before. I'd be needed at the ranch, and if they wanted me, they'd come after me out here. Matter of fact, they'd most likely take to that idea. I knew I was going to have to get someone in town to warn me when they showed up because I didn't want to be riding out here not knowing they were about. There just wasn't any way I'd be able to dodge a fight with them this time.

When we got back, there was a strange horse in the barn. We talked about it some while we were putting up our horses, but neither of us had seen it before. There wasn't a brand on it, but there was a fine rig still on, although the rider had loosened the cinch.

We went in, and there at the table was a man I never saw before. He looked kind of hard up, like he hadn't had a bath or a meal in a week. He was finishing up on a plate of beans. Charlie sat at the table watching him eat. Bule was out riding, because his mare was missing.

I said, "Howdy stranger." I sat down at the table across from him, and the boss came in and sat down by the bed near Bule's bunk.

He looked at me and kept on eating, just mumbling a word of greeting. I stayed silent while he finished, looking at Charlie for an answer, but he just shrugged his shoulder and raised his eyebrows. He didn't know anything either.

Finally he finished, wiped his mouth and leaned back in his chair. He looked over to me and said, "Sorry I couldn't talk, but I've been hungry for days, mister."

"Where did you come from?"

He said, "I left Sante Fe nearly two weeks ago. I was spotted by a band of Apache and they chased me into the mountains. We had word Victorio was raiding around, but we didn't believe it. He must be getting hungry raiding in these parts."

The boss asked, "How'd you got away?"

"I think it was because I was taking them too far away from something. They probably could have got me in a day or so, but they turned back when they saw it was going to be a long chase."

I asked, "Did you get a close look at 'em?"

He nodded his head. "I saw them close enough, mister. Close enough to see the number of them was at least thirty or more."

"Did one of 'em have a funny little hat on his head?"

He gave a start and said, "Why yes! Yes indeed! How do you know that? Have you seen them? Are they here?" In another second he'd have been through the door.

I smiled and said, "No, but we saw 'em. They're camped nearly fifteen miles from here."

He sprang up and said, "That close?"

Before I could say more, he was moving to the door. It was plain he wasn't going to be spending the night. We watched him run to the barn and lead out his horse. That horse was in bad need of a rest, but we didn't try to talk to the man, for he's one of them kind that wouldn't listen. He would never believe that by setting and giving his horse a rest he would be safer than if he was to run now. Not that he was in any danger. I didn't think so. I think that band, if it was Vitorio, was just resting up and would be feeding for a couple days.

He took off and I never saw that man again. I used to wonder how far he got before his horse quit on him. If he got to Reata, it was on foot. Now and then, I used to ask about him in town, but nary a soul ever knew a thing about that man. Could have been he just got lost and wandered off somewhere afoot. If he did that out here, he's found a permanent home. This is no land to be walking in, and some places it's no place to be riding in.

Next day, the boss told us that he was going into Reata. I wanted to go with him, but he took Bule instead. They were going to bring back some extra feed for the horses, plus the boss needed to check on some cows a man had told him about. We wanted to bring our herd up to at least four hundred.

Charlie and me stayed behind and did odd jobs around the house. There wasn't too much to do on the range but check on the cows now and then. Our place was good for keeping the cows from roving too much. It had a pasture, then a drop off, and on two sides of that pasture was some wild country. Those cows could only drift back our way. We figured we'd start branding soon as the boss came back. Another advantage that pasture had was that it was tough for rustlers. They had to drive cows almost within sight of the ranch house.

I decided that it was time for me and the gun I took from that gunman up at the mine to get acquainted. I had cleaned it and played around with it some, but hadn't really put any shooting time in with it. I got it and went off from the house a little distance.

I loaded the gun, eased it into my holster, then drew it out quick as I could. It didn't have the balance my own gun had, and it felt a shade lighter. I worked with drawing that gun for nearly an hour. I got to where I could pull it as fast as I could my own, maybe even a shade faster on account of his gun being lighter, plus it had a shorter barrel. The shorter barrel must have been the weight difference.

I put some empty cans on the rocks about fifty feet away. I relaxed, then jerked the gun out and slapped my palm against it. It got no idea where the first bullet went, but I know it was no where near those cans. I tried again, missed, and then decided that I better just work on moving my hand and palm across the hammer and keeping my aim while I did. I had been throwing my shots to the sky every time I came across the hammer.

In another hour I had it worked out so that I was slapping the hammer and not drawing the gun up, but I still knocked my aim off most of the time. I loaded up to give it one more try. I made a good draw, fast as I ever made, slapped the hammer, and saw rock chips fly. The can fell, but it was from chips, because the shot hit about an inch under the can. It did give me that satisfaction that if it had been a man I'd have dropped him. I tried again and the can went flying. The next shot hit the rocks again, the fourth shot went high, but the last two were good hits.

I gave it up after that, and turned to go back to the house. I stopped quick when something moving caught my eye. I was about to go after it when I saw it was Charlie. He had been spying on me. I don't know why he didn't just come over and watch. I wouldn't have minded, and would have enjoyed the company.

Next day, I rode out to have a look at our cows. They were just grazing peaceful, and I stayed out there a long time, grinning at them and feeling good. I was looking at beef that was mine, that was going to be wearing a "Circle 4" brand before long. That was what we decided to call it. The boss was having irons made up special at the blacksmith's in Reata.

The third day I got worried, because the boss only had to ride a few miles to the other side of Reata to see about those cows. I figured that if he wasn't back the next morning early, that I'd go see about them. I practiced some more with that gun while I was out looking at the cows, and it got to where I felt pretty handy with it, but I still wasn't ready to give up my own gun yet.

It's kind of hard to let go of an old friend that has served you well. I figured maybe in a few more months of practicing I'd maybe take to carrying the other gun, or even both of them. I was hitting everything I shot at by now, but it wasn't any faster than my old way because to get the speed that gunman had, I'd need to have a holster at my side like he did, and with the front cut out. I would maybe try that one day, and suddenly wished I'd kept his holster. For now, though, I'd just do my shooting the way I always did.

Next morning, they still weren't in, so I saddled Mash and headed out. I told Charlie to stay there until someone came back. I got a mile down the trail when I spotted the wagon coming. Only thing, there wasn't two of them, but only the boss. I put Mash into a gallop.

"Where's Bule?" The boss was setting there after stopping the team, and he had a long face. He had also been hurt because his left arm was wrapped in a bandage from the elbow down, plus there was a streak of blood on his left cheek.

He said, "It's bad, Luke. Bule ain't likely to pull through."

I got real hollow inside, like I did when those *injuns* came up on me. I asked, "Who got him? How did it happen?"

The boss shifted his seat some, then said, "Six Texas riders stopped us just outside of town. They was lookin' for you, Luke."

I groaned, because it hurt me that my friend was dying on my account. The boss saw how I felt and said, "Don't go blaming yourself, son. You know how Bule is. He got tough with those riders, and they were *hardcases*, all of them. Bule never had a chance. They got three bullets in him before I hauled us out of there. He did drop one of them, but the funny thing is they never came after us, Luke. They had us, but didn't give chase."

They wanted you to get back and tell me so I'd show myself. They knew I'd come looking for 'em."

The boss looked at me and I saw he had something else on his mind, because when he frowned it always meant he was plumb serious, and he always had trouble talking right out. It was that way now.

His voice got down low, almost a whisper and he said, "Luke...Luke, there's something else, son." He got to looking at me real funny and I got that old empty feeling again because I knew it had to be bad for him to have trouble talking right out at me.

"Boss, get it out. I got things to do."

"Luke, they nearly killed Mary. It was sort of accidental, son. She's hurt bad, too."

I was still for a whole minute, then I tugged my hat down because I was afraid, and I knew it showed. I blinked a few times and took a deep breath and said, "Boss, that ain't...that can't be! Tell me you are joking with me." I was begging for it not to be true, but I knew it was true on account of the way he told me. Besides, the boss don't play jokes like that.

"Luke, it happened a week ago. No one would tell those men where you were, but apparently, they knew about you and Mary. They rode to the Wilson place to rough up Josiah, figuring on you getting word and riding in. One man roped one of the posts holding up the porch. He was just planning on pulling off the porch, but he hadn't reckoned on the whole house being part of the porch. The house fell in while Mary and her mother were inside. They got them out, and her mother was alright, but Mary got a bad knock on the head. She's still unconscious."

I just stared at him. I wanted to cry. It bubbled up in me, but something wouldn't let me. I cried inside, but nothing showed on my outside. I don't know how long I sat there before I asked, "Boss, how come I wasn't told before now?"

He looked at me a long while before answering, then said, "Josiah felt like there was nothing you could do for Mary, and they knew if you came in, it would mean your death, too." He paused to let it soak in, then said, "Josiah said to tell you they'd take it kindly if you'd drop in now and then, same as always."

I got mad and yelled, "Don't that old fool know I loved his daughter! Don't he know I'll follow those men clean back to Texas and across the whole map of the world?" I was standing in my stirrups and tears were in my eyes. The boss sat still and didn't say a word.

I turned my head and moved Mash ahead because I didn't want my tears to show. I stopped and called back, "If I don't come back, give my share of the ranch to the Wilsons."

"Luke, I'm crippled in one hand, but if you'll wait up I'll be back and ride with you. Let me get my shotgun."

I held up my hand, and with my back still to him, I said, "You don't understand. Ain't nobody going to die or get no more hurt on my account. Not you. Not anyone else. I should have taken care of it in the first place. I should have killed Briner when he first come for me."

He did respond, and I pulled away, then reined up and hollered back, "Where's Bule?"

"He's laid up in the hotel, Luke. Doc is caring for him, but I don't think he's going to make it. I'll be heading back into town soon as I get this wagon back."

I booted Mash in the sides and took off on a dead run. I reckon I never felt as empty in my whole life. There was something else in me I never had felt, either. I have been out of my head and didn't care about what happened to me when I was in a fist fight, but I was that way now and it bothered me some. I felt like if there was a whole gang of those Texans standing in front of me I'd ride in shooting and not dodge a one of them.

I went into town and went straight for Bule's room. No one was in there but him, and he was just laying on the bed, covered to his chin, and pale as a gambler's hand. It was like the brown in his skin had just faded right out of him.

I said softly, "Bule, it's me. It's Luke. You alright Bule? Say you're alright, partner."

His eyelids fluttered and he looked at me. His eyes were glazed over, like he had been at the bottle or something. Weakly, he said, "Luke. Glad... glad...you came."

I took his hand and said, "Bule, you ain't goin' to die. You got to help run a ranch. We can't make it work without you, partner. We got to have you there."

He give me a smile at that and closed his eyes. I thought it was the end, but when I looked close I could see his chest moving. I tip-toed out.

Just as I was coming down the stairs, I saw a lady coming up. It was Nellie, daughter of the man we bought the ranch from. She stopped and asked, "How is he?"

I said, "He just went to sleep. But, he's goin' to make it ma'am. He can't die. You just believe that."

"I've been with him for these two days, now. He's just barely hangin' on, Mr. Adams."

I nodded and said, "You just stick by him. You need anything, I'll pick up the tab, and if I don't John Smith will. Don't worry none about money, and I'll see to it you get something for your trouble, too."

She blushed and said, "I don't want money, sir. That's not why I'm helping Bule."

It was my turn to get embarrassed, and I couldn't speak, so I just nodded again and left. I still had to go to the Wilsons. Mary's ma had cared for me when I was laid up and had pulled me through in good shape. I knew it would be a burden on them, but I knew she'd come. They're that kind of folks.

I pulled up and the sight of the pile of rubble and dirt was almost too much for me. I choked back a groan that was partly grief and mostly rage. I didn't see anything else around, so I kicked Mash ahead and went around the hill. There, on the backside of the hill was the family, and they were hard at building a new house. They had most of it done, except the roof and the doors. They saw me and stopped work.

I swung down and as I did, Josiah took my hand and said, "Luke. We missed you, son."

Those tears sprung to my eyes again and I just nodded.

Then Mrs. Wilson came up and I said howdy to her and then the boys. We walked over to the new house and I paid my compliments.

Then, I got something off my chest. I looked square at him and said, "You should have sent for me as soon as it happened, Josiah."

He looked down at his feet and said, "I know that now, Luke. You got to understand that I was full of misery and not thinking too clear." He looked at me and his eyes were brimming when he said, "She loved you, Luke."

I looked away and he added, "It was all I could do to keep the boys home, Luke. I'd have lost my whole family to those men. I didn't want to lose you to them, too. But, I guess I wasn't thinking too good, because if I had, I'd have known that soon as you did hear, you'd have go after them. I tried to tell Mary how you're built, and I went and forgot my own self."

"Where's she at?"

He nodded at the new house. "She's in one of the rooms. Don't go, Luke. It ain't a pretty sight."

I ignored him and walked rapidly to the little house. Inside, against a wall was a bed. Lying on the bed was Mary. She had crusted places on her face, and her head was wrapped in a white bandage. Her eyes were closed. I called out to her softly, "Mary, it's me. It's Luke." She didn't stir.

I couldn't stay and look at her that way very long. Too many emotions were raging in me and all I wanted to do was get on the trail and hurt the men who'd done this.

I went outside and told Josiah about Bule. They hadn't heard.

Lucy said, "Bule's shot?"

"Yes ma'am. Those Texans shot him the other day."

I talked with Josiah for a few minutes longer, and as I left he said, "Good huntin', Luke." I waved and put everything out of my mind except those Texans by the time I got to the gate.

CHAPTER 16

I hadn't seen any of those riders in town, but then I didn't really look for them. I was too busy with seeing Bule was cared for at the time. I figured the best place to start my war was in town. Eventually, they'd come to me. After all, they'd come so far and done so much to get me, I figured if I hung out in plain sight they'd come for me. If ever a body wanted to be found, it was me.

I went to see Bule again. That girl who took care of him and looked to be sick in love with him was there, also. They had him propped up on some pillows, and she was wrapping some new bandages around him. I saw his chest where two bullets had taken him.. Neither one had hit a lung, or he'd be coughing blood and wouldn't have lasted as long as he did. He had a bandage around his head, so I guess one had creased him there, too. I left when he got to groaning because I can't take much of watching someone suffer, especially a partner.

I went over to one of the saloons and looked around. It was still too early for much to be going on, but I went in and got a glass of water. By now, everyone knew about me asking for water, so he just slid it my way when I walked in. I smiled my thanks and drained the glass. There were a couple of miners in the back and they must have been sick or had got fired, because I know they don't give days off up there, except Sundays and this was Tuesday.

Hank, the barkeep walked over and asked, "You looking for those men, Luke?"

I nodded and asked, "You know where they're at?"

He shook his head and said, "Luke, they're mean and they're killers. They come in here nearly two weeks ago looking for you, but none of us would tell. Some would come in every night, play some cards, drink a little, and ride out. No one knows where they made camp."

Well, it was a long time to set out somewhere and camp, so I figured they must have come up with a wagon. I reckon they planned on staying until they got me, even if it was a month or more. Might be I would be better off hunting that camp.

I said, "Hank, do me a favor. I'm huntin' those men, and when I find them it's goin' to be hot. Pass the word to steer clear of any of those men, because when I get to them lead is going to fly and blood is goin' to spill. I don't want innocent blood to spill. You tell your customers that if those men come in here, they should leave. It ain't safe."

I knew that if word wasn't passed that innocent men might get shot. When I braced those men, there was a good chance of someone getting hurt besides those men I was after. Gunfights aren't the kind of fights to be around when they happen. There are too many chances of catching a stray bullet.

I chatted a little more and then left and went to the other saloon. I didn't like this saloon. It was the same one where I had the trouble with Sandy. There was always a rough crowd hanging in here, and it smelled bad besides. I went in and saw men in there drinking and playing cards even at this hour. I passed the word about staying clear of the Texans and left. Then, I led Mash to the livery and asked for some grain and a rubdown for him. I wanted him feeling good for whatever came up.

I walked a little ways out of town, crossed a little gully, and found a big tree. There, I stretched out and relaxed. I couldn't sleep, but I wanted to be fresh as I could when those men came for me. I hoped they wouldn't all come at once. Probably, they'd leave some kind of guard at the camp, but maybe not. Also, they had to be getting tighter with their coin. Man can't keep coming into town, drinking, and playing cards without running short of money, unless he's a card shark. These men weren't that. They were killers, bought and paid for.

Later that evening, I walked back into town. It was the cool part of the evening, with the sun not quite down, when it sends a final splash of red and then purple to let everybody remember that it'll be back. I went to the stables and peeked in. There, on the rack was four strange rigs, and four long-legged horses built for running were munching on some grain. I pulled my Colt, worked it a time or two, then stuck it back loose into my holster pocket. I checked my hideout gun and then went hunting.

First saloon I went to was the quiet one. I didn't figure I'd find them in that one, but I wanted to check it first. I saw the saloon was near empty, so I went on over to the other and slipped through the back door. I saw those four sitting at a table near the center of the room. I took out my gun and walked quickly over to their table.

One spotted me and said something quick to the others. The whole place was quiet now, except for other customers moving back out of the way. There was one townsman sitting with those Texans and I said, "Get out of here. I'm startin' a new game."

That man left pronto and one of the Texans smiled up at me and said, "Wondered where you took to hidin' yourself."

I reckon those gunfighters didn't know what they were up against or they wouldn't have sat there so cool and nervy like that. I said, loud enough for everyone to hear: "You Texans have been huntin' me. You hurt my girl real bad and shot two of my friends. It's war you came for gentlemen, and here's lookin' at you!"

I opened up on them, and my first shot put the one who'd spoke, back against the wall where he slid down, and in half a second, I'd shot the second one. The third man flew backwards out of his chair and piled on the floor, but managed to get a shot at me as he went down. His shot went wild on account of my shot which left him on the floor holding his stomach. The other came up with his hands held up high, yelling something about 'giving up,' but I shot him because there's a time for talking and a time for war, and they'd declared war on me. I just wasn't up to listening.

The whole thing didn't take more then a few seconds.

I turned to the crowd and said, "This war ain't goin' to have no prisoners. You can pass that on if you see any more of those Texans!" Then I stomped out.

I knew the talk might be hard against me, but my thinking on the matter is that when a war is on, there ain't no such thing as fair. You either put your enemy down, or he puts you down. When its just a fight between two men, that's different, except when he's like that Sandy feller, and you know he's going to hunt from behind. Then, there ain't no rules, either. Way I see it, you got to figure that other feller has got only one rule, which is kill you, and if you play by his rule, you lose.

Trouble with most folks is that when they come up against *hardcases,* they got the idea they got to be fair and civilized. Those men were playing a mean game with no rules, except those they make up as they go, one being to kill you any way they can. Even Bule is civilized that way, I reckon. That's what got him shot. If he'd just dropped some of them off as they rode up, using a rifle, he'd likely to have been back on the ranch eating beans and chili peppers with the boss. I growed up different. Pa wasn't a mean man, but he knew when to fight and how to fight.

He taught me to be kind, but he told me that when I come on a snake, I wasn't to give him no warning, but just to go to stomping. Those men back in that saloon had thought I was one of those civilized, rule-bound men. And, I reckon for awhile, I was that. It had got my girl hurt bad and maybe killed and my friend shot up bad enough he might die, too.

And now, there were no rules.

They'd brought a pile of grief on themselves and it wouldn't end until they'd paid in full. Mary used to say that I wasn't no better than them if I wasn't fair. But, the way I saw it, there wasn't no such thing as fair when it come to stopping men who was set on killing you and your friends. To my way of thinking, the world would be better off if they were fertilizer. Least ways, they'd be useful that way.

I went to the hotel, got a room, and began my wait. When those men didn't come back to camp, I figured the others would come after them. I slept light, rose early, and planted myself down front in a chair on the porch. It was the same chair I had words with that time with the outlaw. I soaked up the morning sun and thought some about Mary, then put those thoughts away, and planned what I would do when they came in.

Morning came, but they didn't show. That evening, I got where I could spot them easy when they showed, but they never showed. I was getting impatient, and waiting wasn't in me. I finally went to bed late. Next morning as I was throwing the saddle on Mash, someone came into the stable. I dropped the saddle and whipped out my gun.

"Hold it, Adams! It's me, Williams, the sheriff!"

I put away my gun and picked up the saddle. "You shouldn't come on a man sudden like that, Sheriff. You almost got a new eyeball."

He shrugged and said, "Yeah, it was a fool thing to do, wasn't it?"

"What can I do for you?" I figured it had to do with the shooting the night before. This sheriff was the most tolerant gent I ever met when it came to fights and such. I knew he was a Johnson man, but he seemed to be a decent man. He wasn't in town too often, because he had a ranch here in the valley, and stayed on it most of the time. Only time he came in was when the town couldn't handle things. I reckon this was one of those times.

He wiped his hat onto the back of his head, scratched his whiskered face and said, "Those men you shot in the saloon the other night, the Texans, are they the ones who shot Bule and pulled the Wilson house down?"

I nodded.

He frowned and said, "Well, I guess I can't blame you none for what happened. Only thing, the town is worried and don't want no more of this trouble. They want me to ask you to leave."

I smiled and finished throwing the saddle onto Mash. "As you can see, I was about to do that very thing, Sheriff."

"Good. Only thing, don't come back until this thing is over. I've got some men coming, and I'll chase any rider with a Texas brand clean out of town, and I'll have to do the same to you if you come back."

I just wasn't in a mood for anyone to get pushy with me. He should have just let it lay as soon he saw I was leaving. I whomped Mash in the belly, tugged the cinch tight and said, "I want to tell you something."

I turned and faced him. "I'm going to do what I have to do. Now, if it comes to me having to ride to town, whether it's for shells or food, or to see my partner, then I'm comin' in, and I wouldn't advise any man tryin' to stop me. Just don't be botherin' me because I'm in no frame of mind to be trifled with."

I started to run away, then something came to my mind and I asked, "Did you go after those men for hurtin' Mary and for shootin' my partner?"

"Yes, but they were gone."

Just a minute ago you said if they come to town you'd chase 'em out. That don't sound like "arrest" to me."

He didn't say anything, and I went on. "I think you're playin' a crooked game, Sheriff."

His face flushed and he said, "It all depends on how many men Mr. Johnson sends me. If it's enough and those Texans show, then I'll arrest them. Otherwise, I'll just ask them to leave."

I left town knowing that the Texans wouldn't get arrested, and maybe not even run out of town. I reckon if Johnson wanted them out, they'd be gone, but I didn't see any reason for Johnson to be too partial about my health, or Bule's either. My plan was to look for their camp, because I figured that if they were going to come looking for their partners, they'd have already showed.

I scouted for signs, and finally located some wagon tracks that didn't belong where they were at. I followed them slow, not wanting to come on those riders too sudden. The trail went back into a part of the valley that was pretty wild and had a lot of rocks in it, plus a lot of pine and brush. I'd been in the area a couple of times, and it was a pretty place. There was a stream somewhere back there, but I never located it. I figured maybe they were camped near that stream.

In a couple of hours I saw a trickle of smoke coming from some tree tops about a mile off. I laid back and waited for night. I'd have a better chance of sneaking up on them at night.

It was late when I started moving up. I left Mash after a little ways and walked on in, moving slow and quiet. I could hear voices. It had to be them, because no one else in the valley would be way out here, at least not at night, and not with a wagon. No one but a bunch of Texans looking to shoot me, that is.

I climbed onto a rock and inched my way to the top. I could hear the voices clear, now.

One man said, "I say they're in jail."

"Aw, so what. They were told not to go in after that deal with the girl. It's their own fault if they got arrested."

Then I heard that mellow voice I recognized as Briner's. He said, "They're dead."

"You keep saying that!" Someone was sounding mighty upset at Briner. "There ain't one bit of reason in that. They was four of them, all top men with a gun. They don't come no tougher. You telling us that drifter took all four of them?"

Briner said, "Johnson promised me he'd keep the sheriff out of this. None of those men had gotten their pay for this job, so they didn't run off. I know they're not in jail, because Johnson assured me the sheriff would stay out of things. So, they must have met Adams and his friends. They came off second best."

He sounded pretty calm about it all, but I got to hand it to him, he had it pretty well pegged.

Another voice floated out of the night and said, "I'm getting tired of waiting. Why don't we just ride out to that ranch and take him there. We should have done that in the first place."

Briner said, "You're right, Jack. That was my mistake, but I didn't want those men with him involved. I'm only after Adams."

Somebody said, "Reckon Red got that blue-eyed friend of his involved anyway. Got him so involved he up and died." Everyone had a good laugh at that.

Briner interrupted their laughter. "Yes, and if Red is still alive, he's got me to answer for that when we get back to the ranch." He paused and added, "Like you do for the girl."

My heart skipped a beat, and I was wishing I had a view, because I wanted to make certain I got that man, if I got none of the rest. It was good to know that I had shot the man who had been responsible for Bule's condition.

I wanted to get in closer, and I hoped that they kept on arguing because men who are running at the mouth ain't got too much worry in them, and they don't hear what a quiet man will hear. I wondered if they even had a guard out. The way they were talking loud, I didn't think so, and it just showed me how little they thought of the trouble they'd bought. Like those four in town, they thought they were fighting a farmer or a rancher, or some other kind of civilized man. I would have figured Briner at least would know me better by now. He had to know that when I found out about Mary, I'd come for him.

I waited for the conversation to start up again, and when it didn't I stayed still, not making a sound, waiting patient. I had all night, and the way these men's nerves were on edge with each other, it wouldn't take long for them to start arguing about something again. In a few minutes, I was proved right, because one of them cussed another for taking the last of the coffee, and the other cussed him back, then another man joined in and soon I had all the noise I wanted. I just hoped none of them got shooting mad. I wanted that pleasure myself.

I crawled slowly up closer and got everyone spotted. There were five of them, and Briner was sitting with his back against one of the wheels of the wagon, while two men were hunkered down in front of the fire, and two was standing there arguing. There didn't seem to be a guard, and if there was, he sure was guarding the wrong side of the camp. It's strange how a strong man will get to thinking he can't be beat, and act the fool.

I slid off my rock slow, and then moved in close. I left my rifle sitting by the rock. What I had in mind didn't call for a rifle.

I stepped right out among them, gun pointed straight at Briner. They were so surprised not a soul said a word. They sat there slack-jawed.

"Just rest easy boys and shuck your guns. And don't anyone get jumpy, or I'll start the ball rollin' right now." The growl was in my voice and the promise was there, too.

A couple of them reached for their gun belts to unbuckle, but suddenly, Briner spoke, and his voice had lost that mellow sound. It was hard and kind of excited. "Hang on to those guns, you fools! You give up your guns to this man and he'll shoot you where you stand. If he's here, it means he's killed the others, and if he managed to do that, it wasn't a fair fight. He just bushwhacked them. He's got blood in his eye, boys, and we were stupid enough to put it there."

I smiled, because my idea about Briner not guessing what kind of man he was up against was wrong. The old man had me pegged better than I thought, because as soon as they dropped their guns I really had planned to shoot them where they stood.

It was quiet, except for the camp fire popping now and then. We all stood there just a few seconds, and I saw they had believed Briner, so there wasn't no sense waiting for them to just shoot me down. I pulled the trigger on my Colt, and instead of his head, I caught Briner in the shoulder, because he was moving, falling to one side. He must have seen it in my eyes and knew he was at the top of my list. Then, I caught another on the run and he fell into the fire and rolled out. I dove into the darkness as bullets splattered on rocks near me, humming off into the dark.

I hit the ground, rolled over to my rifle, jacked a shell into the chamber, and planted a shot right into the middle of the fire. There wasn't a soul in sight now, and the burst of light my shot caused when it scattered the fire didn't show anything stirring. It was dead quiet.

I moved back into the night, because the only way now was to circle them. It took some time, and I left some hide in places, but I made it. They were set to wait me out. It's what I'd have done in their place.

I got close enough to make out two shapes beside the wagon, belly down with rifles stuck out. One man was laying kind of funny, it seemed, and it struck me that it might be Briner. He had his rifle laid out in front of him, but one arm was hugging his side.

The only reason I didn't shoot Briner then was on account of him telling the one man about how stupid they were concerning that deal with the Wilsons. I lined up instead, on the shape next to him. When I shot, the shape arched up and gave out a long cry. Briner rolled under the wagon, and I moved away, back on into the night. If I'd stayed, I might have caught a stray because they poured shot after shot into where I had been. I moved back into the night and away from the camp.

It was almost the end of me because one of those two other men had also moved into the night, like all of them should have done. He got a good shot at me and came close to taking my head right off. I heard the shot, felt something brush the side of my face and heard the bullet smash into a rock.

Shots came regular now, some coming close, but most just wild, and not hitting much more than rocks. I kept moving towards my horse, because I figured I had them now. All I had to do was set me an ambush or two and keep whittling until I got them down to my size.

Mash gave me a nudge as I came up and in a flash we were moving quiet out into the night. I'd hole up in some quiet spot near the trail and come morning set my first ambush.

CHAPTER 17

I was wrong. I waited for those Texas men to track me, but they never came. It was two days since I had left the camp, and I had caught nary a sign of them. Finally, I headed back to their camp.

I came up on the camp-site by foot, having left Mash a little ways off. I had to go slow, and it took me nearly an hour. In this country, a man learns to do things carefully or one day he doesn't learn anything ever again. I wasn't anxious to walk into an ambush. I could see the wagon still there, but everything else was gone. They'd cleared out. I saw a fresh grave over to one side.

I went on in, and looked around. They'd taken what supplies were left, and there was only a couple of empty cans laying around, and a sack of flour that was half full, still laying in the wagon.

I could have let this trouble lay, because it was plain they was going to Texas as fast as they could, but all I could see was Mary lying still in that bed with her head bandaged, and the crusty blood on her face, and my partner laying on his bed nigh unto death, pale as dirty snow. I had to go after them. I didn't want them going to Texas and then coming back with fresh men. My Texas past was going to come to an end if I had to follow Briner right into his house. I headed back for Mash on the run because their trail was getting cold.

Four days later I came on fresh sign. Until then, everything had seemed pretty old. I figured them to be about a day ahead. Only problem I had was that I was low on supplies. When I left town, I hadn't figured on chasing that bunch to Texas. I shot a rabbit and a few quail, but life in this part of Texas was awful bare.

I pushed on and sighted them once, but I had to stop and give Mash a rest right afterwards and didn't see them any more. I was tired and Mash was slowing on me. We both needed a good blow, but my need to settle things with those men kept me moving, and I knew that sooner or later I'd reach them. It seemed to me that they were pushing mighty hard, and if they weren't careful, they'd push their mounts right into the ground. That was something I didn't plan on doing.

The wind picked up and made me look for shelter. I came to a sandy place that had a pile of rocks near it, pulled my horse up close to the rocks, and made him lay down awhile. I had to cover Mash's nose with my kerchief, and I buried my face into my hat. The blow lasted about half an hour, then tuckered out. A Texas wind can blow faster than a bullet, and some swear that in a good sandstorm, a man can get a clean shave. I don't know about that, but I know it can skin you real bad. Afterwards, I decided to sit and rest until the sun got red. A man traveling on the desert under a white sun is a fool. Mostly, I had been traveling early in the morning, until the sun got to a blister, and then again in the late afternoon.

That afternoon, about five o'clock, I moved on leading Mash again, walking in front, saving him as I could. Some men would have just rode their horse until it wore out, and then cussed it for dying on them. The *injuns* are about the best there is when it comes to making a horse last. A man can chase an *injun,* but unless you got a couple changes of mounts, you won't catch him. He'll walk most of the way, then, when you think he's played out, he'll jump on his horse and leave you in his dust, laughing all the way.

I'd walked nearly three hours, and the sun was cooled off, and it was laying down purple shadows all over the desert, when I spotted what I took to be a rifle. It had a shiny look to it, but there wasn't enough sun to be certain. I moved aside and out of line with it.

I followed a gully for awhile, then I cut back over towards that shiny spot. The sun was about gone, and I wanted to get to that spot while there was some light.

There was a little tumble of rocks there, and somewhere in that bunch was whatever had give off that little shine to me. I moved ahead without Mash, going easy, not making a sound, carrying my rifle in my left hand.

Then, I saw it. There, laying on top of a rock was this big, empty can. Probably, it had held tomatoes or peaches. I saw another laying in the sand beside it. I slipped on in closer.

Just the other side of this rock, I saw a man laying in the sand on his side. It was Briner. I didn't see anyone else around, so it seemed those men had unloaded their boss, because he was slowing them down with that wound of his. They hadn't even left him a canteen. That was a real loyal bunch of riders he had. The going gets tough, so you drop off your boss and leave him for the buzzards, or in this case, for me.

I remembered my pa, and some of the things he taught me, like staying true to a man I worked for, and giving him all I got, not slacking up on him, and especially not ever leaving a man I signed on with when he was in a tight. Pa always said if I was loyal, then I'd always have somebody backing my play, and I'd get loyalty back one day. He was a firm believer in that 'reaping and sowing' verse in the Bible. I seen it work enough for Pa and for me that I took that saying to heart. It used to be just learning I got from my pa. Now, I suppose it was personal as much as something I learned.

I moved in quiet, my pistol lined out in front. He might be playing possum with a gun in his hand. I reached him, put my hand in his back so he couldn't roll over easy and cocked my gun in his ear.

"Briner, don't move."

All I got was a groan. I rolled him on over careful and I saw his face was pinched with pain, and he was fevered. There isn't much in killing a dying man, and when I saw him, all the hate for him suddenly went out of me. Suddenly, I didn't even feel bitter towards him for bringing all the grief to me that he had. He'd suffered and paid for it, and it looked to me like he might be paying all he had left, which was his life. He'd given a son to his hate, and now his own life. I left and went back for Mash. I hated to have to share my water with a dying man, but I had to do it.

I gave him some water, and that seemed to bring him around. He looked up at me and managed a weak thanks. I laid him back and told him to rest easy. He went to sleep, and I covered him with my blanket. I got out my coat, put that on, leaned against a rock with my rifle in one hand and my pistol in the other and went to sleep.

Sometime in the night he called out for some more water and I give him a couple swallows. He wanted more, but I wouldn't give it to him. He seemed to be out of his fever, and he asked me if I was going to kill him and then go after the other two.

I sat down against the rock I was leaning on and said, "Briner, I will get to those two. I'm burdened with you now, because I can't leave you here, although I ought to. But, I got a limit to my hate, Briner. First place I can drop you off safe, I will."

He didn't say anything at that, but got kind of shy, and wouldn't even look at me. Finally, almost an hour later he woke me again and asked, "Did Ben really try to gun you like you and Mahew told it?"

I asked him who this Mahew was and when he told me, I said, "Oh yeah, that Cat Foot feller. I took a shine to that man. Looked to me to be a bad man to tangle with, but a good man."

He coughed and then said, "Yeah. Top hand, he was. I was a fool not to listen to him."

I found myself pitying him some. I said, "Grief has a way of keeping a man from thinking clear, ."

He looked thoughtful, as though he hadn't heard me. We were quiet for awhile and finally he said, "I suppose I always knew it was that way. Ben was. . . Ben was a good boy until his ma died." I could see the pain of losing that boy was still deep in him.

He went on. "Adams, I never taught him to be low down. He wasn't a mean kid. He just...well, he just got reckless, and got to doing crazy kid things. Fool things. Do you know what I mean?"

I nodded and said, "Briner, I ain't holding a grudge against you or your boy. He paid the price for being foolish, and you paid some of that price. We all paid for it." I didn't tell him that I thought it wasn't just being foolish that got his boy killed, although it was some of that, but there was a lot of mean in that boy. I saw that in him.

He just looked at the sand awhile, then fell back into his blanket. I went back to sleep. Come morning we'd ride out and keep moving until the heat came on us.

I had trouble getting him out of his blanket in the morning. He kept trying to get me to leave him, so finally I just picked him up and dumped him onto Mash. It hurt him some, and I hated to do it, but there was no other way, and he was holding me up.

After we got moving and he was settled into the saddle good, I asked, "Which one of your men hurt Mary?"

He said, "Adams, I am truly sorry for that. That crazy kid had no call to do what he did. I planned to make it up to that family when I got back. I thought maybe I could drive up some cows for them, if you think that'd be all right."

I nodded my agreement, then asked, "What about that kid? Did I get him yet?"

"No, he's with Miller, my cook. I think he's going to kill Miller when they get out of this desert. Miller tried to stay back with me, but that kid didn't know his way out of here, so he made Miller go with him."

"What's this kid's name?" I wanted to know who it was I had to kill.

Briner shifted some in his saddle and frowned. "I don't know his real name. Everyone always called him 'Duece' and that's the way I wrote his name in my book."

I asked, "How long since they left you there?"

"Couldn't have been more than a few hours before you found me. I know it was late morning when they pulled out. We'd camped there that night."

"What kind of shape is their mounts in?"

Briner managed a weak laugh. "Pitiful. Your horse here has more in him than all three of ours. That fool kid pushed us through all that desert like he had fresh mounts waiting up ahead. I tried to talk to him, but he wouldn't listen."

"There was five of you. I saw one grave back there. Where's the other man?"

Briner coughed and said, "You got two of us. We put them both in the same hole."

That meant I had two men to catch, not three. The odds were about even, now. We stopped in a few hours and I put Briner in some shade by a big rock. We didn't talk much and I let him have another swallow of water. I gave Mash some, then took one precious swallow myself. We dozed there in the heat of the day until late. Then, I got Briner back on Mash and we headed out again. I was stumbling some now and then, and I knew I was coming to the end of my rope. It looked like if I didn't catch those two soon, I'd just have to trail that one to wherever he took me. I might be a long time coming back to my ranch.

That night, we slept in a gully. It was a sleep of exhaustion, and if Briner or anyone had wanted to take me, this would have been their best chance. I wouldn't have heard a whole army ride up. It was what I needed, though, because when I woke, I felt like a lot of my strength come back. We started out early.

We covered a lot of ground, but not as much as if I'd been riding alone. I had a pair of feet that was on fire, and I knew they were swollen and maybe even bleeding inside the boots, but I just picked one up and put it down, picked the other up, and put it down, and never give any more thought to anything but moving on ahead.

Briner quit talking and took to slumping over Mash's neck. If he didn't get some attention to that shoulder soon, he wouldn't make it. Close to noon, I pulled into some rocks, and as I did, Briner fell out of the saddle. I dragged him into the shade of the rocks and give him a big swallow of water. That brought him around. He tried to tell me to go on without him again, but he was too weak to argue with me. We stayed there in the shade until late afternoon, and although I wanted to stay through the night, I pushed on because Briner was fading fast.

We hadn't gone more than a mile when I spotted them. They weren't moving, and it looked as if they'd made camp already. Likely, their mounts had played out on them. I looked over at Briner, but his head was slumped down on his chest and he didn't see a thing. I tugged on the reins and led Mash down into a gully out of sight of those two. I didn't say anything to Briner.

I left Mash standing with Briner sitting in the saddle and crept ahead. There, sprawled out on the sand lay two men. One was laying on a blanket with his hat over his face. The other was in the sand and on his stomach.

I stepped out and jacked a shell into my rifle. Neither man stirred. They were both out like I was the night before. I smiled, and then winced, because it cracked the skin on my lips, which were all dried and blistered. Then, I stepped back and went and got Mash. Those two weren't going anywhere.

I got Briner, laid him out on a blanket under a little piece of brush on the edge of the camp, stripped Mash down, and give all of us another drink of water. I took the canteens off those other horses. Two was empty, but that third had most of a canteen left. They hadn't even bothered to unsaddle their horses.

I woke Briner, because I wanted him as a witness. Then, I woke the one he pointed out as Miller. His face went white, and his eyes widened more than I thought a man's eyes could open. I explained things to him, and once he knew he would live, I saw tears of relief spring to his eyes. He went over to Briner and gave the old man a long drink of water.

I went over to that other man, the one called Duece. I took out my pistol, then kicked him in the side so it would hurt. He come flying off his blanket, and I slammed him along side the head with my fist. He fell into the sand, rolled over and got his eyes full of me standing there with my big Colt cocked and pointed straight at his head. He was snarling like some kind of mad dog, and I thought for a minute he was going to run right into the face of my gun, he was so mad and wild. Watching him, I got the notion that this was a man who wasn't all right in the head. He was mean, like a dog gets mean when it has the sickness and froths in the mouth. I'd seen men like this one before. I felt a rage come up in me, and an anger at Briner for hiring such a man to come for me.

I made him stand up, then I said, "Your name Deuce?"

He just glared at me and I went on: "You hurt, maybe killed, the woman I'm to marry, and you helped shoot up and maybe kill my partner."

He didn't even look at me, but glared at Briner and said,"Mister, you ain't in the Territory, you're in Texas. You best let me go and ride on out of here." He give a little sneer, looked at Briner and added, "I'll even take care of him for you."

I shook my head. "Yeah, you would. Only thing, you're about to go on trial. You ain't exactly got the time."

"What trial? There ain't a court for a hundred miles, and there ain't a judge in three hundred miles."

I took a few steps forward, put my hand in his chest and shoved. He staggered backwards to the edge, caught himself and stood still staring at me with eyes full of hate. Then, in the best 'judge' voice I could muster, I said, "I find you guilty, Deuce-whatever-your-name-is, of maybe murdering Mary Wilson and helping to shoot my partner, Bule. On behalf of them and those we don't know about who you probably shot in the back, and on behalf of those who, if you lived any longer than today would probably be murdered, in the name of and on behalf of the Territory of New Mexico and the State of Texas, God and anyone else I might have missed, I hereby sentence you to death at the hand of Judge Colt."

He got a funny look on his face, pointed his finger at me, then yelled, "You ain't got no ...." I shot that little killer where he stood, while he was still talking. I was in no mood to hear the likes of him. He fell backwards and slid head first down to the bottom of that sandy wash.

I should have buried him, but he'd caused me too much grief, too much hurt and trouble. Maybe I was wrong for being so sudden and for taking the part of the law like that, but I was on the ragged edge. I was trail-worn and bone-tired. That little killer standing there snarling like a mad dog and me knowing that he was the one who hurt poor Mary was more than I could take. Even my ma, if she'd been alive and standing there, wouldn't have talked me out of that killing, though I know she'd have tried. The regrets would come, I knew, but right then, there was no stopping me.

I left Briner and Miller there in the desert. We didn't part friends, but at least we weren't enemies any more.

I took a good rest before I went back. I laid around, mostly, and got Mash good and fat. We stayed in a little town that seemed like it was ready to blow away. Wasn't much there, and I was glad when I left. I made good time back and headed for the hotel soon as I pulled into Reata.

The clerk told me they'd took Bule out to the Wilsons, so I left town on the run. As I come through the gate, I saw one of the boys and he disappeared on the run. By the time I got near the house, the whole family was outside and there in front leading them was my partner, Bule. It was a wonderful sight, and I admit I got a little choked up.

And then my heart leaped, because I saw Mary hobble out on crutches. It was more than I could take. I'd tried to steel myself against the hurt when they'd tell me she was dead, and this plumb took my breath away. I'd been prepared for the worst and was seeing the best. My eyes were pretty full of water by then, but I wasn't ashamed of it. We hugged for a long time, swaying together, weeping, feeling each other's pain and joy.

I knew my Texas past was gone and she knew it, too. All I had ahead now were good friends, a good woman at my side, and a lot of work.

That suited this cowboy just fine.

We all talked for a long while after that, and I made them get the buggy ready because I figured Bule was ready to head back to the ranch. Lucy tried to talk us out of it, but we wouldn't mind her. I made sure Mary understood that as soon as I got Bule back to the ranch, her and I were going to sit down and talk serious. I told her I had something real important to ask her, and I wanted to be sure she didn't run off and get married to some crazy miner before I got back. She hit me with her crutch.

On the way back, Bule asked, "Luke, what about Briner? I know you got those Texans even if you won't talk much of it, but what about Briner?"

I looked at him and said, "Partner, Briner drove me out of Texas, and then I run him out of the Territory, and now we've both decided that we're quits. That kid of Briner's caused us both a lot of grief. Things are settled between us."

We got to the ranch late and I learned then that we had some more problems. The boss and Charlie had been riding all the time, trying to keep the rustlers scared off. They had three run-ins with them. Seemed like I had me some more trouble, again.

Some men are just born to it .

THE END

LIKE THIS BOOK?

If you enjoyed this western fiction story, then you'd love reading more by this author. He has several western stories available on Kindle. Check out the website http://westernfiction.com for more titles. And, for sure take a look at the novel Bloody Wes Teague.

BLOODY WES TEAGUE
by
Voyle A. Glover

Any man raised in the West in the mid 1800's knew hard times, particularly if he was raised in a dirt poor cow town with a father as Marshal. Weston Teague grew up in hard times, saw tough men up close and watched in horror as his father was gunned down before his eyes. He made a vow that day to always take another man's threats against him seriously. His father had ignored a man's threat. Teague vowed he'd never do that.

But he did, many years later in another place, another time. It would cost him dearly.

Teague met Abitha Claymore on a cattle buying trip to Colorado. She is the daughter of a rich New York rail road man. When Teague shows up in New York City to court her, Claymore opposes the marriage and even tries to have Teague shanghaied. But, the local city thugs hired by Claymore had never met a man as quick and as tough as Teague. Claymore reluctantly gives his lessing to the marriage.

But James Wood, the foreman of Claymore's Colorado ranch, didn't give his blessing. Indeed, prior to the wedding, Wood makes a threat to kill Teague, but because Teague was in the city courting Abitha Claymore, he chooses to ignore the warning, agreeing with Wood that there would be a "more convenient time" for them later. It would be a deadly mistake.

Teague returned with his new bride to the newly opened Wyoming Territory and his ranch. In less than a year, Abitha was expecting their first child.

She was not expecting James Wood in her first trimester.

Wood arrives on the ranch leading several other riders while Teague is in town to handle the building of a town house for his expectant wife. The riders force Abitha and her maid onto horses and kidnap them, heading back to the Colorado ranch. Wood knows Teague will follow.

He does. But, Wood will come to wish he hadn't.

This is a romantic, action-adventure in the tradition of Louis L'Amour, with some slices of history thrown into the mix. For more, see http://westernfiction.com/teague